HIDDEN CREED

Prairie Wind Publishing
Omaha, Nebraska

HIDDEN CREED

Attention: Permissions Coordinator
Prairie Wind Publishing
15418 Weir Street
Box 207
Omaha, NE 68137

This is a work of fiction. Names, characters, places, and incidents are a product of the author's imagination. Locales and public names are sometimes used for atmospheric purposes. Any resemblance to actual people, living or dead, or to businesses, companies, events, institutions, or locales is completely coincidental.

Ordering Information:
Quantity sales. Special discounts are available on quantity purchases by corporations, associations, and libraries. For information, please email the Sales Department at sales@pwindpub.com

Interior design and formatting: Prairie Wind Publishing
Book cover design: Prairie Wind Publishing & Shae Marcu (Shae_Retouch on Fiverr)
Jacket photograph: Dissolve Filmmaker ™

FIRST EDITION

ISBN: 978-1-7320064-3-0 Hardcover
ISBN: 978-1-7320064-4-7 eBook
ISBN: 978-1-7320064-5-4 Paperback

Printed in the United States of America
10 9 8 7 6 5 4 3 2

ALSO BY ALEX KAVA

RYDER CREED SERIES

Breaking Creed
Silent Creed
Reckless Creed
Lost Creed
Desperate Creed
Hidden Creed

MAGGIE O'DELL SERIES

A Perfect Evil
Split Second
The Soul Catcher
At The Stroke of Madness
A Necessary Evil
Exposed
Black Friday
Damaged
Hotwire
Fireproof
Stranded
Before Evil

THE STAND-ALONE NOVELS

Whitewash
One False Move

NOVELLA ORIGINALS WITH
ERICA SPINDLER AND J. T. ELLISON

Slices of Night
Storm Season

SHORT STORY COLLECTION

Off the Grid

DEDICATION

In Memory of
Sandra K. Rockwood
August 28, 1937 — December 20, 2019

*The rest of this journey won't be
the same without you.*

AND

In Memory of my boy, Scout,
(March 1998 to May 2014)
who is the *true inspiration* for this series.

HIDDEN CREED

ALEX KAVA

There are two kinds of secrets.
The ones we hide from others,
and those we keep from ourselves.
—*Frank Warren*

Chapter 1

Blackwater River State Forest
Sunday, June 14

The scream sounded human.

It pierced through the darkness and sent a chill down his sweat-drenched back.

It's not a person, he reminded himself though his jaw remained clenched. Tonight the rocking of the boat made his stomach lurch.

The scream came again. Closer.

This time he recognized the bird and tried to calm his nerves. The Eastern screech owl was one of the first voices after dusk. That sound usually didn't bother him. Tonight he was on edge. Every sight and sound and smell set him off. Earlier he'd twisted around so suddenly he almost tripped over the bag at his feet. What would it take for him to lose his balance and go over the side?

The water wasn't deep but the current was swift. And it was dark…so very dark.

Settle down.

Why was he so jumpy?

Then slowly, the other night creatures began their symphony.

He couldn't see them in the dark forest, but he knew their voices—each and every bird, insect, reptile or animal. He could pick out and identify the rasps and the whistles, the tick-tick-tick and the whirs. He could tell the difference between a bird-voiced tree frog and a barking tree frog. He knew to steer clear of the bellow-hiss of an alligator. He could even recognize the huff-huff grumble or jaw pop of a black bear alerting trespassers to its presence.

In a matter of minutes the creatures filled the thick, moist air with their songs. He couldn't even hear the water lapping at the boat as he steered against the current.

The squawks and chuffs and trills calmed him. And finally he felt some relief.

Maybe he needed to lay off the drugs for a while. He kicked at the two-liter plastic bottle squashed against the black bag at his feet. He didn't like when the meth started messing with his mind, inviting the voices back inside his head. Maybe that was why the screech owl's scream unnerved him. It sounded an awful lot like a woman's scream, one in particular that was still caught in his memory forever.

He shook his head, a quick shake back and forth as if the motion could send the audible snapshot back to a locked compartment.

He lifted his ball cap and mopped the sweat from his face with his forearm then raked his fingers through wet hair. The humidity was so heavy that a fog hovered over the water. He couldn't see the moon but it was bright enough to give the darkness a misty, silver haze.

Branches stretched above him, swaying in the breeze. They looked like long arms reaching down to snatch him up.

Another shake of his head. His mother always called this the witching hour. She had a whole lot of crazy superstitions.

Superstitions. That's all they were.

He needed to settle the hell down. He knew this creek by heart. There was no one else around for miles. No screams. No arms grabbing at him out of the mist. He tried to concentrate on the melody of the creatures. The rhythm of the croaks harmonized with the wheezes and gurgles.

He adjusted his trolling motor, anticipating exactly where the current began to increase. Instinctively, he knew when to duck his head before he came to the tree trunk that leaned so far over the creek, it looked as if it could topple into the water at any moment. It created a natural blockade that required looping wide and squeezing along the bank. Without seeing them, he avoided the tangled roots. He steered around the shallow spot that could snag his boat and wedge it into the sandy bottom.

This place was sacred to him. It was a safe haven. He'd found solace and solutions as he floated on these waters. Numerous times the forest relieved him of his problems. He knew he could leave them behind to be swallowed up in the clay and hidden by the shadows of the tall, longleaf pines.

By the time he reached the clearing he was drenched in sweat. The fog pushed down on his shoulders before he yanked at the bag. It was heavier than usual tonight. He hoisted it over the edge of the boat, bending it in two and leaving it while he crawled out onto the sandy bank.

He yanked off his ball cap and slipped on the headlamp. He flipped the switch and bobbed the light around. The stream caught a pair of eyes before the animal scuttled off. He snapped the lamp off and tugged the cap on over the contraption. It was difficult to see through the gray mist with it on or off. And it was almost impossible to hear anything over the symphony.

Fallen leaves lifted and jumped near his boots, coming alive with tiny tree frogs. He grabbed the black bag and pulled one end until the other plopped to the ground, sending a mass of creatures skittering. It took him too long to yank and drag.

Thirty minutes later he was ready to empty the bag.

It moved.

He froze, feet planted, heart pounding. Was his mind playing tricks on him?

He stared at the black bag, holding his breath and keeping every limb, every muscle, every finger as still as possible. It was late. He was exhausted. Maybe it was the drugs. He'd experienced hallucinations during binges. They were wild and surreal.

He focused his eyes, willing the silvery mist to allow him a better view.

This was crazy. He was driving himself crazy.

He reached for the shovel again, and this time there was no doubt.

The bag was moving.

What was inside was not dead…yet.

Chapter 2

Blackwater River State Forest
Monday, June 15

Ryder Creed couldn't keep up.

He watched Brodie glide between the tree trunks like she was riding the breeze. Tall and willow-thin, his sister reminded him more of a skinny teenager than a twenty-seven-year-old woman. After being held captive for sixteen years, Brodie was still playing catch-up physically and mentally. In many ways, she was very much like the eleven-year-old Creed remembered.

That last image of her skipping in the rain toward the rest area bathrooms had been imprinted on his mind. For a long time, it brought sadness and then despair. All those years in between he didn't know whether she was dead or alive. Turned out she was imprisoned in an earthly purgatory.

He pushed the image away. He needed to concentrate on here and now; on the new challenges that Brodie faced. Besides, she and Grace were leaving him behind.

The vines and holly bushes grabbed at his pant legs. There was no trail that he could see, and yet, Brodie slipped through the forest with little hesitation as if she were following an invisible path.

"Hey, wait up," Creed called to her.

She stopped and spun around to face him. Her thin shoulders bunched up then heaved with an exaggerated sigh of impatience.

"You're such a slowpoke," she said.

Creed wiped at the smile before she noticed it. What he'd forgotten of their childhood, she remembered keenly as if most of it had occurred just last week.

Slowpoke. Did anyone even use that word anymore?

She had always been faster than him as if carried by the wind. He was three years older and stronger, but any footrace left Creed in the dust. Out here, where the pine trees grew thick and close with low-hanging branches, being over six feet tall and broad-shouldered left him at a disadvantage. He had to go slow and weave between the spaces, snapping branches to cut a new path. He wondered how Brodie even knew where she was going. Though he shouldn't have been surprised. She spent a good deal of time in the forest exploring.

Their fifty-acre property backed up to Blackwater River State Forest and shared an invisible border. Most of it was undeveloped like this stretch. Depending on the time of year and the amount of rain, streams and creeks cut through, sometimes restricting access to certain portions and other times, providing empty riverbeds to add to the adventure. But it also made it easy to get lost.

Creed had made sure Brodie took a dog with her and a well-stocked daypack every time she ventured out on her own. Even now, he could tell that the holster around her waist held a canister of bear spray.

Just then the scrub grass parted, and he saw the tip of Grace's tail. The little Jack Russell terrier came backtracking to see what the holdup was. She cocked her head at him. He couldn't help thinking she seemed to mimic Brodie's impatience.

Creed adjusted his daypack and squeezed through the narrow passage. He surveyed the tree bark before placing a hand on the tree. Oak snakes could blend in easily.

"Have you been this way before?" he asked, stepping over downed branches that hadn't slowed Brodie.

"No, silly. What kind of adventure would that be?"

"Then how do you remember where you hid the target scent for Grace to find?"

The target scent was a Mason jar with cheesecloth stretched across the top and secured with a rubber band. Inside was a bloody sock.

"I don't have to remember. Right, Grace?" Brodie said to the little dog. "Grace, go find." She waved her hand, and Grace took off.

Normally, he wouldn't let his dogs off leash in the forest—too many unpredictable obstacles. Grace was the exception. She watched out for Creed as much as he did her. She wouldn't let him out of her sight for long. They'd been through too much together. Most recently, a tornado had swept them up into the heavens for what Creed thought might be their last, wild ride.

The top priority of a dog handler was the dog's safety. That was one of the reasons he'd started placing GPS devices inside the pockets of his dogs' working vests. Creed wanted to call out for Grace to go slower.

To his surprise, Brodie beat him to it. "Grace, slow down."

Up ahead in a clearing he could see Grace stop and look back at them. She pranced in place, waiting. Threw her head up and nosed the air.

"You seem distracted," Brodie said over her shoulder, keeping ahead but at a slower pace for his benefit. "Are you thinking about Maggie?"

"Maggie? What? No."

Maggie O'Dell was an FBI agent he'd worked with on several cases over the last two years. In fact, it was Maggie who helped find Brodie. Each time Creed and Maggie grew closer, Creed swore he became more confused by their relationship.

"Aren't you looking forward to seeing her?" Brodie wanted to know.

She was coming to Pensacola but for another case. What else? They were supposed to have dinner together while she was here. She always seemed in a hurry to head back. It had become a sort of dance. One step forward, two steps back.

"Of course, I'm looking forward to seeing her. Maggie and I are friends."

This time Brodie stopped to look at him, and he almost ran into her.

"Just friends?" she asked.

"I think you've been reading too many romance novels."

"And I think *you* haven't been reading enough of them."

But suddenly, her hand shot up to shush him. She tilted her head to listen.

"I think she's close to finding it," Brodie whispered, and with that, she turned back to their adventure with Grace.

Relieved to change the subject, Creed followed. He stayed close, watching and fascinated by this woman in front of him who seemed to know exactly where to skip, step and duck. She was braver than he gave her credit. And she was getting stronger every day. To Hannah's two little boys, Brodie was a superhero who removed spiders from their bedroom and snakes from their backyard with her bare hands.

That always made him smile. He could still remember Isaac and Thomas, their eyes huge and mouths open as they watched Brodie slap a spider with the palm of her hand.

He needed to stop worrying about her so much.

For weeks, Brodie had been nagging to be included in one of his training sessions. But he could see now that she had already learned from simply observing.

Over seven years ago, Creed and his business partner, Hannah, had created a training facility where they rescued abandoned dogs and turned them into scent tracking heroes. That Brodie showed an interest, pleased him. When she first came to live with them just six months ago, she was afraid of dogs. Her captor, Iris Malone, had used dogs to stop Brodie from escaping. A scar on her ankle was a vicious reminder.

Now, Brodie stopped in the middle of the clearing. Creed saw Grace dart off into the trees in the opposite direction, but Brodie stayed put. She turned slowly, surveying the area, glancing around.

Creed came up beside her but kept quiet.

He could hear a faint buzzing sound. Instinctively, he reached up and adjusted the red kerchief around his neck. Brodie had a matching one. Both were soaked with a concoction Hannah had created that acted as an organic mosquito repellent. It usually worked wonders. All his handlers used it, and so did their dogs. But it wasn't mosquitoes he was hearing.

"I think she might have missed it," Brodie told him. She pointed off to the left of where Grace had disappeared. "I came from the other direction when I planted it, but I'm pretty sure it's on the other side of that ravine."

She glanced back at Creed, apologetic and a bit embarrassed. The expression on her face was almost childlike. He hated that sometimes she still looked as if she expected to be punished.

"I should have taken a turn before that huge oak tree," she said. "I forgot about the ravine. No way we can cross it from this side."

Then panic flooded her face. "You don't think Grace would try to cross the ravine?"

Before he could answer, Grace came back out from between the trees in the exact spot where she'd disappeared.

"She's okay," Creed told Brodie, pointing to the little dog and hoping to calm his sister.

Then he did a double-take back to Grace. She was staring intently at him. She was alerting that she had found the target.

"Is it possible your directions are mixed up?"

Brodie looked at Grace and knew exactly why he was asking. Instead of answering immediately, she surveyed their surroundings again, turning her entire body to take it in. Her eyes came back to Grace.

"I guess I could have come all the way around," she said.

Grace was getting impatient, stomping her front paws and wagging her head over her shoulder as if to direct them.

"Okay, girl," Creed told her.

He started to unzip his daypack to get her reward, but Grace darted back into the trees. Brodie didn't hesitate. She hurried to follow. Creed felt his phone vibrate against his hip and stopped to check the text.

Okay, so maybe he was anxious to see Maggie. They talked frequently but he hadn't seen her since March. Before he could grab the phone, he heard a rustling sound then a thud.

"Brodie?"

She didn't answer. Creed rushed into the trees. He punched branches out of the way as he ran. Vines threatened to trip him. Twigs whipped into his face.

"Grace! Brodie!"

They couldn't have gone far. He skidded to a stop and twisted around. In his hurry, had he taken a wrong turn?

More rustling.

"Oh no!"

It was Brodie.

He had gone too far. He backtracked to her voice.

"Are you okay?" he yelled. "Is Grace okay?"

He came around a thick stand of trees and finally saw them. Brodie had fallen, her hands and knees coated with mud. Grace stood beside her, agitated and whining. She looked from Brodie to Creed and back. Her eyes darted in sync with her front paws dancing in place.

But as Creed came closer, his stomach did a nosedive. It wasn't mud. Brodie was covered in blood.

Chapter 3

"It's not mine," Brodie told him, sitting back on her knees but holding up the palms of her hands to show him.

Creed hurried over, giving in to his panic. He was so concerned about Brodie, his eyes searching for injury, that it took him a minute to see what had caused her fall.

The body was buried in a shallow grave. Really only half buried, face down, arms flung up around the head. Matted hair was caked with blood where flies had already settled and had begun their work. Blood pooled on top of the leaves and dirt. The thick humidity kept it sticky enough to cling to Brodie.

"Are you okay?" he asked reaching out his hand to help her up.

When her eyes met his, he held them looking for shock and horror and was surprised to see neither.

"I guess this is what Grace was trying to show us," she said. "Not the Mason jar."

She ignored his extended hand, standing up without effort. She was careful where she stepped. Creed couldn't tell if she was being reverent to the dead, or she simply didn't want to slide in the mess again.

"Are you sure you're okay?" he asked a second time.

"Yeah, I'm okay." Brodie nodded.

She stared down at the body while holding her hands up in front of her as if she had just washed them and was trying not to drip before reaching for a paper towel.

"Who do you think he is?" she asked.

Creed thought it was an interesting question. Brodie wondered who the victim was while his mind sorted through the process of the killer. How did he manage to drag a body all the way into the forest then only half bury him? Actually, there was an awful lot of blood. Did the murder happen right here?

His eyes started scanning the landscape around them. Was it possible the killer was watching?

The flies told him this didn't just happen. But the sticky mess that covered Brodie's hands and knees meant it had been recent.

"We need to be careful," he told her. "So we don't disturb any evidence."

"Okay."

He caught her glancing at her hands, and this time, she winced. From his daypack he pulled out one of his extra T-shirts. During the summer he usually rolled up and stuffed several inside to change when the humidity left him soaked in sweat.

He offered her the shirt, but Brodie only stared at it.

"Go ahead and use it to wipe off."

"But it'll stain your T-shirt."

"I have dozens of them. Go ahead but don't toss it. We'll take it with us just in case."

As he was zipping up his pack, he noticed Grace wasn't at his feet waiting for her reward toy. She'd found the body and alerted, yet she'd disappeared again.

Before he called out, he saw her tail poking up out of the scrub grass about thirty feet away. He watched the tail wag, go straight then curl over her back.

The realization hit him. Grace didn't want her reward yet, because she wasn't finished.

"Brodie, did you hide the Mason jar at the base of a tree?"

He looked back at his sister. She hadn't taken her eyes off the dead body. But now she glanced up.

"I wedged it inside the branches of a cedar tree."

Grace nosed through the grass just enough to find Creed and stare at him. Brodie twisted around and noticed the dog's alert. Her head swiveled, taking in the clearing and the surrounding landscape. Creed did the same and was quick to realize there wasn't a cedar tree in sight.

He pulled his cell phone from his pocket. Just a few minutes ago it had vibrated with a text message, but now there were no bars. It wasn't unusual in the middle of the forest for cell reception to come and go.

To Brodie he said, "Do you think you can find your way back to the house from here?"

"Of course, I can. I'm not lost. I just took a wrong turn. I haven't been on this side of the ravine before."

He held back a smile at her long explanation. A slight relief swept over him. Brodie sounded like her ordinary self, again, even a bit indignant that he'd ask the question.

"I'll try to text Hannah," he said and checked his wristwatch. They had walked for almost a half hour. "I'll have her call the sheriff. Probably the medical examiner, too. They'll need you to guide them back here. Can you do that?"

"Sure. You're not coming?"

Creed looked for Grace. She'd already moved to another area. He slipped his hand into his daypack and his fingers searched for the surveyor flags he always carried with him.

He nodded at Grace as he said to Brodie, "She's still working."

He waited for his sister's eyes then waited to see the acknowledgment that she understood. This time he saw a hint of alarm.

As Brodie disappeared into the trees Creed texted Hannah.

WE FOUND A BODY IN THE FOREST.

He started examining the spot in the scrub grass where Grace had alerted. It was about three feet away from the base of a huge, old oak. He was careful not to disturb the layers of leaves and pine needles under his boots.

His cell phone pinged with Hannah's response.

LORD HAVE MERCY. ARE YOU SERIOUS?

YES. CALL WHOEVER WE NEED TO CALL. BRODIE'S HEADING BACK TO LEAD THEM HERE.

OK!

HANNAH. GRACE ISN'T FINISHED. THERE MIGHT BE MORE.

OH MY DEAR LORD!

He pocketed his phone and focused on the terrain under his feet. With the side of his boot, he swept the bed of leaves bringing them to life as tiny tree frogs jumped out of the way. Underneath, a tangle of tree roots snaked out of the ground, resembling gnarled fingers. Tall patches of scrub grass grew in between. He couldn't see what had drawn the dog's attention, but that wasn't unusual. In the past Grace had alerted to bodies buried as deep as seven feet down.

He bent to place one of the fluorescent flags in the ground when he noticed a crevice. Where two roots formed a V the dirt had caved in and left a deep hollow. Creed poked the flag in the dirt about six inches away then tugged a flashlight out of his pack.

This time he squatted closer and shot a stream of light into the fissure. The sight startled him, jolting him back on his heels. He took a deep breath and repositioned himself. Before he could take a second look, Grace appeared at his side.

She nudged his forearm with her nose. Whatever was down below no longer interested her. Instead, she was poking the air with her nose, glancing up into the treetops and shifting from one front paw to other. She had more to show him.

"Just a minute," he told her. "I need to take a look at what you found here first."

Carefully, he brushed some of the leaves out from between the web of tree roots. As he plucked and swept, debris crumbled and fell, leaving a wider gap to the hole below. It also gave him a much better look at the smooth gray-white orb half-buried about a foot down.

This time there was no mistake. He was looking at the top of a human skull.

Chapter 4

Blackwater River State Forest

If it hadn't been for the voices he would have walked right into the path of these intruders.

At first, he wasn't sure they were real. He hadn't slept much last night. Whenever he closed his eyes all he saw was that black body bag moving again and again. His night fevers created something different crawling out each time. Sometimes the contents slithered out. Sometimes it burst through the bag.

After hours of tossing and turning in sweat-drenched sheets he started second-guessing himself. Had it really even happened? Or had the drugs infected his mind so deeply he could no longer tell what was real and what was simply a figment of his imagination?

When he couldn't find his favorite ball cap, other memories started flooding back. He could remember how his heart felt like it would pound its way out of his chest. The humid air suffocated him. By the time he stumbled back to the boat he could barely breathe. He remembered being halfway down the creek when he raked his fingers through his hair and realized the cap was gone.

Damn! He loved that cap. Tampa Bay Buccaneers. His favorite team.

As soon as he finished his morning route he drove back out and headed up the river. He needed to make sure last night actually happened. If nothing else, he'd retrieve his ball cap.

The forest was over 200,000 acres. He'd chosen this area because of its isolation. It was on the northwest edge of what was officially Blackwater River State Forest, bordering private property that was just as undeveloped. All of it was so thick and wild he never saw anyone. Even the forest creatures treated him as if he were a novelty.

And yet, someone was here!

Not just in the forest, but right at the clearing. His clearing! His sacred grounds. How was it possible that they had stumbled across this secluded area?

He had learned long ago how to be invisible, a difficult and cruel lesson for any child. Make yourself small so the other kids won't notice how different you are. Stay quiet and don't argue, so grown-ups won't point out how stupid you are. Nod. Sit back. Instructions from a mother who thought she was protecting him.

Now, being invisible was a part of his daily life. He didn't mind that most people rarely saw him even when he was in the same room with them. Being invisible was his superpower.

In a matter of seconds he backtracked then weaved around the intruders. Through the sliver of trees he could see at least two figures: a man and a woman. Was it possible they had gotten lost?

Without alerting them he managed to come back at them from the other direction. It wasn't until he was sitting ten feet up, hidden in the canopy of a tree that he noticed something else.

A dog!

It was small and hardly threatening. But dogs could smell things. Could it smell him?

His past experience with dogs had left him with a scar over his eyebrow. Dogs never treated him like he was invisible.

This one was definitely onto him, sniffing everywhere—the air, the ground, and the grass.

He tried to listen in to the conversation, but the forest was too loud. Insects were buzzing and hissing. A woodpecker drilled. While the canopy of leaves created a safe barrier for him, it made it almost impossible for him to hear everything they were saying. He plucked only a few words out of the air.

"find your way…sheriff…guide back…"

The realization rushed over him in a wave that sent a chill down his sweat-drenched back. He craned his neck to see her leave. Here, this close to the river, the swamp hardwoods were large and so tightly packed that their branches overlapped. He shimmied and glided from one treetop to another then another with only a swish and a whir.

By the time he dropped to the ground he was far enough away from the clearing that he knew the man and dog couldn't see him. With only a glance, he saw the red kerchief weaving its way through the thick woods.

The woman was about fifty feet ahead of him.

If she never left the forest, she'd never be able to bring back the sheriff. That seemed like an easy task.

He'd make her disappear…just like all the others.

Chapter 5

Brodie wiped her hands on Ryder's T-shirt. She kept it balled up in one fist then the other, sometimes stretching it between both hands. Sixteen years of being held captive had taught her how to hide her hunger, how to see in the dark, and how to sleep through pain. She had also learned how to hide her emotions and feelings. She had told Ryder that she was okay. But honestly…she wasn't okay.

Having a dead man's blood on her hands reminded her of the man she had killed. Aaron Malone wasn't much older than Brodie, and she had taken his life. That was eight months ago, and yet, sometimes it felt like it was just last week.

It didn't take much to relive it. She could conjure up the image easily. How much pressure it took to stab the scissors into his neck. How the blood spurted out. It hit her in the face as she hung on, even when he tried to buck her off of his back.

Seeing that man half buried with the back of his head bashed in…no, she wasn't okay.

She thought she was safe in the forest. It was the one place she could walk for hours and investigate and enjoy. Ryder had insisted she take one of the dogs. He had a whole kennel full of different sizes. And a couple of them had enthusiastically taken on the task of protecting her. But Brodie worried about the dogs running into snakes or bears or bobcats. All those things that Ryder had warned her about. Brodie was willing to take the risks, but she didn't want the dogs to run into wild animals. Still, wild animals were one thing.

Killers? She hadn't expected that.

This changed everything.

She shook her head and increased her pace.

That's when she heard a twig snap. It was close and off to her right. Brodie froze. She let her eyes slowly scan around her.

One of Iris Malone's punishments was to leave Brodie in the dark. Sometimes she left her for days at a time. Brodie quickly learned that her other senses came to life when she couldn't see. Suddenly, she could hear rats skittering between the walls. Mildew that she didn't notice before stung her nostrils. She tasted even the slightest bitterness of the drugs added to her food rations. She could feel the electricity of an approaching thunderstorm long before the clouds rolled in. She could sense things that others didn't notice.

And she was certain now that someone was following her.

She started walking again, pretending she suspected nothing. She continued to swing the T-shirt with her left hand as her right hand sneaked up to her utility belt. Carefully, she slid the bear spray into her palm. Without looking, she closed her fingers around the canister and flipped the safety tab to the side.

She left the path and purposely slithered between the tall, longleaf pine trees. Here, the trunks grew so close even Brodie had to weave her thin body between them. The brush grew wild and scraped noisily against her pant legs. It would slow her down, but it was also a shortcut.

Most importantly, Brodie counted on the person not following directly behind her. She expected him to continue to track to her right.

Directly to her right, Brodie remembered a wide swatch of elbow-deep shrubs that she knew to avoid. The plant was deceptively attractive with reddish stems and glossy dark, green leaves. This time of year there were even pale, yellow clusters of flowers. The shrubs grew between the pine trees so dense that if you accidentally walked into the middle of them, it was impossible to not get the oil from the leaves on your clothes. And it was worse, if the oil got on your skin. More people were allergic to poison sumac than both poison ivy and poison oak.

She heard the swish and crackle behind her, and yes, to the right. She picked up her pace, her feet skipping over fallen branches hidden in the thicket. The subtle scuffs and shuffles turned into thrashing. The person was no longer hiding, and he was coming fast.

Brodie didn't slow down to look. She ran.

She leaped over obstacles. Zigzagged between trees. In places, her shoulders scraped against bark. Twigs grabbed and whipped her in the face. Vines snagged her feet. She pushed up the incline ignoring the stitch in her side.

Now, the footsteps pounded behind her. No longer was the person bothering to sneak. Snaps and cracks grew louder and closer.

At the top of the incline, Brodie reached for then grabbed the slender trunk of a young pine tree. She lifted her feet off the ground and let the momentum spin her, allowing her to take a sharp left. As soon as she dropped to the ground it was a race downhill.

She leaned into the slide, keeping her balance and using the humidity-drenched leaves to increase her progress.

Finally, through the tops of the trees she could see the roof of the fieldhouse. It was impossible to hear anything behind her. Her heart thumped against her ribcage. Her breathing came in rapid gasps.

Feeling safe at the base of the tree line and back on Ryder's property, Brodie slowed down. She still had the bear spray canister gripped in her left hand as she pivoted around.

There was no one.

She looked up at the top of the ridge where her skid marks began. All she saw was the blur of blue fabric before it turned and disappeared into the forest.

Chapter 6

Pensacola, Florida

FBI agent Maggie O'Dell parked the rental car in front of Storage Unit B12. The place was quiet. Even the guard hut had been empty when she tapped in the code to lift the security gate. So she was surprised to see the woman leaning against a Lexus SUV parked just across the lane.

Her short hair was flame red. Maggie guessed her age at somewhere in her forties. Dressed in a T-shirt, faded jeans and Birkenstocks, she was petite, but judging from her stance—crossed arms, one foot kicked back against the bumper—Maggie knew there was nothing diminutive about the woman's self-assurance.

She lifted her chin to Maggie as a greeting but didn't move or even lift her designer sunglasses.

"You the FBI agent?"

"Yes," Maggie said as she glanced around.

She had expected Escambia County Sheriff Clayton to meet her. He was the one who had requested her presence. But Maggie hadn't seen any signs of him or his vehicle as she drove up and down the lanes that gave access to the hundreds of storage units. Maybe he sent a staff member to open up the door.

"Have you worked with Clayton before?" the woman asked.

"About three years ago. Is he on his way?"

She shook her head. "He's a bit squeamish when it comes to stuff like this."

"I'm sorry, are you from the sheriff's department?"

The woman finally pushed off the bumper.

"Medical examiner's office." She walked over and extended her hand as she slipped the sunglasses to the top of her head. "Vickie Kammerer. Call me Vickie."

"Maggie O'Dell."

"So three years ago? You probably worked with Dr. Tomich."

"Yes. How is he?"

"Retired," Vickie said as she took out a key and unlocked the padlock. She slid the bolt back then grabbed the handle at the bottom of the garage door. It groaned then squeaked as it slowly started rolling up.

"Nice guy." Vickie was still talking about Dr. Tomich and appeared oblivious to the pungent odor that immediately began leaking from the open space. "First time I met him he scared the crap out of me." Her eyes were taking in the unit's contents as far as the sunlight reached. She continued, "You know he has that crotchety, old man stare that feels like daggers."

"So you've worked with him?"

This time she looked over at Maggie as if suddenly realizing something. "No. I'm sorry, I probably wasn't clear. I replaced him."

"You're the medical examiner?" Maggie heard the slip of surprise before she could stop it.

"Yup."

The woman didn't look offended, but Maggie noticed a slight grin at the corner of her lips when she turned back to the storage unit.

"That's okay," Vickie said. "I didn't peg you for an FBI agent."

She pulled her phone out of the back pocket of her jeans and started taking photos without stepping any farther inside.

"We get together for lunch," she said.

"Excuse me?" Maggie asked.

"Dr. Tomich and I. We get together for lunch every month that has an R in it."

"An R?"

"His idea, not mine. A quirky way of saying he doesn't like to go out much during the hottest months."

Maggie noticed the whole time Vickie talked she continued to take photos. Maggie stepped in beside her and started examining the inside of the unit for the first time.

It looked like a mad scientist's closet. There were dozens of plastic specimen cups, racks with test tubes, several five-gallon buckets with lids, foam takeout containers and stacks of trash bags. Many of them had cracked or leaked, contributing to the foul odor.

And yet, in the back corner she could see a mop handle with a bucket full of cleaning supplies. Alongside stood a tall stack of paper towels, each singly wrapped. And each had a bold, black banner with the price of 59 cents that she could read all the way from the door.

"Clayton told me to wait for the FBI before I got started," Vickie said. "Why the federal interest?"

Before Maggie could answer, the medical examiner asked, "Does it have anything to do with that case three years ago?"

This time she stopped snapping photos and gave Maggie her full attention, waiting for the answer.

"How much do you know about it?" Maggie asked as she noticed one of the buckets had a label that read: TISSUE SAMPLES.

"Dr. Tomich told me some of the details. Clayton mentioned that this might be connected, so I pulled up the file. Let me see if I have this right. Three years ago, some guy who called himself Joe Black sold body parts to doctors to be used for educational purposes. Legal at the time. Not a lot of restrictions. However, there were speculations as to how bad-boy Joe acquired the body parts."

She glanced at Maggie for confirmation. Then she chin-pointed to the contents of the unit. "Flash forward to last week when a Pensacola man buys the abandoned contents of a storage unit for $900 at auction. He opens the door and immediately smells something funky. Then he finds what he thinks might be a human heart in a Tupperware container. Freaks him out. Clamps the door shut and calls the cops."

The medical examiner paused as she tucked her phone away and pulled on latex gloves. She handed a pair to Maggie and said, "I immediately thought of organ harvesting. Or at least the leftovers. Hearts are worthless unless they're transplanted in a very short time frame."

She looked over at Maggie and asked, "Isn't that what you're thinking?'

Maggie accepted the gloves and began tugging them on as she scanned the mess. There had to be dozens of disposable takeout containers. Seeing them here and suspecting what was inside them made her stomach flip.

One of Maggie's first cases involved a killer who enjoyed placing assorted parts of his victims in takeout containers and leaving them in public places. When he discovered the name of the newbie FBI agent tracking him, he started leaving pieces of victims for Maggie. Victims she knew. Actually she didn't really *know* the victims, but they had all come in contact with her. And that contact—that brief acquaintance— had made them targets.

"Actually my first thought was a serial killer," Maggie finally said.

Vickie raised her eyebrows. Maggie shrugged and added, "Occupational hazard. Serial killers are sort of my specialty."

"Sweet! Mine used to be floaters."

Maggie's turn to look surprised.

"I started my career in Minnesota. Land of 10,000 lakes. Seemed like we were constantly fishing a body out every other week."

Vickie put her hands on her hips, not in a hurry to do anything more for now.

"I got the impression that Sheriff Clayton thinks these are Joe Black's leftovers," the medical examiner said. "But you don't?" she asked.

"It's possible. But Joe was a lot neater," Maggie said pointing to a supersized soda cup. It had tipped over, spilling its contents. The blob was shriveled and unrecognizable. "He also had a fetish for cling wrap."

"And yet, you came all this way."

Maggie checked again, looking to see if the woman was offended by having her own county sheriff call in the FBI. But Vickie Kammerer appeared only curious. The medical examiner's phone started ringing. She grabbed it out of her pocket and glanced at the screen.

"My staff. I need to take this," and she headed back across the lane as she answered the phone.

Maggie took the opportunity to pull out her own phone and began snapping some shots. She took a few steps closer then zoomed in to take a shot of the only organized part of the unit—the back corner with all the cleaning supplies and the neatly stacked paper towels. She couldn't help thinking there weren't near enough paper towels to clean up this place.

Even Albert Stucky would be appalled at this mess. Stucky was the serial killer who had precisely extracted his victims' organs and neatly tucked them into takeout containers. Then he left them to be found on café tables and counters in truck stop diners.

"I gotta go," Vickie said. "Dead body in the forest. Maybe two. Sorry, I can't leave you here without someone from my office."

"Two dead bodies?"

Vickie stopped at the storage unit's padlock to glance over at Maggie. "I'd never hear the end of it from local law enforcement if I bring along an FBI agent."

"How about one who specializes in serial killers?"

Chapter 7

Baptist Hospital
Pensacola, Florida

Kayla Hudson waited in the hallway while nurses settled her son in the hospital room. They'd just brought him back from the regular barrage of tests including a CT scan to rule out anything else. Ten-year-old Luke slept through all of them, waking up only once to vomit.

There was a time when all of this would have sent Kayla over the edge of panic. That wasn't to say his seizures didn't scare her anymore. This morning when he stumbled into the kitchen she had been sitting with a cup of coffee. His blood sugar had been in perfect range when she tested him earlier that morning at one o'clock. She didn't even wake him anymore when she gently took his finger and pricked it.

Even as he reached for the cereal, he simply looked half asleep. The cereal didn't make it into the bowl. Luke collapsed. Lucky Charms went skidding across the tile. In seconds her little boy was convulsing, his jaw clenched so tight she couldn't squeeze the glucose gel past his teeth. She knew to call 911 as she raced to the drawer for the glucagon kit. Her hands still shook every time she prepared the syringe.

Kayla had confessed to her sister that she worried she'd never get good at this. Her sister simply told her that she didn't need to get good at it. It wasn't a skill that she needed to master. She just needed to do it. Kayla knew her sister was right. Panic only made the situation worse. Luke needed her to react quickly and do what was necessary.

She still remembered his first seizure. Remembered exactly how it felt, like someone had ripped into her chest and grabbed her heart in a fist. The fear paralyzed her so completely she couldn't breathe, let alone move. If Kayla's sister hadn't been there…

She didn't want to think about it. She couldn't think about it, or all she'd do was beat herself up. Or remember how much she missed her big sister. And none of that helped Luke right now.

She made sure her cell phone was still on vibrate before she checked her messages, though there was no one she expected to hear from. No one she could call.

Stop it! She told herself. *You're starting to feel sorry for yourself, and this isn't about you. It's about Luke.*

But the truth was she missed having someone take care of her. At least worry about her. Was that so wrong?

Luke's father had been serving in Afghanistan when Kayla first learned why their sweet, affectionate Luke had suddenly become belligerent and moody. How did she *not* notice that he was always so thirsty, or that he was getting up three or four times a night to go to the bathroom? It was the weight loss that freaked her out. Shopping for school clothes, she realized his usual size was too big when she was expecting him to need a size larger.

How could she not know that her child had type 1 diabetes?

Her sister helped her through it. She went with Kayla and Luke to the doctor. Came over every day that first week to help with the insulin shot. She was there for his first seizure.

And Eric? He was 8,000 miles away, wishing he could be home. Always ending their video chats or phone calls with that exact phrase, "Wish I could be home with you guys."

But then, when he finally came home for good last February, he couldn't handle it. He couldn't give his own son an insulin shot. Couldn't prick Luke's finger or remember to bring Skittles. He said the grocery store was too crowded, too loud, so he couldn't even deal with that one simple chore. Eventually, just picking Luke up from school became a problem for one reason or another.

One by one, everyday tasks were removed from Eric's list of what he could do, and what he couldn't do. The tough, brave soldier couldn't handle or remember a lot of things, at least not without the drugs. And then he couldn't handle anything at all because of the drugs.

No, Kayla didn't understand PTSD. How could she be expected to take on one more thing? Her sister had just passed away before Christmas, and it felt like something had ripped inside of her. But she'd looked forward to having her husband back. She looked forward to having a partner to relieve some of the daily stress.

Instead, what she got was an addict who didn't leave the couch except to go play cards with his veteran buddies. And without her sister to lean on, Kayla felt more alone than she had when Eric was in Afghanistan.

Maybe it wasn't his fault. When he first came home, he tried. His contribution? One of his veteran buddies had offered a dog for Luke.

A dog!

Like she didn't have enough bodies to take care of. Eric made it sound as if the dog would be able to help with Luke. Like it would relieve them in some way.

She had never heard of such a thing, but even after she read up on it, she still didn't believe it. She dealt with the day-to-day realities of Luke's diabetes. Eric didn't deal with it at all.

But Eric had agreed to take this dog without telling her. Agreed to it back in February then completely forgot about it when his addiction took over his life, and he no longer ventured out of the house. In fact, the only way Kayla knew about Eric's agreement, was a phone call updating her about the dog's progress, and that she'd be ready in the fall just as planned. Luke overheard, and father and son were so excited, how could she say no?

In a surprising turn, it had spurred Eric on. Last week he'd finally agreed to check into a rehab center. He found a doctor he trusted and a facility that was only thirty minutes away.

She should have been happy her husband wanted to get better. And she was. Yet, she couldn't help wondering if Eric would be any help taking care of the dog.

Still, Kayla thought she'd be sad leaving him at the facility. Sad that he'd be locked away in some stark and sterile rehab center. But the place was nothing like she expected. It was immaculate with sunny rooms, manicured grounds, a restaurant-style cafeteria and a solarium looking out over a huge swimming pool. Instead of feeling sad, Kayla caught herself feeling jealous. Here Eric was copping out by getting addicted to drugs, and what does he get? Something that looked like a vacation at a five-star resort.

Kayla? Back to being mom and medic 24/7. Back to being alone.

"Mrs. Hudson?"

Kayla startled at the nurse's voice.

"Luke is awake. He's having a snack. I can stay with him if you'd like to go get a cup of coffee or something to eat. I know you must be exhausted."

Kayla glanced at the nurse's name badge while thinking the woman was probably Kayla's age, late twenties, early thirties. But that's where the comparison ended. The nurse had an air of confidence, was tall, pretty and blond with a figure men would notice even under her scrubs. All of that was the exact opposite of Kayla.

"Thanks Taylor." Kayla turned to look down the hallway. "Are you sure they'll let you do that?"

"We're pretty quiet today."

"Downstairs was crazy busy," Kayla told her as she walked to Luke's doorway and found herself crossing her arms over her bulging mid-section as she walked by Taylor. She knew they'd want to keep Luke for a while and check for slurred speech or incoherence. The seizures were physically exhausting for him though he didn't remember them.

Her sister always insisted that was a blessing, the fact that Luke couldn't remember why his body ached afterwards. Kayla thought it was ridiculous to think any of this could be considered a blessing. But that was her big sister, always looking on the bright side.

Now without her, Kayla struggled to find those imaginary blessings or bright sides. How could she, when her husband had decided to checkout on them? How could she, when she couldn't stop her little boy from collapsing right in front of her, no matter how many precautions she took?

She glanced inside the room. Luke was sitting up watching the television up in the corner and sucking on a straw.

"Hey Luke. How're you doing?"

He smiled around the straw while he raised the glass a little. He took two seconds to say, "chocolate shake," then continued to suck it down as if he thought it was the best milk shake he'd ever tasted.

"I'm going get a snack for myself. Be right back, okay?"

He nodded, and his eyes darted back to the television. She should have felt comforted that he adjusted to these emergency hospital visits so well. Instead, she hated that they were becoming a regular part of their lives. More and more it was difficult to remember what their lives were like before the diabetes.

Kayla thanked Taylor, and she tried to not hate the woman because she was pretty and fit. Kayla knew she wouldn't be overweight if she had some time for herself. She headed for the elevators. When she was safely inside and all alone, she leaned her head against the wall and allowed a sigh of relief.

Things would get better. She could do this. She could be strong.

Those were her sister's words, not Kayla's. Her sister who believed in blessings and mantras. None of which saved her from the cancer.

The elevator dinged and the doors opened to another bright sterile hallway. Kayla wandered out. The early morning adrenaline rush was gone, leaving in its place a mind-numbing fatigue. She ran her fingers through her tangled, shoulder-length hair and tried to remember if she'd even brushed it before Luke's seizure.

Things would get better. She could do this. She could be strong.

Who was she kidding? Even she didn't believe that bullshit anymore.

Chapter 8

Baptist Hospital
Pensacola, Florida

Taylor Donahey was relieved the mother agreed to leave. It gave Taylor an excuse to stay away from the other nurses. Her second week on the job was not going so well. She was a trauma and surgical nurse with a tour of duty in Afghanistan under her belt. Her last assignment had been in an ER back in Virginia. Fresh trauma was her specialty. And where did they put her?

On the pediatric floor!

Maybe it was preparation for getting her son back. A lesson on being around kids, because she definitely didn't specialize in kids. Or perhaps it was punishment for deserting him all those years ago.

This wasn't punishment though. She liked Luke Hudson. He reminded her of William, though Luke was four years older. His grandparents were calling him Willie.

She winced at the nickname. Was there any going back? Maybe she no longer had a right to how he was addressed.

"I'm getting a dog," Luke told her out of the blue.

From his chart, Taylor knew he'd crashed early this morning. Juvenile diabetes. He'd arrived by ambulance and had gone through a barrage of tests. And yet here he was, cheerful and optimistic. She'd forgotten how innocent and genuine children could be. How resilient. Could she really expect to drop back into her son's life? She knew so little about him. How could she ever be a good mother to him?

"Boy or girl dog?" she asked, thankful for the diversion.

"Girl. She's a black Lab-ra-dor retriever."

He said Labrador slowly, pronouncing each syllable carefully so the word sounded like three instead of one. It was obviously something he was still getting used to.

"Do you have a name for her?"

"She already has a name. I'll find out when I meet her. But I don't get to meet her until this fall. She's not even two years old yet. She's twenty-two months old."

Taylor checked his monitors and cleared his tray. They had sent up instructions that included watching for slurred speech, so this conversation was helpful.

"Do you have a picture of her?" she asked to keep him talking.

He shook his head. "No, they don't let you have pictures before you meet. I have to pass some tests before she gets to be mine. My dad says I have to show that I can take care of her. I have to spend a whole week at her training facility working with her. If I do a good job, then she gets to come home with me. She's gonna help me with my diabetes. I can hardly wait!"

"Oh, so she's a medical alert dog?"

"Yup. That's right. She's still in training."

"I've read about those dogs," she said. "They're very smart."

"My dad said she'll even get to go to school with me."

"I bet your mom's looking forward to having a dog help you."

And that's when his smile slid completely off his face. He crinkled his brow, and he shook his head.

"I don't think my mom likes dogs. She said they're messy and they shed a lot."

"Oh, well…" Taylor was caught off guard. "I bet when she sees how smart the dog is she'll change her mind. Sounds like your dad thinks it's a good idea."

His expression stayed serious. It didn't matter what his dad thought. He didn't need to say it. His face made that clear. Sometimes she hated how transparent little kids were.

Change the subject, Taylor.

What did she know about little boys? Hell, was there anything she knew about kids?

It wasn't that long ago she was helping piece them together. Young men. Boys really. Eighteen, nineteen years old. Convoys or helicopters brought them in with arms blown off or half their faces missing. Shrapnel—nails, bolts, and twisted wire—in their guts.

Sometimes her nightmares took her back inside the mobile units that pretended to be surgical wards. She'd spend an entire night trying to stop the bleeding. She'd toss and turn while she searched for their missing pieces. Patching up one boy only to be replaced with another.

Their eyes were always the same…always pleading.

After a while even the vodka didn't help. The only thing that seemed to help was putting on a pair of running shoes and hitting the pavement.

Running.

She was forever running away from her nightmares, away from her problems, away from her obligations.

"My dad had to go away for a while," Luke's voice startled her back to the present. "Just so he can get better. Not like when he went to Afghanistan."

"Your dad was in Afghanistan? Army?"

He nodded and sat up. Proud. A much better subject for him.

"I was in Afghanistan," she told him.

Luke gave her a suspicious look. "Really?"

"Yup. As an Army nurse."

"Wow!"

And suddenly he had all kinds of questions for her, while Taylor wished they had kept talking about dogs.

Chapter 9

Blackwater River State Forest

Anger fueled his hike back through the woods. A couple of times he had to stop and get his bearings. The woman had steered him off course. He thought for sure she had panicked and had started running headlong with no idea where she was going. He thought she'd get lost. Turned out she knew exactly where she was going. And she had dragged him through an area he wasn't familiar with.

But now he knew where she had come from.

As he slid the boat into his usual hiding place he wondered if the woman had realized her mistake. He trudged the rest of the way to his pickup and felt the tension in his shoulders ease just a little. He was still in a pickle.

His mother's phrase. He didn't have any idea what it meant, but he knew exactly how it felt.

Sometime later today, his sacred grounds would be crawling with law enforcement officers. They'd find what was left. Maybe even start digging to see if there was anything else. He needed to think. He needed a plan.

When his cell phone rang it made him jump. He yanked it out of his pocket bringing with it twigs and leaves. His shirt and pants were covered in forest debris, and he swept it off. He brushed more off the back of his neck and plucked it out of his hair.

Ordinarily, he'd let it go to voicemail, but he recognized the number and knew better.

"I'm a little busy," he said in place of a greeting.

"Udie, my man, you sound like you're in the middle of the woods."

The guy was always cheerful, always on. Most people would recognize it as being fake, but this guy was so full of charisma and confidence, you found yourself hoping some of it would rub off. The man was older, accomplished, knew things and had everything Udie could only wish for. Somehow the guy had found out that Udall was his middle name and began calling him Udie. He managed to take the embarrassing family label his mother had shackled him with and turn it into a fun, cool nickname.

"Actually, yeah, I'm out in the woods."

"You're in luck, my friend. Turns out this could be a double for you this week."

"A double? No. Wait."

"This one's back to the usual. Nothing special. I should have him ready to go by the end of the week."

"Yesterday's was a little too special. It wasn't a simple drop-off. You left him unfinished." Udie let the anger drive his confidence. He had to, because otherwise, he'd never be able to confront this guy. He liked the man, respected him, and wanted him to like him. But all hell was about to break loose.

"Hold on, Udie." The singsong tone had an edge. "What's going on? What do you mean he was unfinished?"

"The guy wasn't dead."

"What?"

"He was only mostly dead."

"What the hell are you talking about?"

Udie leaned against his pickup. He'd never heard the guy upset. He was always cool and calm, and now he was mad at Udie. He regretted telling him.

"Where is he now?"

"I took care of it." He didn't want the guy to worry. He wanted to be his partner. He needed him to know he could count on him.

"You took care of it?"

"Yup. No worries." Udie had heard the guy use that phrase before, and he hoped it would calm him.

"You took care of it," he repeated. Not a question.

"That's right."

Silence.

"I guess I owe you one."

Udie wouldn't tell him about the man and the woman and the dog. About the cops. How could he? That would ruin everything. No more drop-offs. No more connections. Somehow, he'd need to take care of it. All of it.

And his sudden confidence propelled him to add, "Yup, you do owe me. Double."

"Thanks, Udie."

He wiped the sweat from his forehead, grabbed the new ball cap from the seat of his pickup and pulled it on. The guy had never thanked him before, and Udie smiled. Maybe he would end up teaching this guy a thing or two instead of the other way around.

Just when he thought he had a handle on things, the guy said, "I'll give you a call when to pick up the next one later this week."

Chapter 10

K9 CrimeScents
Florida Panhandle

Brodie wished she hadn't upset Hannah. Although the woman usually appeared calm, Brodie knew her level of worry and stress by how many "Lord have mercies" she used.

By the time she reached the house, Brodie had caught her breath, but she was still clutching the bear spray in her fist when she came in the back door and into the kitchen. Hannah took one look at her and her eyes went wide.

"Lord have mercy, what happened?"

She tossed the baking sheet onto the top of the stove with such urgency that one of the biscuits, fresh out of the oven, slid off and hit the floor. Hannah grabbed it before the two dogs at her feet snatched it up.

"I'm okay," Brodie told her, realizing that Hannah must have noticed the canister squeezed between her fingers.

But that wasn't what had gotten her attention. Hannah didn't even notice it. Instead, she started opening drawers, gathering items and pointing for Brodie to come in and sit down on one of the stools by the counter.

"You didn't need to rush," Hannah told her as she plucked twigs and leaves from Brodie's short hair. Then she ripped open a package of cotton balls and removed the cap from a bottle of alcohol. "That man's gonna still be dead whether you ran or walked."

Hannah dabbed one of the cotton balls with alcohol and started gently wiping Brodie's cheek. Only then did Brodie notice the rips in her shirtsleeves. Ryder always insisted she wear a loose cotton shirt over her T-shirt whenever she went into the forest, no matter how hot and humid it was. Long cargo pants. No shorts. Hiking boots and socks. Even with all those precautions, she saw that her shirt didn't just get caught and ripped, so did her arms. In some places the scrapes were deep enough to bleed.

"There was someone in the forest," Brodie told her.

"I know, Sweet Pea. Rye texted me."

"No, I mean someone followed me."

Hannah's fingers stopped. She tilted her head to look directly into Brodie's eyes.

"Did you get a look at who it was?"

Brodie shook her head. "A flash of blue is all. He was trying to sneak at first. When I started running. He did, too. He was pretty fast."

"Oh my good Lord."

"He chased me all the way to the edge of the ridge. You can see the roofs of some of our buildings from up there. I think that's what stopped him."

Hannah caressed Brodie's face, but the lines in her forehead didn't relax.

"A good thing you're faster," she said then grabbed her cell phone off the counter. "I better warn Rye."

"Do you think the person who chased me killed that man?"

"I don't know, Sweet Pea."

But Brodie thought Hannah's eyes believed it was.

Now as they waited for the sheriff and medical examiner, Brodie watched Hannah make lunch as if they were expecting invited guests. Ryder had explained to Brodie when she first arrived about Hannah and how she believed food was therapy; even medicine. She administered it sometimes with wise advice. Ryder said that both the food and the advice came from the heart, and that Hannah had nourished dozens who had found their way to her kitchen whether they were lost, on the run, or injured. It was one of the things Brodie understood, took comfort in and had come to rely on.

"Will Ryder be okay?"

Hannah's eyes flickered to the cell phone next to the jar of mayonnaise. Her fingers never stopped spreading and layering.

"He knows how to take care of himself," Hannah said, "But I'd feel better if he told me he was okay."

Then she glanced up at Brodie and added, "Probably poor cell reception inside the forest."

Brodie nodded in agreement while thinking this was just another reason to not carry a cell phone. Everyone wanted to her to have one. She was convinced the mobile device provided a false sense of security. It certainly wouldn't have saved her earlier. Still, she was fascinated by the dependency and hypnotic effect it had on people.

She did agree there were some advantages, just as Hannah's phone buzzed.

"Sheriff Norwich is here," Hannah said. "Looks like the medical examiner is right behind her."

With only a glance and a tap of the phone's screen Hannah could see anyone who turned into their long driveway. Brodie knew it was something called an app that Ryder had set to buzz when the security cameras sensed motion.

Ryder had cameras all over the property. He showed her how easy it was to look in on the dogs out in their yard or inside the kennel. He could see them on any of the monitors inside the buildings or by pulling up the app and seeing on his cell phone's screen. The cameras were under the eaves, on fences and even in the trees.

All the security was in case of bears or bobcats, he'd told her. But Jason slipped once and admitted the cameras were meant to warn them of any human intruders as well.

She didn't understand why they were so careful about telling her this. It actually made her feel better. Brodie still worried that one day Iris Malone would find her and drag her away, again. Or pay someone else to do it.

Of course, she never told Ryder or Hannah or even Jason about these hidden fears. They'd just worry more, and that was the last thing Brodie wanted them to do.

She helped Hannah pack the sandwiches and bottles of water. They were almost finished when Sheriff Norwich knocked on the back door.

"Come on in," Hannah called out as her hands continued working.

Brodie immediately felt her insides tense. She still wasn't comfortable meeting people for the first time.

The stocky gray-haired sheriff came in and held the door for someone.

"Hey, Hannah. Have you met Dr. Kammerer?" Sheriff Norwich asked.

A petite woman with red hair came in, followed by yet another woman. But this one, Brodie knew.

"Maggie!" she said before Hannah could answer the sheriff.

"Good Lord, girl! What are you doing here? We didn't expect you until this evening." Hannah rushed over to hug Maggie.

"Hannah, Brodie, it's so good to see you again."

"Oh, isn't this special," the medical examiner said. "You all know each other. And here I was worried about bringing a fed to the party."

"Good to meet you, Dr. Kammerer." Hannah smiled at her as she gestured toward Brodie and added, "This is Brodie Creed. She's going to guide you all to the scene."

Then Hannah turned to Sheriff Norwich, and her face went serious. "Someone chased Brodie on the way back."

"Did you get a look at him?"

Brodie liked the sheriff's eyes. They were almost the same gray as her hair, but warm and gentle. Not at all what she'd expect from the color.

"No, ma'am. Just a blur of something blue. He was very fast."

The woman nodded as if she understood exactly what it felt like to be chased through the woods.

To Hannah, she said, "A couple of my deputies are about an hour out. I don't want to wait for them. I can give them GPS coordinates, but I'm not sure that'll make it easier for them. Is there any way we can guide them to the site without sending Brodie back?"

"Sure we can," Dr. Kammerer said.

She already had a backpack on and slipped it off. Brodie liked the medical examiner's voice, rich and full of confidence and certainty even as she made them all wait while she unzipped and sifted through the contents. Brodie recognized trowels sticking out of one overstuffed pocket.

"We'll blaze a trail," the medical examiner said, pulling out and showing them a can of fluorescent spray paint.

Chapter 11

Blackwater River State Forest

Ryder Creed had already planted five surveyor flags, and Grace still wasn't finished. The bright orange stood out against the green and brown like flowers that didn't really belong this deep in the forest.

Other than the skull, they'd found another body on the far edge of the clearing. Even if Grace hadn't pointed this one out, Creed would have followed the swarm of flies. This one wasn't even buried. He was on his back as if staring up at the sky. Staring up at the sky before the maggots took over.

Creed wondered if the killer purposely left his victims out in the open so the forest's scavengers would have easy access. Was he counting on nature to clean up his mess?

Grace had also led him about twenty feet into the forest. At first glance, Creed thought it looked like someone had left a pile of old, dirty clothes then covered it with branches and debris. Rain and animals had poked and pulled enough for him to recognize canvas pants. There was no shape to the fabric, and the clothes had sunk partially into the ground. Judging by the slight depression Creed guessed the owner's remains were probably still inside or what was left.

Creed had noticed that was something killers didn't seem to realize. Some were very careful to not leave a mound of dirt, thinking it would be an obvious telltale that a grave was underneath. Most didn't account for the body's decomposition. Investigators rarely looked for mounds of dirt. Instead, they searched for concaves in the landscape, places where the grass didn't grow as tall or maybe didn't grow at all.

He knew more about killers and victims than he cared to know. Being a K9 handler wasn't just about taking care of the dog. Creed had learned about decomposition and bones. How long a body lasted on top of the ground was different than underground. Water played an entirely separate role if a victim ended up in the river or at the bottom of a lake. That was another thing people got wrong. A dead body didn't automatically float to the surface.

When Creed taught new handlers, he emphasized that the dog didn't do all the work. It was a team effort, which could be tricky. The handler was an extension, not a guide that gave instructions. In fact, Creed usually asked for very little information from investigators. Knowing too much could result in the handler throwing off the search, especially if the dog wasn't following the already established evidence or preconceived notions.

But the one thing Creed drilled into his handlers was that their main priority was to watch out for and protect their dog. That meant foreseeing obstacles or threats. Floodwaters hid all kinds of debris traps. So did the floor and the trees of a forest. Snakes, spiders, bears, alligators could surprise a scent dog that was focused on and working the scent she was asked to find.

Sometimes the dog became so focused she pushed herself beyond physical limits. A handler needed to know how to rest the dog, cool her off, protect her paws, and even rehydrate her if necessary; all of that without getting in the way of continuing the job.

But handlers also needed to know which way the wind was blowing, how the humidity could push down a scent, which direction a missing person with dementia would instinctively go.

Of course, nothing taught better lessons than experience. Creed had lost track of how many searches and recoveries he'd done over the last seven years. He'd started the business in search of Brodie, hoping he'd someday find her remains. Never in his wildest dreams had he expected to bring her home alive.

He was so grateful to have her in his life again. But he realized he'd replaced relief with a new concern, a new responsibility. He wanted to protect her. Keep her safe. Make sure she was okay. He wanted to make sure the PTSD wouldn't destroy her chance for happiness; that her nightmares wouldn't prevent her from having a regular life. It was a struggle for him to do that and not smother her. He didn't want her to feel like a butterfly captured in a jar.

At the thought of Brodie, Creed pulled out his cell phone. She should have made it back by now, but there were no messages from Hannah. He had wandered out of range.

"Grace."

Immediately he heard a rustling in the shrubs.

"Come on, girl. Time for a break."

As they treaded back to the clearing his cell phone started pinging. Text messages came in, one after another. All of them from Hannah. They came in rapid succession as if to match the urgency of her words.

SOMEONE FOLLOWED BRODIE.

CHASED HER.

SHE'S OKAY.

BE CAREFUL.

His eyes darted through the trees. How did he miss someone watching them?

Grace had tried to get his attention, nudging his arm when he found the skull. But she was used to other people being around the search sites.

Now, he kept her in his peripheral vision as he continued to scan the surroundings. He pulled out her collapsible water bowl and filled it for her then drank the rest of the bottle as he listened.

Birds chirped. Mosquitoes buzzed. The breeze rustled leaves. He didn't hear anything that didn't belong. Except for the steady drone of flies.

Creed glanced down as a couple more messages came in from Hannah.

SHERIFF NORWICH JUST ARRIVED.

M.E. IS HERE, TOO.

I'LL LET YOU KNOW WHEN THEY HEAD BACK IN.

He brushed his hand over his bristled jaw trying to relax it. He could take care of himself and Grace. But Brodie…he should never have sent her back by herself.

Chapter 12

Blackwater River State Forest

Maggie O'Dell was grateful she'd packed hiking gear. Even in the middle of June she'd learned from past experience that trips to the Florida Panhandle or Alabama could mean unexpected adventure. She rubbed her arm. The ache had finally receded, but the memory was still fresh. In March, just outside of Montgomery, Alabama, she'd gotten trapped in the basement of a meat and three when a tornado plowed through the restaurant.

A fellow FBI agent, Antonio Alonzo had given her a framed drone shot of the wreckage. He had presented it to her as if it was now supposed to be a symbol of inspiration or a trophy of survival. She'd put it up in her basement office at Quantico. But every time she looked at it, all she could feel was the suffocating claustrophobia, the debris raining down and the electrical charge that was still so strong she could taste it.

Right now, she told herself that she should be pleased to be outside in the open air despite the humidity. But the truth was, this forest brought a whole other set of memories.

Several years ago a madman's scheme had brought Maggie and her FBI partner, R.J. Tully to Blackwater River State Park in search of his buried victims. But it was only a trick. There were no bodies. What he really wanted was to hunt Maggie down and bury her deep in the woods.

Ironically, that case was the first time she and Ryder Creed had worked together. Maggie didn't dwell in nostalgia. She wasn't superstitious either. But she was having an overwhelming sense of déjà vu right now, and she didn't like it. Maybe it wasn't a bad thing. It put her senses on high alert.

"Brodie, are you certain there's not an easier path?" Sheriff Norwich asked, her breathing labored.

Only ten minutes into their hike, and Maggie saw the sheriff's chin-length hair was already wet and sticking to her neck. The branches had snagged and tilted the woman's ball cap enough times for Maggie to pull her own down tighter onto her head.

"The shorter path is steeper," Brodie explained. "This one at least has these animal paths."

Maggie glanced back at Vickie, who was bringing up the rear, spray can in hand. For a second they exchanged the same unspoken thought, *what paths?* There wasn't a section yet that didn't require high-stepping brush and dodging low-hanging branches.

One thing Maggie was sure of, Brodie knew this trail well and was forcing herself to slow down. Their pace, especially Sheriff Norwich's, was holding the young woman back. Several times Brodie had skimmed over the shrubs and glided between the trees, getting ahead of them so far, she needed to stop and backtrack, or wait in place. It was easy to see the forest was second nature to Brodie, but she was uncomfortable in her role as guide.

It was if Brodie didn't realize that her knowledge of their surroundings wasn't common sense for the rest of them. Halfway through, she started pointing out things, matter-of-factly: a snake camouflaged on a tree's bark; a tangle of shrubs with sharp thorns; an area of poison ivy and a huge spider's web.

"Don't break the spider web," Brodie insisted. "Duck under it if you can. They catch mosquitoes and yellow flies."

Maggie tugged at the bandana on her neck, realizing she hadn't felt a single bite. When Hannah handed them out to each of them, the fabric was still damp with the magic concoction she had created to repel biting bugs. Unfortunately, Maggie knew all too well, it couldn't prevent snake or scorpion bites or even fire ants. Taking a hike in a Florida forest was definitely different than her regular jogs through the woods in Virginia.

The canopy above created more shadow than allowed light. Maggie tucked her sunglasses into her shirt pocket. The bandana wasn't the only thing damp. Her T-shirt stuck to her skin, and her holster harness started to feel like a straitjacket. The humidity was so thick it made it difficult to breathe, and she was in good shape. Maggie worried about Sheriff Norwich. The woman was stocky and perhaps in her late fifties, maybe sixty. The forest was alive with the sounds of birds and frogs and yet, Maggie could hear Norwich's raspy breathing from three feet behind.

By contrast, every time she glanced back at Vickie, the medical examiner looked unfazed even with the loaded backpack. Once when they stopped for a water break, Vickie joked that she had gotten used to the fact that she couldn't just drive up to a crime scene. Although they all agreed that this killer had gone above and beyond most others.

In fact, Maggie had dealt with all kinds of places killers dumped their victims. From one who displayed his victims on DC's monuments in full view of tourists to another who encased them in fifty-gallon drums then hid them in an abandoned rock quarry.

As a criminal profiler she was supposed to take as much information as she could gather and come up with a mental and physical profile of the killer. But the farther they walked and the thicker the forest became, she realized it didn't take an expert to know one thing for certain.

Without seeing the crime scene or examining a single victim, Maggie knew if the man who chased Brodie was the killer, he definitely wouldn't be happy to see a parade of investigators invade his burial grounds. Question was: what was he willing to do to stop them?

Chapter 13

The more Creed discovered, the more he wished Brodie wasn't coming back with the investigators. Maybe he could figure out a way to send her back without looking dismissive or overprotective. There was enough here to challenge a seasoned law enforcement officer, let alone, someone who had never experienced a crime scene.

Grace kept alerting. She hadn't stopped since Brodie left.

Creed was beginning to think this place looked like a scene from the Body Farm. The original project at the University of Tennessee took donors' bodies and deposited them out in open fields, sometimes in the trunks of cars or submerged them under water. It allowed forensic students to examine corpses at various stages of decay. It supplied criminal investigators with data they'd only been able to piece together in the past.

From what Creed could tell, this killer might have been dumping bodies here for years. Creed didn't have a law enforcement background, but he'd witnessed the different stages of decomposition. He had seen how maggots could devour a victim's identity. And he knew that wildlife could leave experts wondering whether the killer had disarticulated a body or animals had helped themselves to parts.

The skull Grace had found down in the hollow space below the tree roots, looked like it had no tissue or hair left. Creed knew that hair was one of the last things that stayed attached, although it was also one of the things wildlife scavenged for nests and dens. From what he had seen, the skullcap was all that was left. Which could mean the body had been dumped here years ago.

The killer had obviously taken drastic measures to transport his victims deep into the forest. He wanted them hidden, and yet, Creed was surprised by the malicious disregard in the way he'd left them. Granted it was difficult to dig a hole in the middle of a forest with tree roots trailing everywhere. But even in the clearing where it would have been easier to dig, the bodies were barely covered or left in the grass.

Creed knew how isolated this area was. There were no hiking trails. He was pretty sure it wasn't detailed on any maps of the forest. He practically lived next door and had never ventured this far into these woods.

Creed stood back, exhausted. He needed Grace to stop again. He called for her to join him in the shade. Reluctantly she came, her front paws shifting and waiting for permission to resume. The scents were overwhelming, and she wanted to keep working. She was impatient with his enforced limitations. But they were approaching the peak of the day, and his main concern now was keeping her hydrated and her body temp down. Even in the shade it was impossible to escape the heat. The humidity kept it stuck to his body. There wasn't a hint of a breeze.

He checked the ground around them for fire ants. He brushed his fingers through the dried leaves and pine needles, scattering the tiny frogs hidden underneath. Then he gestured for Grace to sit while he pulled out her collapsible bowl, along with a bottle of water. Again, he filled the bowl and put it down for her as he drank the remaining half.

He scanned the surroundings, continuing to search for the watcher. His eyes stopped and settled on the body Brodie had stumbled over. The flies were unrelenting, newcomers descending, crawling and disappearing into the victim's hair or between the folds of clothing. Other flies were already busy laying their eggs.

Burying a corpse under a pile of debris or deep in the ground delayed decomposition. Leaving it out in the open, or partially exposed, allowed the elements of nature to eliminate, devour, disassemble and scatter it. Until there was nothing left. The insects, birds and wildlife were all willing accomplices. Creed was certain it was exactly what the killer intended.

He pulled his phone from his pocket. No matter how excited and capable Grace was, the heat and the amount of remains would require another dog.

To Hannah, he texted:

I'M GONNA NEED JASON AND SCOUT.

He barely pressed send and his phone pinged with an incoming message. Grace's ears pitched forward, and she looked over her shoulder. She heard something other than the phone. Creed thought he heard it, too.

Two more pings.

The messages must have gotten delayed from the on-again, off-again reception. Either his message or his movement had triggered them. Now in the clearing they were coming all at once.

That's when he heard and recognized Brodie's voice. Grace stood and turned in the direction, tail wagging, but she stayed next to Creed.

He could see flashes of red, bobbing between the trees. Hannah's red kerchiefs. He glanced down at her messages.

THEY'RE ON THEIR WAY.
THE M.E. BROUGHT SOMEONE WITH HER.
I SENT SANDWICHES AND MORE WATER.

That was Hannah, making sure they were all fed.

JASON AND SCOUT WILL COME LATER
AND LEAD THE DEPUTIES.

Creed was still smiling about Hannah packing lunch for everyone, when he looked up and saw just who Dr. Kammerer had brought along.

Chapter 14

"Maggie, how in the world did you get roped into this?" Creed asked as he shook the other investigators' hands before giving Maggie a hug. "I didn't expect to see you until dinner," he said quietly, close to her ear. Close enough that his lips brushed against her skin.

If she was embarrassed by his display of affection, she didn't show it. She hugged him back then smiled at him when he pulled away. He held her at arms length to get a good look at her.

"Seemed like a good day for a hike," she said, mopping her face with the sleeve of her shirt. Then she kneeled down to say hello to an impatient Grace.

"It's never a good day for a hike in the middle of June," Sheriff Norwich said.

"Actually, it's my fault. I brought her to the party," Dr. Kammerer said. "That was before I realized the crime scene was literary in the middle of the forest. But I have to admit, it doesn't smell as bad as I expected."

Creed kept his eyes on the sheriff. She was red-faced and breathing heavy even as she guzzled water. He pulled out an instant cold pack from his emergency gear. Punched the bag in the center then shook it. He wrapped it in a cloth and handed it to her.

"Hold this in the palm of your hand," he told her. "Or put it against your cheek."

Creed looked for signs of heatstroke. Her shirt was drenched with sweat. That was a good sign. Perspiration helped cool the body. Dogs didn't have that mechanism. When Norwich still didn't take the pack, he added, "You can fold it over the back of your neck. Just for a few minutes."

She continued to stare at it for another second or two, but as soon as her fingers touched it, her eyes lit up.

"You are a lifesaver," she told him, shoving it under her collar.

He hoped it was soon enough. Heatstroke could hit quickly in dogs. He didn't have as much experience with people.

"So give me a rundown, Mr. Creed," Dr. Kammerer said. She was examining the site, hands on her hips and turning in place.

"Call me Ryder."

"Fair enough. Then call me Vickie." She waved her hand over the area. "I'm seeing lots of flags. Your girl was busy."

"Her name's Grace."

At the mention of her name, the little dog understood the medical examiner was talking about her, and she pranced in place. When Vickie offered her hand, Creed gestured to Grace that it was okay to go to her.

"Aren't you a good girl," the woman squatted down to Grace's level and scratched behind the dog's ears, even as she glanced up at Creed for an answer.

He'd worked with Sheriff Norwich, but this was his first time with the medical examiner. She was new to Florida's District 1, but Creed had heard good things about her. Before he responded, he looked over at

Brodie searching for some signal, a hint of how she was dealing with all of this. He stopped himself from wincing at the sight of the new scratches on her face. As far as he could tell, she seemed anxious to hear about Grace's findings, too.

"Two bodies." He nodded in one direction then the other. "There appear to be other remains in various stages of decomp."

The flags could be seen not just in the clearing, but between the trees inside the woods. Their bright orange stood out, but what they marked remained hidden.

"Grace alerts to decomp?"

"Actually any human remains."

"Bones?"

"Yes," Creed answered.

"Recent as well as old?"

"She wasn't specifically trained for old, but she found a skull down in a hollow underneath some tree roots." He pointed back over his shoulder.

"Impressive," the medical examiner said.

"It's still going to be too much for her in this heat. I called in another dog and handler."

Creed watched her eyes, looking for resistance. He'd worked with medical examiners and coroners who were happy to have a dog locate a body but then wanted the rest to be left for the crime scene techs.

There was something that flashed in Vickie's eyes as they darted away from his. Creed didn't think it was resistance. Instead, she looked like she was only now realizing the magnitude of what they might find.

Finally her eyes returned, and she said, "How many victims do you think are here?"

"I can't tell you that," Creed said. "But one thing is certain. Grace isn't close to being finished."

Chapter 15

Pensacola, Florida

Kayla Hudson barely got Luke home from the hospital, and her phone started ringing. It was a number she didn't recognize. Immediately, her mind went to the negative. Did one of Luke's tests show something else?

"Hello?" she answered.

"Kayla, I'm glad I got a hold of you."

It was Eric, but he was whispering. She could hardly hear him.

"Eric, I thought you had to schedule phone calls."

In all honestly, she hadn't really listened to the rules. She figured it was about time he took responsibility for remembering what the hell he needed to do. After all, she wasn't going to be there to make sure he followed all the things they asked of him.

"They don't know I have a phone." Still a whisper. "I borrowed it. Listen, you have to get me out of here."

This, she did remember. They warned her that he might be asking, maybe begging for her to pick him up.

"That's against the rules, Eric. You did agree to do this on your own. In fact, you chose this place."

"I know, I know. But something's not right."

She rolled her eyes and stopped herself from saying anything.

"Remember the guy that was here with me? My roommate, Simon?"

She remembered that he had a roommate. She didn't remember his name. The guy who wore black-rimmed glasses that he constantly shoved up the bridge of his nose. He stared at her the whole time she was there and never said a word even after introductions. The guy was definitely not right. Kayla chalked it up to the drugs or the withdrawal. Supposedly, he was a veteran, too, but to Kayla, he looked like some loser who probably still lived in his parents' basement.

Eric had gone silent, and she pulled her cell phone away from her ear to see if she'd lost the connection.

"Sorry, someone walked by."

"So what happened to Simon?" Kayla asked.

"That's the thing. He's gone."

His whispers were muffled now, and she wondered if he was hiding in a closet or worse…under the covers.

"What do mean, gone?"

"They said he's been dismissed."

"He's probably gone home, Eric."

"No way. The guy's mind is like gumbo soup. He can't put his socks on unless someone helps him. He doesn't even know what you call socks."

She'd never heard Eric like this. He didn't just sound paranoid, he sounded afraid. During all of their phone calls while he was deployed in Afghanistan, Eric had probably been scared at times, but he'd never once let Kayla know or hear it in his voice. This had to be the drug withdrawal.

"Shhhh…" Eric shushed her, and she wasn't even talking.

But then she heard another voice and realized he was trying to hide the phone.

"How are you doing today, Eric?"

Wherever the phone was hidden, Kayla could easily hear the thunderous voice that stood above it.

"I'm fine, Doc." And Eric did sound surprisingly fine.

"I was told you're not taking your meds. Is there a reason for that, Eric? You know you can't get better unless you trust me."

"Just really nauseated. I thought they'd make me throw up."

"Oh sure. I can order some injections instead."

"No, no," Eric answered quickly, and Kayla recognized her husband's panic slipping again. "The pills are good. I should be okay for the bedtime dose."

"One other thing. I didn't realize you're married. You never mentioned it."

"Didn't I? Is that a problem?"

"No problem. Most of the guys recommended by veterans' organizations don't have any family."

"If you're worried about whether I can pay—"

"Don't worry about it," the doctor told Eric, but even through the muffled phone, Kayla sensed it was, indeed, a problem.

Immediately, she wondered how much the ritzy resort-style place would cost them. Eric promised it was covered. She missed the rest of the conversation as she calculated in her head what the daily rate might be.

"Kayla, you still there?" Eric sounded more like himself now.

"How much does this place cost, Eric? You said your veteran's benefits would pay for it. Why does he care if you're married?"

He was quiet again. She was probably too loud.

"Kayla, listen to me," he finally whispered.

She expected him to go into a long explanation of how he had all this covered. That she needed to trust him. Don't worry about it, just like he told the doctor about the pills.

But instead, she heard the fear again when he said, "Get me the hell out of here."

Chapter 16

Blackwater River State Forest

Maggie devoured the last bites of Hannah's sandwich despite the putrid smells surrounding her. She hadn't eaten since early morning before she caught her 6:00 am flight, so when Brodie asked if anyone was hungry Maggie wasn't shy about accepting. She sure had come a long way since her first crime scene when she needed Vicks VapoRub and still ended up tossing her cookies.

She washed down the sandwich with warm water while taking in the scene. And all the while, she kept wondering how long it would be before Ryder Creed's indigo blue eyes wouldn't completely disarm her. It wasn't just his eyes. It was that hitch of a smile and the feel of his carefully manicured, bristled jaw.

She was a seasoned professional, an expert in her field. She chased serial killers, for God's sake, and yet this man had the ability to make her feel like a silly, lovesick schoolgirl.

Just minutes ago, she'd watched him as he disappeared into the forest with Sheriff Norwich to show her the spots where Grace had alerted. He left Brodie and Maggie in the shade to finish their sandwiches and make sure Grace did the same with her own lunch. The little dog's ears twitched, still listening to his voice despite her nose in her bowl.

"Grace doesn't like to be without him," Brodie said.

Maggie knew the feeling, although she hoped she wasn't as transparent as Grace. Fact was, she had been looking for an excuse to see Ryder for months now. They talked on the phone regularly, but of course, that wasn't the same. And she wouldn't dare ask him to come to Virginia. He had Brodie to look after and so many other responsibilities with a kennel full of dogs.

At least that's what she told herself. Maybe a part of her worried that if she asked and he said "no," it would forever change things between them. "Things?" She wasn't even sure what to call it.

From a distance it was easy to say she liked her life just the way it was. She was busy putting together a new investigative crime unit. The new FBI director had chosen her specifically, and so far, he had given her wide latitude. It was one of the reasons she was personally able to respond to Escambia County Sheriff Clayton's request.

The storage unit's contents were strange enough to warrant a look. So she'd arranged the trip along with dinner with Ryder. She knew she could tack on a couple of days off, if need be. She thought she'd play it by ear. See if the storage unit required a closer look. Or decide if she had the courage to stay and spend more time with Ryder.

Her brother Patrick, a firefighter who shared her home, was off duty for a week and had already agreed to take care of her dogs, Jake and Harvey. There was nothing stopping her from staying. Nothing, except herself. Then she looked into those indigo blue eyes, and suddenly, she couldn't remember why she was tiptoeing around her feelings.

Now she saw the medical examiner gesturing for Maggie to join her. Earlier, Vickie had handed out shoe covers and latex gloves. Maggie pulled them on now.

"You two good?" she asked Brodie and Grace before she left.

Brodie nodded. Grace was still focused on Ryder's voice.

When Maggie joined Vickie, she immediately wished she had waited a few more minutes.

"Maggots," she sighed as she watched Vickie scoop up a handful and drop them into a specimen cup already filled with isopropyl alcohol. "I hate maggots."

"Really? I would imagine you see a good deal of them on a regular basis."

"Doesn't mean I have to like them."

"Sometimes they can tell a piece of the story that we'd never know without them."

Maggie couldn't argue with that. As disgusting as they were, what they devoured, and when they devoured it, could end up providing important evidence.

"But these aren't quite maggots," Vickie said. "In this heat, that means he hasn't been dead for long. Possibly less than twenty-four hours."

The medical examiner marked the specimen cup, stood up and backed away. Then she said, "Tell me what's wrong with this picture."

Maggie noticed the woman was quieter out here in the field. The chatter from the storage unit was long gone. There was a serious calm to her now. Maggie thought she seemed contemplative but with a slight edge. Something had unnerved her.

Maggie came in for a closer look. The man was lying face down. The wound on the back of his head had still been bleeding when he arrived at this site. The blow may have been administered here. There was enough blood on the leaves and surrounding dirt to support that theory.

Sandy dirt covered him up to his waist. The grave was shallow, almost as if the killer had only dug the length and width of the body, about a foot deep—if that—rolled the body in and didn't bother to cover it entirely.

That's what it looked like at first glance.

Then Maggie saw what Vickie was alluding to, and she winced. Why hadn't she seen it immediately?

The man's arms were up over his head, his elbows bent. But the arms hadn't simply flung up as his body was rolled over and into the grave. She squatted down and leaned over him. She swatted at the flies, but it didn't make a difference. They weren't leaving.

Carefully with gloved fingers, she lifted one of the victim's hands. It was stiff with rigor mortis. She glanced up at Vickie who noticed.

Without prompting, the medical examiner said, "So he's been here less than thirty-six hours."

But Maggie wasn't focused on that. Instead, she was shocked to see the scratches in the dirt. They confirmed what she already suspected. Leaves were clutched in his hand and dirt embedded under his fingernails.

She stood back up, and her eyes darted around. Sheriff Norwich was at the other end of the clearing and on her cell phone. Maggie could hear her giving instructions. Ryder and Grace were with Brodie in the shade and out of earshot. She turned her back to all of them and looked directly at Vickie.

"He was still alive when the killer buried him," Maggie said.

Chapter 17

"Did the killer not know?" Maggie asked, "Or maybe he didn't care."

"Motive is your department," Vickie said as she unpacked another specimen cup and several evidence bags. "There could be other injuries."

Maggie walked the length of the body, examining and searching.

"Doesn't look like there are any drag marks," she said.

She could see the scuff in the dirt where Brodie must have stumbled. Her footprints were much smaller than the other ones trampled all around the grave. She glanced back at Ryder and saw that he wore his low-profile hiking boots. They'd be easy for the crime scene techs to discount. The other prints were distinctive, too. Footprints—because of sole patterns and debris stuck in the treads—could be as incriminating as fingerprints.

"If you eliminate Ryder and Brodie's shoe prints, it looks like there's only one pair," Maggie said.

"Which means this gentleman didn't walk to his grave." Sheriff Norwich had finished her phone call and wandered close enough to hear.

"Sheriff," Vickie said, "you're right. But it looks like he wasn't dead when the killer buried him."

Norwich blinked several times before her head pivoted and her eyes darted down.

She looked up at Maggie and asked, "Do you think he knew his killer? Was this personal?"

Maggie understood what the sheriff was asking, almost hoping. If it was personal, it might mean that this man wasn't a random victim. Sometimes it was easier to find a killer when there was a connection.

"Even if it was," Maggie told her, "it doesn't explain the others."

Norwich drove her hands into the pockets of her uniform's dark green trousers and shook her head.

"I have a CSU tech and a deputy on their way. Jason and Scout are bringing them in. Sounds like the spray paint is helping."

Vickie grinned even as she sunk a thermometer into the brown mass of maggots.

"We're going to need an easier way in and out of here," Norwich said. "I can't imagine hauling equipment and personnel back and forth through that jungle."

She stepped back away and gestured to Ryder and Brodie.

Maggie knew Ryder and Norwich had shared some harrowing experiences during the Alabama tornadoes in March. Earlier, she wasn't surprised to see him administer first aid to the sheriff. It was part of his nature. However, she was surprised to see the proud and tough sheriff accept. There was obviously a mutual respect between the two. But given all that, Norwich missed what Maggie saw just now. Ryder hesitated with a quick, involuntary glance at Brodie.

Ever since they arrived on the scene, Maggie could see he was uncomfortable and concerned about Brodie being here. She knew firsthand what the young woman had gone through. Only eight months ago a crazy woman and her son were still holding Brodie captive. Brodie's tall, thin body was still recovering from the effects of malnutrition and also the damage from the drugs her captors used on her. Maggie didn't pretend to guess her mental state, but Brodie certainly didn't appear upset.

Ryder instructed Grace to sit, and he attempted to leave Brodie, along with the dog, in the shade. But Norwich waved for Brodie to come over too. She stepped away from the body and shielded it with her own. Maybe she wasn't entirely oblivious to Ryder's concerns.

"You two know this area. Do you know of any paths to a road?"

Maggie watched as Brodie shook her head then said, "I've never been in this area before today."

"I might be able to figure out what direction the killer came from," Ryder said.

"You can tell us that?"

Maggie started smiling even before Ryder told Norwich, "I can't, but Grace might be able to."

Chapter 18

Creed wasn't sure if this would work. He'd never asked one of his dogs to follow scent beginning from footprints alone. Using a piece of clothing worked best, especially fabric worn close to the body. An individual's scent—including skin rafts, sweat, body chemistry and even traces of hygiene products—was a combination specific to that person.

Footprints carried some of that scent, too, but he was simply hoping they highlighted where lingering scent might still be in the air. Following the footprints would also indicate where odor molecules might have collected on grass or shrubs.

There were a lot of prints pressed into the dirt. Some were so distinctive he could see the tread pattern of the sole. Grass and debris had been trampled. Leaves were smashed into the soil. But the tracks appeared to go in every direction.

To Vickie and Maggie he asked, "Most of these prints look like they were made by one person. Does that sound possible?"

Maggie nodded and said, "We were just talking about that."

Both women had stepped aside to let him and Grace have access and to watch. Norwich and Brodie had come over, too. Usually he'd ask people to back all the way up, but truthfully, Grace didn't mind as much as he did. Too often people watched like they were expecting to witness a magic act. This audience didn't fit in that category.

"Are you telling me she can sniff out where the killer came from just by using footprints?" Norwich asked.

Creed was disappointed to hear doubt in her voice. Just three months ago Sheriff Norwich had watched Grace find a baby still in his car seat. A tornado had thrown the child over three hundred feet and left him in the middle of a field under a line of downed pine trees. So he was disappointed to think Norwich might still be one of the "magic" believers.

"Footprints can leave a trail of scent," he explained. "But they can also point out where he was and where his scent might be lingering." He looked to Maggie and Vickie again. "It depends how long they've been here. Do you have any idea?"

"We still have rigor mortis," Vickie told him. "So less than thirty-six hours. Also the masses of blowfly eggs are only starting to become maggots. In this heat, that could mean less than twenty-four hours."

"Odor molecules diffuse into the air," Creed continued. "Humidity keeps them closer to the ground. These steps might still have a faint scent. His last steps will have a stronger scent. And remember, he was here again today. Chances are, he came back into the forest the same way."

"I forgot about that," Norwich said.

Creed didn't like to think about it. That the killer came back to the scene of his crime, saw them—spied on them—and followed Brodie.

Chased her.

His footprints and scent were definitely here but narrowing them down and getting Grace to find the path to his arrival could be challenging. Especially since the guy may have tracked all around the site before he took off after Brodie.

Creed found one of the prints that was deeply embedded in the soil and called to Grace. He gestured and pointed directly to the ground, asking her to sniff it. Her nose immediately started twitching. Like bloodhounds, Grace worked the scent with her nose. But instead of sniffing close to the ground, she poked the air checking for matching scent clinging to the landscape. He pointed to the next closest print. And then another.

The air was filled with different scents. Grace had been overwhelmed all morning, finding and alerting. But those were decomp odors. He was asking her now to separate out and search for an individual's specific smell.

Grace snuffled the surrounding trees and shrubs. She stopped at one spot where the grass was smashed down from something that had been placed on top of it. Perhaps something belonging to the killer.

They had gone over almost a dozen prints when he finally decided it was time. Grace definitely had identified this new scent.

Creed glanced around and found his audience had stayed in the shade about twenty feet away. He gestured to Sheriff Norwich.

"Usually when I ask one of my dogs to follow an individual's scent, I know the name of the person lost or missing," he told her. "I call the scent by the person's name."

"I remember your handler, Jason doing that," Norwich said. "That young girl we were looking for last fall."

"I'm going to call this scent Predator."

Grace's nose was still working. Only now, she had moved toward the opposite side of the clearing. She didn't need a name. She was already tracking. But she still looked up at him and waited for the command.

"Grace." He pointed to the last set of footprints beside her. "Grace, this is Predator."

She watched him and poked her nose in the air. Her front feet shuffled back and forth, impatient and ready.

"Grace, find Predator."

He could hear the sheriff breathing hard behind him. Creed slowed his pace to keep just a few steps in front of her while Grace bounded so far ahead, he lost sight of her. He let Grace go off-leash, and now he was second-guessing that decision. What if the killer was still lurking around here? If Grace found him...

Just as he felt a chill at the back of his neck, he caught a glimpse of Grace's tail. She realized she'd lost him and was backtracking to get him. She darted through the trees. When she saw him, she waited but threw her head back like she was impatiently pointing out the direction.

"This doesn't feel like an easier path," Norwich called to him. Her hands were on her hips and her face was red, again.

He stopped and put up a hand to tell Grace to stay.

"Should we stop for a water break?" he asked the sheriff.

It couldn't have been more than ten minutes that they'd started on the trail. And the farther they went, the more it looked like a real trail. Creed could see broken branches and shrubs. The grass was worn down. Leaves and pine needles had been swept away. In places there were drag marks made by something heavy and over a foot wide. If he had to guess he'd say a bag...a body bag.

"This is the way he came," he told Norwich.

"Well, I hope this is leading us to a forest service road."

Creed didn't answer. He suspected the sheriff wouldn't be excited to see what waited for them on the other side of the trees. This parcel of the forest hadn't been developed by the state park. It created a wild barrier that kept tourists and hikers from wandering onto private property like Hannah's and his. There were no roads that he knew about. At least none that showed up on maps.

Grace took off again, but this time more slowly. Before they reached the edge of the tree line, he could smell and hear the water. They walked out of the woods and into the glaring sunlight. The sandy shore extended for about thirty feet. Grace pranced to the riverbank, turned and looked Creed in the eyes.

She was standing beside skid marks in the sand. Fresh skid marks from a flat-bottomed boat that had banked here many times and recently.

"Coldwater Creek," Creed said.

He glanced at Norwich, and he knew immediately she wasn't pleased.

Chapter 19

Brodie was torn whether to go with Ryder and Grace or stay. Ryder was worried about her. He wouldn't dare say that, but she recognized the look in his eyes. He wasn't a very good pretender. Even as kids he couldn't lie very well. Brodie could. She could keep secrets, too. And after sixteen years of tamping down her feelings, she had learned how to keep her emotions hidden, too.

Besides, she liked watching the medical examiner work. She was organized, efficient and completely unaffected by the grossest stuff. That last part was what clicked with Brodie the most, because she found herself being totally fascinated by the gross stuff.

She read constantly. Just since she'd come to live with Hannah and Ryder, she'd worked her way through half of their personal libraries. Jason brought books to her, too. Usually well-worn paperbacks with dog-eared pages. She loved every single one. Lately, she'd been reading some of Hannah's favorite romance authors, but mysteries and thrillers were her favorites.

In Brodie's mind, mysteries and thrillers were the kind of stuff Ryder and Jason did all the time. Up until now, they hadn't allowed her to tag along. Fact was, she could see Ryder trying to figure out how to send her home. How to protect her. When he first found out she was wandering into the forest alone, he almost yelled at her. She could see him holding it in.

All of them had been going out of their way to be polite, to treat her like she was something fragile, like she might at any second break into a thousand pieces. Isaac and Thomas, Hannah's two little boys, were the only ones who treated Brodie like she was simply a member of the family. Except when they needed a spider killer. Then they treated her a little bit like she was a superhero. That, she didn't mind.

Maybe that was why Brodie liked the medical examiner.

Vickie.

She told Brodie to call her Vickie.

Vickie was treating Brodie like she was…normal. Like she was here to help, and she was perfectly capable of doing just that.

"Your brother started putting surveyor flags where Grace alerted," the medical examiner said as she pulled out a handful of flags from her backpack. "If you see anything that doesn't belong in the forest—a soda can, a shoe, a bone—don't pick it up. Just stick a flag in the ground next to it."

She handed some of the flags to Brodie and Maggie.

"I need to wait for the CSU tech before we move the body," Vickie told them. "Try to stay away from the footprints over here. Those are probably our best for casting. I'm going to check out some of the spots where Grace already alerted. I could use both of you to help."

Vickie started loading items into her backpack, so they could move into the forest. Brodie had caught a glimpse of all those flags Ryder had planted. She was curious and excited to be included. But her eyes darted back to the man's body. Her knees were still stained with his blood.

"Do you think the person who killed him knew he was still alive?" Brodie asked.

When neither woman answered, she looked up to find Vickie and Maggie staring at her.

"Why do you think he was still alive?" Maggie finally asked.

"It looks like he was crawling out of the dirt." Brodie's eyes skipped from Maggie to Vickie. "Did I get that wrong?"

"No, we believe he may have been buried alive," Vickie said. "You have good instincts."

Brodie beamed inside and allowed the smallest of smiles.

"So here's the thing," Vickie said, "there are other bodies dumped here. We start with that premise."

"And that the killer is disorganized, possibly erratic," Maggie added. Her stance was ready and alert.

Brodie noticed Maggie's eyes scanning the forest. She wondered if the FBI agent was looking for evidence, or did she suspect the killer was still lurking somewhere in the trees.

"We also need to remember that the forest tends to have a whole bunch of scavengers that can make a crime scene even more of a jigsaw puzzle," Vickie said.

"Ryder and Jason said they've seen black bears," Brodie said. "They make me carry bear spray."

"Smart," Vickie nodded. "Bears can be a pain in the ass. They can crack long bones and decapitate a body."

"Can you tell whether a bear's done that or the killer?" Maggie wanted to know.

"From my experience, bears knock it around. Sometimes they take it with them. They tend to take pieces to a creek or a stream."

Now Brodie could feel Maggie watching her. She was pretending not to. She was a little better than Ryder at pretending, but not much. She didn't want Maggie to worry about protecting her.

"Coyotes will go uphill," Vickie continued. "Raccoons like to dine on the spot. But sometimes they'll drag a snack up into a tree." Her head pivoted upward and started swiveling as she examined the treetops.

Almost instinctively, Brodie noticed that she and Maggie also looked up. Within seconds Brodie saw the bird's nest. Something dangled from the twigs. Bright yellow. It didn't look quite right.

"How about that?" she asked, pointing to the nest.

Vickie came over and stood directly under the branch then said, "I think it might be a thread."

"Should we knock it down?" Maggie asked.

"No, no," Vickie waved her off. "No need to damage someone's home."

Brodie realized the medical examiner was serious even when some of the things she said sounded like a joke. Or sarcasm. Brodie hadn't quite grasped sarcasm yet.

Vickie grabbed her backpack and began shifting contents until she found what she wanted. The foot-long rod extended and kept extending until it reached the branch. On the end, it looked like a big set of tweezers, and Vickie could control them from where she stood. In no time, she pinched the yellow strand and gently tugged it free.

"Definitely a thread from some kind of fabric," she said as she weaved it into an evidence bag.

"That's a pretty nifty contraption," Maggie told her.

Vickie started breaking down the magic rod and she grinned.

"All it takes is falling out of a tree once." Then she turned to Brodie and said, "You have a good eye for this stuff."

Brodie shrugged, trying to look nonchalant when she really wanted to smile and maybe even skip a little. She wanted to be good at something other than surviving.

Chapter 20

Blackwater River State Forest

Jason Seaver used his forearm to club and snap yet another branch out of the path. Every once in a while his prosthetic arm came in handy. Although, he would need to be more careful. The new sensors were working, and he was starting to actually feel the contact of the wood.

"Almost there," he called over his shoulder to the sheriff department's men.

The CSU tech named Hadley had no problem keeping pace, though he was an older guy. Older by Jason's standards meaning anyone over thirty-five.

Deputy Danvers was closer to Jason's age. He guessed maybe twenty-four or twenty-five. And yet, Danvers was the one falling back and holding his side. His dark green uniform shirt had sweat stains that had long ago run into each other so that the whole shirt looked soaked. It didn't help that his sheriff's department ball cap sat crooked on his head and kept getting knocked off. Twice Jason looked back to see the dude trailing off the path just to grab the cap off a branch. Hadley didn't have a problem with his own, and Jason's K9 CrimeScents' ball cap stayed planted.

At least Danvers agreed to take one of Hannah's kerchiefs, but only after too much hesitation. Jason didn't like that the guy looked at her like she was some crazy witch doctor. That red kerchief was going to save Danvers' lily-white ass, along with his arms, neck and face.

Scout had picked up the scent as soon as they got into the forest. The fluorescent splashes of spray paint simply became affirmation that they were, indeed, on the right path.

He was so proud of his dog. And thankful that every day he woke up to this bundle of happiness—all lean, sixty-five pounds of him. As soon as he noticed Jason's eyes open, Scout gave him a slobber kiss then head-butted him. He wanted to get up and get on with the day. The dog loved doing exactly this.

So of course, Jason stifled a cringe when the first thing Scout found on the site was a discarded fast food bag, bulging enough to mean there was probably leftover food inside.

They had barely gotten to the scene. Barely gone through all the introductions when Scout poked his head up from a clump of scrub grass. Jason understood this area in the woods was in the opposite direction of where Creed and Grace had posted over a half dozen alerts.

That Scout found it and found it first, was a sore spot for Jason. It was his fault his dog alerted to food. He'd made the mistake of giving Scout little treats when he first started training him. Creed had warned that scent alert dogs needed an award other than food, and Scout now worked hard for the love of his rope toy. He loved to play as much as he loved to work. The dog could hardly contain himself when he knew Jason had the drool-stained toy inside his pack or pocket.

But Scout hadn't made a false alert to food in a long time. He hoped this wasn't some kind of setback. He almost didn't want to tell anyone, but they were all there. The medical examiner had just specified she wanted anything and everything that didn't belong in the forest.

"This is great," she told Jason. Immediately, she unfolded an evidence bag then gingerly lifted the fast food's crumpled bag into it. "We haven't found signs of anyone else in this area other than the killer," she explained. "There's a good chance this was his."

"So *the killer's* scent might still be on it?" Jason was starting to feel better. "Maybe it's his scent that Scout is alerting to and not the possibility that there's a couple bites of a double cheeseburger still inside."

"Oh, I hope there are remnants of a burger. Even fries."

He raised an eyebrow at her. She seemed a bit quirky, and he wasn't sure if she was making a joke.

"DNA can be pulled off food items. A half-eaten hamburger would be excellent."

She patted Scout. "Good boy!"

Chapter 21

Creed pulled a small notebook from his daypack and wrote down the GPS coordinates on two separate pages. He tore out one and handed it to Norwich.

"I think I can come up with a place to launch a boat if nobody else can. I just need to look at a map."

"Yes, thank you. That would be very helpful." But she still gave him an exasperated look as she got on her cell phone.

Within minutes she was instructing someone about getting a boat and body bags when Creed led Grace into a shady spot. He pulled out her collapsible bowl and filled it with water. Drained a bottle himself. He swept off a fallen log and sat down, suddenly exhausted. Grace had to be, too. They'd been out in the heat since early morning. Jason and Scout would need to take over, because whether Grace agreed or not, the little dog was finished for the day.

Coldwater Creek was just one of the many streams, tributaries and creeks that flowed through the forest. Blackwater River was the biggest of them, but Coldwater Creek had its own challenges. It was some of the swiftest water, spring-fed and remarkably cool no matter what time of year. The creek also had plenty of debris obstructions depending on the time of year and recent rains. Logjams in the narrow curves could surprise even the seasoned of boaters. And there were a few holes in the shifting sandy bottom that were deep enough to suck a kayak down without warning.

Creed could feel just a hint of coolness coming off the water. Shadows were lengthening even out here in the open. Longleaf pines and huge hardwoods stood tall on both sides of the creek. The other bank was only about twenty feet away. Gnarly roots poked out of the earth like some river monster crawling out of its den.

The water was clear but tea-colored, stained from the tannin found in the surrounding trees' bark. The current ran quick here, and it would push a boat downstream. But coming up, would definitely take a motor. And it would require some navigating because even Coldwater Creek branched off into tributaries that could lead to nowhere.

So he wasn't surprised when he heard Norwich's disappointment.

"Tomorrow? It's barely three o'clock."

The dead would still be dead tomorrow, but he understood her frustration.

He could see her shaking her head as she listened and paced in the sand. She looked up at him and shouted, "Thunderstorms rolling in. Lots of wind and lightning."

What else was new? This was the Florida Panhandle. It wasn't unusual for storms to break out any afternoon in June. The sky would suddenly go dark. Rain would pour down, sometimes even as the sun still shined. Twenty miles away it might not even be cloudy.

But lightning? This part of Florida had the most each year. It could be dangerous to be caught in the middle of it. Trees were particularly susceptible to strikes.

He pulled out his cell phone and tapped out a quick message to Jason and Maggie warning them of the forecast. All three of them had gone through the Alabama tornadoes in March. They weren't likely to look at stormy skies ever again in the same way.

Creed sat and stared at the marks in the sand where a boat had pulled up and beached. It had done so, over and over again and as recent as hours ago. At least the killer was gone for now.

But suddenly, Creed felt a prickle along the back of his neck. He stood up. Then he told Grace to stay while he walked farther downstream along the creek edge. It was impossible to see from here, but Creed realized the man could have other spots where he came ashore. By now, he probably knew this area well enough that he could sneak up on the crime scene and do it from several different ways. Creed had seen enough pieces of this man's handiwork to know what he was capable of doing.

He walked back to Grace while a knot started forming in his gut. He didn't like that his property was less than half a mile away. How close had Brodie come to running into this guy during her walks through the forest? He hated the thought of her being chased. It didn't matter that she was okay. It still felt like he had let her down. Dangerously so.

Ever since he found her and brought her home, all he wanted to do was protect her. And somehow, he'd managed to put her in the middle of a madman's path. A killer who wasn't happy that they'd stumbled onto his dumping ground.

And the worst part? Now the guy knew where they lived.

Chapter 22

Pensacola Beach, Florida

Taylor Donahey was annoyed at herself. Here she was again looking and waiting for a text message from a man.

She had finished her shift and drove straight home to her apartment on the beach.

On the beach!

She still couldn't believe that part. Granted, it was tiny. One room made up the living space. A counter that could seat two, and certainly no more than three, separated the kitchen. Not like she knew two other people she could invite for dinner. But hopefully someday, and soon, William would join her for a meal. Then she realized she didn't even know what his favorite food was. There was so much she didn't know about her little boy.

It was too early to hope for a sleepover, and her in-laws wouldn't be crazy about the arrangements. They certainly wouldn't like the fact that there was only one bedroom and a foldout sofa. But she'd already decided she'd give William her bed. Taylor had slept on army cots and in the back of Humvees. Even a Serta plush mattress hadn't stopped the nightmares, so a lumpy foldout sofa wouldn't make a difference.

What the place lacked in space it made up for in view. The apartment was above a marina shop. It had its own entrance, even a small balcony that looked out over the boats. And just beyond that was the Gulf of Mexico. She could sit out and watch the sun sink into the sparkling emerald waters.

Her first two nights she woke up out there, disoriented by the sky full of stars and trying to remember where the hell she was. She kept reminding herself that vodka was not her friend, although most nights, it was her only friend.

She'd found this apartment on her own, unlike the job. The job had been arranged. It was a part of the favor-packet, the one she'd signed with the devil. She was proud of the fact that she had managed to get this place on her own. She was driving by when the marina shop owner was literally putting the "apartment for rent" sign in his window.

He looked a bit like Zeus or what Taylor imagined the Greek god would look like. Howard was a giant of a man with longish white hair to match his beard. He wore white trousers and a button-down shirt splattered with colorful images of fish.

He told her he was picky about who lived above his shop, and he honestly appeared unfazed by her feminine wiles. Yes, that was a silly thing to call it, but Taylor was well aware that she was a master at the art of shamelessly flirting. Just when she was certain she'd overplayed her hand, she let it slip that she was a nurse. Her occupation seemed to please him.

"It might be nice to have someone around who didn't wince at the sight of blood."

She wasn't sure what he meant. She didn't ask. Didn't really want to know. It got her the apartment. He even helped carry up her bags. The duffel with the army insignia raised his eyebrows.

"Afghanistan," she said.

That was all she had to say. She could immediately tell it was enough to be golden in Howard's view.

Partly, that was the problem on night one. He'd invited her down on his dock for a nightcap. She already knew there was nothing seductive or manipulative about his offer. It was simply an old army war veteran wanting to have a drink with another. How could she turn him down when she knew she'd just landed the best rental deal on the beach?

Besides, it turned out that Howard was one the last decent, honorable guys she'd met in a long time. Especially now that John Lockett hadn't even bothered to leave her a voice message. A man she thought might genuinely be after her heart, not just her body.

She'd met Lockett back in Virginia just before she'd left. They'd dated for two weeks. Two weeks that weren't just about sex. Then a couple of days ago he showed up in Pensacola. Him and that big, ole dog.

"I can't stop thinking about you," he told her.

They'd taken a walk on the beach. Had a lunch of grouper sandwiches at Peg Leg Pete's. But she didn't invite him back to her new apartment. She tried a second time to make him understand that she wanted to be in her son's life again, and she couldn't have any other distractions.

He wanted to help. Promised to not be a distraction.

She told him she'd think about it. She left Peg Leg Pete's taking a detour to walk on the beach again. She wasn't in love with Lockett, but he was a decent guy. Maybe she needed to give him a chance. Before she got back to her apartment her cell phone started ringing, and for a second or two there was a flutter in her stomach that tried to convince her to let him stay.

But it wasn't John Lockett. It was the devil, reminding her of their deal. Reminding her that she had promised to stay out of trouble. That if she wanted his help to get her son back, she'd need to "clean up her act."

Derrick, the devil, wasn't wrong. She did attract trouble and most of it the male persuasion. Hell, he was evidence of that, wasn't he? A smooth, charming, silver tongued…forked tongued devil.

But John Lockett wasn't like that. And how did Derrick even know about Lockett? Did he have someone following her? He didn't call Lockett by name, but he knew she was having lunch with someone.

She didn't dare ask that day. She didn't ask any questions. Instead, twenty minutes later she called Lockett, telling him he needed to go back to Virginia. She thought she'd been gentle, using phrases like, "I hope you understand" and "maybe in the future."

She wasn't sure why she still expected him to call her. Just to let her know he arrived back in Virginia safely. What would it matter?

Why did it matter?

William mattered. He was *all* that mattered.

That's what Taylor needed to focus on. That's what she wanted more than anything else. And evidently, she was allowed one wish and only one wish from the man she knew could help make her wish a reality.

For too long she had wanted to correct the biggest mistake she'd ever made…giving up her son. Deep down she understood there'd be a tremendous price to pay for that.

That was a couple of days ago. She checked her phone again. Lockett should have arrived back in Virginia by now. Would it have killed him to let her know he was okay?

She changed into shorts, sports bra, T-shirt and running shoes, anxious to clear her mind. She grabbed her phone to slide it into a zippered pocket, when suddenly she stopped.

Taylor stared at her cell phone. Was it possible he was tracking her? Why hadn't she considered that before?

This was ridiculous. Maybe it was time to force his hand. Make him put up or shut up. She'd been here for three weeks. Two weeks on the job. And Derrick still hadn't arranged for a meeting with her son's grandparents. How many more hoops did he expect her to jump through? How long did he think he could dangle her hopes in front of her without delivering?

In Afghanistan she had dodged sniper fire and listened almost nightly to IEDs going off outside the wire. There were times when she wore her shoulder holster with her 9-millimeter handgun even during surgeries. She wasn't easily intimidated. Maybe he needed a reminder.

This new hospital assignment didn't include being on call. She shut the phone off and carefully placed it on the kitchen counter as if it actually might be a tracking device.

Then she left the apartment, and this time she headed in the opposite direction from the one she usually took. Perhaps she'd just happen to run into the devil and make *him* squirm for a change.

Chapter 23

Blackwater River State Forest

Brodie wanted to be with Jason, but she knew Scout couldn't be distracted while he worked. So she stayed focused on the medical examiner. She enjoyed watching how Vickie and Agent Maggie worked together. It looked like they'd been doing it for years, but Brodie was sure the two women had only met this morning.

They approached each flag with the same process, no matter what the contents were that the flag marked. In one spot, Brodie couldn't see anything in the grass. That didn't surprise her. She understood that Grace could smell things that might be buried deep underground. What did surprise her was that Vickie took photos of each site, whether or not there was anything visible on the surface.

She was careful and deliberate, getting down on her knees and gently waving her hands through the grass then raking the top of the dirt with gloved fingertips. A couple of times she found pieces so small Brodie had no idea how Vickie knew they were important.

Maggie stood on the other side of the medical examiner, ready with assorted evidence bags. Vickie asked for a specific size, Maggie handed it down to her, and Vickie placed an item. Then she lifted it up to Maggie and told her what to write. Maggie sealed each envelope or bag and set it aside to be picked up later.

Brodie recognized that the medical examiner's process included working the crime scene in a counterclockwise motion. When finished, she left the flag in the ground but took out a black marker and drew a letter and a number on it. Brodie could see the letters and numbers matched the ones Maggie put on the evidence bags.

They took breaks in between with both women wiping the sweat from their faces and drinking a whole lot of water. Brodie didn't mind the heat. She'd spent days on end locked in airless closets, dirty sheds and a damp basement. Now, with her hair cut short she no longer had to worry about wet strands wrapping around her neck like a noose.

She wore loose-fitting T-shirts and lightweight cargo pants, most of which didn't cling to her. And shoes! The miracle of shoes. She had lived years without anything protecting her feet, and the scars were still an unpleasant reminder.

Brodie joined Vickie and Maggie and gulped down another bottle of water, because she knew it was good for her, even though she could go longer without it. One of Iris Malone's punishments was to withhold food and water. It was probably the cruelest of her punishments. Brodie's stomach would hurt so bad that by the time the woman left a cup of water and a slice of bread, Brodie's insides rejected both. She'd gulp down the water and before she finished the bread, all of it came back up.

Brodie's therapist, Dr. Rockwood, told her it was okay to remember those things. "But don't let them hurt you anymore. Don't let Iris Malone have any more power," she had said just as recently as last week when they did their weekly Zoom chats. "Every time you remember something bad, follow it up with something that's now good in your life."

There was so much good. If only she trusted that it wouldn't all go away. Ryder seemed to think that he needed to protect her from everything as if he could make up for what she had gone through. She didn't know how to convince him that what she'd gone through had actually made her stronger.

Nevermind. Dr. Rockwood's assignment was an easy one, and Brodie quickly thought about Hannah's chocolate chip cookies, how they smelled and tasted fresh out of the oven. Probably an odd thing to think about surrounded by what smelled like rotten garbage. Which made Brodie also grateful for Hannah's red kerchief and her magic concoction. The flies and mosquitoes buzzed everywhere without landing on her. Swarms of flies were like black clouds over certain areas, and they were approaching one of those right now.

It wasn't until they reached the third flag that Brodie felt a gasp escape her throat. Thankfully, neither of the women acknowledged it. And Brodie didn't feel embarrassed when she noticed Maggie take two steps back and wipe a hand under her nose.

"More maggots," the FBI agent muttered under her breath.

This man wasn't buried at all. Instead, Brodie thought it looked like he was simply lying down under the tree, right in the middle of tall grass that grew around him. Vines had begun to climb over him.

But the flies…masses of flies…and maggots. Bunches of the black insects squirmed covering his eyes and nose. His mouth, too, because his lips looked like they were moving.

It was disgusting, and yet, Brodie couldn't take her eyes away.

Vickie waved a hand to disperse some of the flies, knocking them away. She bent over the body with an empty specimen cup ready to fill.

As she plucked a handful of maggots, the flies were back swarming the plastic container. She popped the lid on and stepped away. Then she pulled out a bottle of isopropyl alcohol. Brodie had seen her do this before. It seemed to be the only thing that killed the chunky inchworms. But this time Vickie stopped. She left the lid on and held up the specimen cup to get a closer look.

"These guys are smaller," she said.

Maggie and Brodie leaned in for looks of their own. Brodie realized she wouldn't know the difference.

"Does that mean something?" Maggie asked.

Vickie shrugged and said, "They're moving a lot slower, too."

"Heat and humidity?" Maggie suggested.

"No, I don't think that's it. Toxicology might have an answer."

Maggie's cell phone chimed. She pulled it out of her back pocket and looked at the message.

"Ryder says there are thunderstorms coming our way."

Brodie noticed the FBI agent wince as she looked up. It was almost impossible to see anything other than slices of sky through the thick mass of branches and leaves, but Brodie knew why Maggie looked anxious. She figured it was the same reason Grace now got scared at the sound of thunder. It was only three months ago that both of them had been battered by tornadoes.

"If that's the case," Vickie said, "there's one other thing we need to get before the rains wash it away."

She gestured for them to follow her. Brodie caught Maggie biting her lip as she glanced up at the sky again

Chapter 24

Brodie came up beside Vickie. They stood over the flag stuck between giant tree roots that snaked out of the ground in different directions. Scrub grass shot up in places clinging to what little dirt there was.

"Ryder mentioned a skull somewhere down here," Vickie said. "I want to see if I can grab it before the rains move it."

She took a couple of photos then pulled on gloves and kneeled down. Brodie watched her readjusting herself. The roots didn't make it easy to work. She gently wiped away some of the debris, sending little green tree frogs jumping. At least there weren't any flies to compete with here.

Vickie pulled out a small flashlight and started shooting the beam down into holes between a web of roots.

"There it is," Vickie said and handed the flashlight up to Brodie.

"Can you hold this at an angle and shine it right there." She pointed exactly where she wanted the stream of light to hit.

Brodie got to her knees, too, then shifted to her feet. The roots were impossible to kneel on. When Vickie moved out of the way Brodie could see the round white orb. The light made it stand out against the dark debris and muck that surrounded it.

Vickie pulled her glove higher up her arm. She had to push more dirt and grass away from the hole to make room for her hand. She sat down, then stretched out on her side.

From behind them Maggie said, "Can't you use your handy contraption?"

"Won't fit."

"How do you know there's not an animal down there?" Maggie asked. "Or a snake?"

Without glancing up at the FBI agent, Vickie said, "Not helpful."

She repositioned herself then plunged her hand inside the hole.

There wasn't enough room for Brodie to shine the light around her. Nor was there enough room for Vickie to see, once her arm plugged the hole. She'd need to find the skull by feel.

The medical examiner released a sigh of frustration. Her loud huff startled both Brodie and Maggie.

"My arm's too short," Vickie said, looking up at Maggie's arm.

"No, don't even ask," Maggie told her. "This is where I draw a line."

"I can do it," Brodie said.

Both women looked at her. They exchanged a glance and Maggie said, "Brodie, you've been a great help, but you don't need to do this. I'm sure the CSU tech will have a way to get it."

"She's right." Vickie waved her gloved hand at her as if it wasn't a big deal. But only minutes, ago the medical examiner was concerned the skull might be taken farther underground by the rains.

"I really don't mind," Brodie told them. "This person has a family somewhere. They might still be wondering what happened to him...or her." When they didn't respond she added, "And I have really long, thin arms."

It was Vickie who gave in. Maggie's only response was to glance up at the sky again.

The crisscross of roots jutting up and over made it uncomfortable to lie down. Vickie found a way to insert the flashlight into a neighboring hole that lit up the hollow. It ended up not being much help, because in order to extend her arm, Brodie had to shift to her belly. Her cheek rubbed against the gnarled roots. She could smell mold and dirt, but none of this was worse than what she'd experienced living at the whim of Iris Malone.

By the time her fingers felt the smooth bone, Brodie was shoulder deep in the burrow. Her hand wasn't big enough to secure it in her palm. She tried to wrap her fingers around it but couldn't get a grip. Then her forefinger poked and looped through something. In her mind she realized it might be the eye socket.

"I got it!" she said, forcing the image away and finally getting a hold on it.

Maggie and Vickie helped pull her up. She hadn't noticed how far she'd dived in. They had to untangle some roots so the skull could come through.

There was a rumble of thunder. They hadn't even heard Ryder and Norwich return.

"Brodie, what are you doing?" Ryder wanted to know.

Chapter 25

Creed almost panicked when he saw Brodie stretched out on the ground. Even after he realized what she was doing, he wasn't happy about it. He couldn't believe the medical examiner allowed her to help like this. And he couldn't believe *Maggie* allowed it.

But Brodie raised the skull to show him, and she was absolutely beaming. She continued to surprise him.

Besides, there were other things to worry about. By the time he and Norwich got back at the clearing, the sunshine had already begun disappearing. Norwich's CSU tech and deputy were unrolling lightweight tarps and pulling out bungee cords. They'd secure the tarps as best as possible over the victims' bodies and the other visible remains.

Creed knew Mark Hadley, the crime scene tech. Hadley had been at the Santa Rosa Sheriff's Department for a least a decade. The two had worked alongside each other several times before. Hadley was quiet and serious, but always kind and respectful to Creed's dogs. They exchanged a nod.

He wanted to ask Hadley why he hadn't retrieved the skull, instead he asked, "Need some help?"

"Nope, we got this," Hadley said, shooting a look at the deputy already helping him as if he hoped that was true.

Norwich's deputy looked a bit young to Creed. His eyes were too wide. His head swiveled, taking in everything as if it were brand new to him. Half of his shirt was tucked in. The rest puckered out of his waistband, bunching up and spilling over his holster. It was also sweat-drenched. Creed couldn't help thinking if the man needed to grab his weapon in a hurry he'd probably end up with a handful of wet shirttail.

Norwich introduced him as Deputy Danvers. Now back inside the forest, she seemed a bit frazzled as soon as she realized she'd lost any reliable cell phone reception.

Creed's first priority was to get his crew out of the forest. Grace's ears had been pinned back for the last ten minutes or so. He knew she could smell the approaching storm. Ever since March when the two of them got caught up in a tornado, Grace had become anxious when the ozone changed. She was already exhausted from the heat.

In his daypack he included a mesh travel pouch that Grace fit into. It had an adjustable strap that went over his head and crossed his body. He'd used it to carry her before when she was injured. He was taking it out now and hoping she wouldn't put up a fuss.

Scout bounded out of the trees, excited and panting. He brushed against Creed's leg, started to nose Grace then backed off. Even he could sense her distress.

"Scout and I marked three possible sites," Jason said coming out of the trees. "Are we sure this is only one guy?"

"Good question," Maggie said, overhearing from behind them.

Brodie and Vickie were with her. Each of the women carried more gear than they came in with, duffel bags that held the evidence samples they'd collected. Creed could see more blue tarps beyond the trees. The splashes of blue looked like a tossed campsite.

He could feel the wind pick up, and instinctively he turned to Maggie, checking to see if she was okay. When she caught his look, she held his eyes. It was only for two or three seconds, but enough time to see her concern. The panic would still be fresh.

He wanted to reassure her that it was only a thunderstorm. Not a tornado. But they were in the middle of a forest where lightning strikes could topple a tree or set it on fire.

"We need to move, people. Now!" Norwich told them, taking charge, despite her face painted red and dripping sweat.

That was the thing about these late afternoon storms. The wind would kick up. The skies would darken, but the heat and humidity never relented. In fact, after the downpour it would be more oppressive, adding moisture to the already saturated air.

"Can you get us back out of here?" Norwich asked Brodie.

Creed noticed that his sister, who had been bright-eyed and excited all day, suddenly looked exhausted. Before he could say anything, Jason stepped up.

"Scout led us in here," he said. At the mention of his name the big dog wagged, tail thumping one tree and another. "He can get us back. Isn't that right, boy?"

Ropes of saliva drooled from his smile as he took Jason's hand in his mouth. Creed couldn't help thinking these two had come a long way in two short years.

Jason, Scout and Brodie took the lead. Creed offered to bring up the rear. He placed Grace inside the mesh carry bag, and she was content to snuggle against his hip. With every low rumble of thunder he could feel

Grace's body stiffen against him. He should have gotten her home sooner.

He kept a hand pressing her close to him and making sure none of the branches scratched or snagged her or the bag. It slowed him down, but Norwich slowed his pace even more. She was five feet in front of him, and he could hear her heavy breathing. She grabbed onto tree trunks to pull herself along and keep her balance. Any minute now the downpour would start, a new threat to upending her already shaky foothold.

They had trailed back so far that he couldn't see the others. Her men knew better than to backtrack and check on her. Actually, Creed was surprised that Norwich didn't leave Deputy Danvers to guard the crime scene. Perhaps protocol didn't allow it when lightning was concerned. Maybe it didn't matter. If the killer returned overnight what could he do? Mess up the scene even more? Drag bodies out? He supposed anything was possible. Norwich obviously wasn't willing to risk the safety of one of her deputies out in the middle of a storm.

The rumble of thunder had become constant, so when the crash came, it jolted both Norwich and Creed.

He heard her mumble something, but the wind kept taking it away from him. It couldn't be much farther, yet he didn't recognize anything. As the forest darkened, it was getting difficult to see ahead. The only way he knew they were still on the right path were the broken branches, shrubs stripped of leaves and the stomped down grass from those before them.

Creed could hear the rain before he felt it. The thick canopy overhead acted as a barrier, delaying the droplets. Above them the storm heaved and howled. Then the deluge came and there was nothing to slow it down. After a day of skin slick with sweat and heat, the rain was shockingly cold.

He put out a hand against Norwich's back to steady her. The ground had flattened but the pine needles and leaves that covered the forest floor would quickly turn it into a slippery slide. He caught her elbow and braced her up. His other hand stayed on Grace, cradling her against his side. He could feel her trembling through the thin mesh fabric of the carrier.

Norwich leaned her back against a tree. She hesitated. Face down. He couldn't see her eyes. Couldn't hear her through the pounding rain. Using his arm she pushed forward only to slide back against the tree.

Then suddenly, Creed felt a hand on his shoulder.

Maggie!

She wrapped her arm around Norwich's waist. The sheriff allowed it and draped her arm around Maggie's back. The trail was too narrow to walk side by side. Maggie sidestepped, pulling the older woman along. Creed was able to hold Norwich's other arm. Between the two of them they kept her upright and moving along.

To Creed, it felt like a long slog. It was impossible to see. His hiking boots became heavy and caked with mud, concrete blocks threatening to trip him. The flashes of lightning stayed above, a constant strobe light. But the cracks of thunder vibrated all the way down to the ground. It felt like it rocked the earth below his feet, adding to the unsteady trek that was already an obstacle course with the gnarled roots and fallen branches.

It must have lasted only fifteen or twenty minutes. By the time they reached the edge of the forest, the sun replaced the lightning with streams breaking through the clouds. Rain still fell. Softer, gentler now. The wind had quieted. Creed noticed birds were chirping again. But a new rumble in the distance behind them announced it might not be over.

The others were waiting for them despite the kennel and house now visible and less than a hundred feet away.

"Well, this day just gets better and better!" Vickie said.

Finally out of the woods, Maggie and Creed eased their grips on Norwich at the same time. And the sheriff collapsed to the ground.

Chapter 26

Later Creed would learn that six of the seven of them knew CPR. That should have been comforting. If only Norwich would have responded. The trek through the storm had seemed like an unending journey but waiting for the LifeFlight helicopter felt like an eternity.

Creed was surprised that Jason had been the first to react. He'd immediately dropped to his knees. He was still counting and doing chest compressions while Creed gestured, pin-wheeling his arms to direct the LifeFlight crew to the open field close by. Vickie had joined Jason on the other side of Norwich. She was doing the rescue breaths while Jason continued the chest compressions.

Hannah had brought out a blanket and towels. But everyone stood stock-still, watching, waiting. All of them soaking wet.

Creed squatted down next to Grace and Brodie, but he didn't take his eyes off of Norwich's body. In his head he heard a mantra pounding against his temples: *Breathe, breathe, breathe!* It was taking too much time. Way too much time.

The paramedic and flight nurse took over. When Jason stood up, he stumbled a bit. Scout, who had been staying back, because Jason had told him to do so, went to Jason with head down, humbled and quiet as he brushed against Jason's leg.

Creed moved closer to Grace, still sitting back on his haunches. He leaned over and put a hand on Brodie's shoulder. He couldn't stop thinking how red Norwich's face was as soon as she'd arrived in the forest. Her breathing was heavy even back then. He should have known. He thought she might have been suffering from heatstroke, but she seemed better after the ice pack and some water.

He looked up at the sky. The clouds were rolling in again. The crew told him they had a small window of time. Creed knew they meant the storm, but he knew it was a small window of time for Norwich, too.

Actually, Creed had been surprised they sent the unit, and he wondered what Hannah had told them. As soon as Norwich collapsed, Creed had called Hannah instead of 911. *Knee-jerk reaction.* And he wasn't sure his signal would last long enough for detailed instructions or explanation.

They should have stayed put. Hunkered down and waited out the storm. Hurrying back had only made it worse.

He felt Maggie's presence before he saw her. Just like in the forest. She squatted down beside him, leaned against him as she put her hand through his arm. Then she said as if reading his mind, "You couldn't have known."

Was he that transparent? Or did she just know him too well.

He overheard the flight nurse tell Jason he'd done a good job. Then he heard her say they had a pulse.

There were no sighs of relief. No celebratory cheers. No one said a word. All of them seemed to know a pulse meant nothing.

All of them except Brodie.

"Is Sheriff Norwich going to be okay?" she asked.

No one answered. They watched as Deputy Danvers helped the flight crew carry the stretcher across the meadow to the waiting helicopter.

Creed leaned over Grace, and this time he wrapped an arm around Brodie's shoulder.

"I don't know," he told her. "I hope so."

He glanced over at Hannah. Spiritual inspiration was supposed to be her wheelhouse.

"She's in the best possible hands," Hannah said. "We're not doing her any good by standing around. Y'all look like you've been swimming in the mud. Come on and dry up a bit."

Then she headed for the house, and one by one the rest of them followed.

Chapter 27

K9 CrimeScents
Florida Panhandle

Creed knew there was nothing that would have made Hannah happier than to soothe their souls with her food. She invited everyone to stay for an early dinner, but the blank eyes and exhausted faces reiterated that it had been a long day. The shock of watching Sheriff Norwich's incapacitated body being carted away had not worn off.

They mumbled plans for the next day then shuffled off: Danvers and Hadley together back to the sheriff's department; Vickie with her evidence bags to the medical examiner's office; Jason and Scout to his trailer; Brodie upstairs to her room; and Hannah to her kitchen. Ryder, Maggie and Grace were the only ones left on the front porch of the big house. Without the other vehicles, Norwich's Sheriff's Department SUV stood alone under the shade of a magnolia tree.

Creed offered Maggie to stay, even suggesting one of the many bedrooms in the house if she wasn't comfortable in his loft. He was being a gentleman, when he really just wanted to take her hand and lead her to his bed. But every step of the way in this relationship, Creed had allowed Maggie to call the shots. It wasn't something he was used to, but it seemed like the right thing to do.

No, not just the right thing, but the necessary thing.

When she didn't automatically leave with the medical examiner, and asked if he would drive her, Creed hoped it was because she really wanted to stay. Now he wondered if she had simply been worried about him. Her remark earlier about Norwich not being his fault, stuck with him. He was a big boy. He didn't need anyone worrying about him.

Maggie insisted all of her things, including a change of clothes, were in her rental car. They had originally planned to have dinner this evening in Pensacola, but the day's detour had put a damper on that.

Then a fleeting thought gave him pause. Maybe this was her way of inviting him to her hotel room on the beach. Maggie O'Dell was complicated. He knew there were emotional scars—from her childhood and from her marriage—that hadn't fully healed.

By now, he'd hoped they were beyond playing games. They had shared their pasts, their secrets. They had even saved each other's lives. They obviously trusted each other with everything. Everything except their hearts.

When Maggie suggested Grace come along "for the ride," Creed tamped down any last hopes for romance or an overnight stay.

Grace was much better after the storms had cleared, and after she had a meal in her belly. But she still insisted on going along. Ever since the tornado, she didn't let him out of her sight. Hannah said the little dog cried if he left her behind. Cried like Hannah had never heard her cry before.

She'd always been attached to Creed since that day he'd found her, half starved and abandoned at the edge of his property. People had long ago gotten into the habit of leaving their unwanted dogs at the end of his driveway. That was how Scout came into their lives, too.

Creed caught Scout's owner dumping the mother dog late at night into the ditch. Good thing Creed had caught him, because the man also had a burlap sack filled with her puppies that he was going to dump in a river.

That was almost two years ago, and Creed could feel the anger sizzle in the pit of his gut. At the time, he let Bolo, a Rhodesian ridgeback, hold the man down and scare the crap out of him while Creed rescued the female black Labrador and the bag with her puppies. Scout was one of five. Since then, the mother made her home in their kennel, as did his siblings.

Creed had given Jason the pick of the litter when Jason first came to work and live at the facility. But the others were being trained as medical alert dogs. It was a rare training opportunity, since it was best to start with puppies. Creed and Hannah's rescues usually came to them a bit older.

In fact, Scout's sister, Sarge would be ready to go to work this fall. Jason and Hannah were training her for one of the vets who played poker with Jason at the Segway House. Eric Hudson's little boy, Luke, had type 1 diabetes.

So many of their searches included death and destruction, it would be good for all of them to see more positive results.

There were still a few hours of daylight, so Creed asked Maggie if they could take a detour.

"I promised Sheriff Norwich that I'd find a place for her team to launch a boat," he told her. "That'll be the best way for them to bring out the remains."

He remembered an old two-track off one of the gravel roads, but it was a long time since he'd used it. The path was easy to miss. No signs. Overgrown grass and a line of trees hid the area. There wasn't an official boat launch, but the clearing provided plenty space once you made it through the entrance.

The two-track was bumpier than Creed remembered. Deep ruts were filled with the recent rain. After a short drive through the woods, a sandy beach appeared. As he parked in the clearing, he could see tire tracks cut into the tall grass. Marks were left in the sand, too, where someone had backed a boat trailer right to the water's surface. It was the perfect place to launch a boat without dropping off a steep bank.

Both of them got out of Creed's Jeep at the same time without a word.

Then Maggie asked, "Do a lot of people know about this area?"

"Locals do," Creed said. "It's not a secret. Most of the canoeing outfitters use Blackwater River. They usually start up north in the park. Current brings them down river."

"Going from here to the crime scene is against the current?"

"Yes."

"And this isn't Blackwater River?"

"Coldwater Creek."

They stood shoulder to shoulder looking out over the water. The creek was wide here, but Creed remembered that it quickly narrowed.

He glanced at Maggie. Her eyes darted around, searching the surrounding woods and the tree line on the opposite bank. Only now did he notice her shoulder holster and that the snap over her weapon had been undone.

He'd forgotten what she had gone through two years ago when a madman managed to coerce Maggie and her FBI partner into the forest.

He'd planned to hunt them down. If Creed and Bolo hadn't found him first, the guy might have succeeded. It was one of those scars. One that he knew about.

"You were clear on the other side of the park," he tried to reassure her.

She didn't look at him. Only nodded, acknowledging that she knew exactly what he was referring to.

They both heard the sound at the same time. Half whine, half growl. When Creed looked over his shoulder, he saw Grace with her nose and paws up against the back window, staring in the direction of the sound. Then she started frantically scratching at the window.

"That wasn't human," Maggie whispered, and Creed saw her hand on the butt of her gun.

Chapter 28

Between the long shadows Creed could barely make out the eyes and snout peeking through the shrubs. He approached cautiously, aware of the mud sucking at his boots, and of Maggie two steps behind him.

"It's a dog," Creed told her over his shoulder, keeping his voice low and calm. "I think he's injured."

The eyes watched. There was no attempt to run away. Perhaps the injuries wouldn't allow it.

Creed had slowly moved within three feet when the animal lunged out of the brush. Jaws snapped. Nostrils flared. Its stocky, muscular body pushed up but not far.

Creed heard a click behind him. He gritted his teeth and stopped himself from looking back at Maggie.

"You didn't just pull your gun," he said, keeping his tone calm and steady, despite his irritation.

"He's ready to attack," she countered, not as good at disguising her panic.

"Put it away and back toward the Jeep."

"But you don't know—"

"Put your gun down and back away."

She didn't move for several beats, and just when he thought he'd need to tell her again, she started leaving.

The dog hadn't come any closer. But now, Creed could see the bloodstain on his tan-colored coat. Blood covered the dog's chest and shoulder. He was soaking wet from the rains but still bleeding. And despite being injured, he was intimidating as hell.

"It's okay," Creed changed his cadence, making it friendly and reassuring.

The dog watched, eyes wide. His black muzzle swung back and forth then jerked down. He was trying to keep the flies off of himself. But he didn't attempt to come forward. He was panting and waiting. Clearly trying to figure out if he'd need to defend himself, again.

"Just stay," he said, and immediately he saw a hint of recognition at the word.

Creed backed slowly away. The dog held himself up to watch as Creed turned and opened the Jeep's tailgate.

"I thought he might bite you," Maggie said, clearly feeling the need to explain her actions. "He looks like a pit bull."

"He probably will bite me," Creed said, "But I don't want you shooting him. It looks like someone else already did that."

He pushed aside a duffel bag and started digging for another that was stashed to the side. Grace wagged at him but kept her perch by the window, more interested in the dog, as if her job was to keep an eye on him.

"What can I do to help?" Maggie asked.

He glanced over. Her holster was still undone. She noticed and deliberately snapped the flap closed.

"We'll need to get a muzzle on him."

He pulled it out and showed it to her. He also brought out a bite sleeve, towel and a slipknot lead. The dog had a thick collar on to match his thick neck, but a clip-on leash would be worthless.

Creed moved Grace's dog crate forward, turning it so it faced the window she was looking out.

"Time to get inside, Grace," he told her as he gestured to the zipped open door. Reluctantly, she obeyed. He secured the closure and placed the crate against the side door, so she could continue watching the big dog.

Then he slid out a spare crate that had been laying flat on the bench. He unfolded it, making sure the sides were secure, and it wouldn't collapse on itself if the big dog thrashed around inside. He positioned this crate as close as possible to the open tailgate with the crate's door facing out.

Tucked along the inside wall of the Jeep, he pulled out a narrow ramp. He secured it over the bumper, positioning it so it came right to the open crate. Using his boot, he tested its strength. He wasn't sure if the dog was able to walk on his own. From his limited view, Creed guessed he had to weigh fifty to sixty pounds. Creed had carried dogs heavier than that. But this one had a body-builder physique, and Creed was getting ready to trigger its fight or flight instinct.

He prepared himself as best as possible. The bite sleeve covered his entire left arm. It was military grade, a low-profile construction that could fit under a shirt. Compared to commercial ones that looked like the arm was in a cast, this one was sleek and thin. He adjusted the Velcro straps and could easily bend his elbow. The cuff came down to the palm of his hand but kept his fingers free.

Creed picked up the slipknot lead.

"I'll distract him. Be sure and keep a wide loop," he said as he showed her, making a lasso of the slipknot. "Slide it over his head from behind his head. If he looks at you, he'll need to tip his head up. Slip it over without getting your hand close to his mouth. Then tug it tight. Don't pull on him too hard. We don't want to hurt him any more than he's already hurting."

"You did see that he has a massive head and jaws, right?"

"Yes, I did notice that."

He handed her the lead, watching her eyes.

"And if he bites you?" she asked.

"He probably will. I'll be offering this arm to distract him," he said, flexing the bite sleeve and holding his forearm out. "Don't worry about it. He can't bite through this. Eventually, he'll let go. If you miss slipping it on, just wait a few seconds, and we'll start all over. Just keep calm. Don't fight him. If nothing else, we'll wear him out."

She hesitated while she looked over the corded lead, letting her fingers get a feeling for how it worked.

Finally she looked up. Her eyes met his, and she said, "You've never done this before."

"Not even once."

And he had no idea if it would work. He had only used a bite sleeve once while in Afghanistan. Since then, he'd wrestled with plenty of injured dogs, but not one with jaws strong enough to break bones. Most of the dogs he'd helped or saved were too hurt to fight him.

"What do you think?" he asked. "Can we do this?"

She took the lead, played with the slipknot again then said, "Piece of cake."

Chapter 29

One of Maggie's own dogs was a huge, black shepherd mix. Her friend Lucy Coy, who had rescued the dog in the Sandhills of Nebraska, insisted that if Jake wasn't part wolf, he certainly had the spirit of one. Maggie had seen the dog jump out of nowhere and viciously attack a man.

Of course, it was a bit different. The man was trying to kill Maggie. Jake had saved her life.

Still, she knew and respected the damage a powerful dog could inflict. If this injured dog knocked Ryder off his feet and started to attack him, there was little Maggie could do to stop it. At the risk of disappointing Ryder, Maggie wouldn't hesitate to shoot the animal. Ryder's life or the dog's life? As far as she was concerned, it was an easy choice.

But as she watched Ryder, looking for his instructions and letting him guide her with subtle head gestures—a tip of his chin, a flick of his eyes—she found herself becoming mesmerized by his movements.

And so was the dog.

Ryder possessed a rare, quiet confidence that didn't intimidate or bring about any sense of confrontation. Even when he was telling her to put away her weapon, there was nothing demeaning or threatening in his tone. Training dogs had made him very good at draining the emotion from his voice.

How many times had she heard him say it?

Emotion runs down the leash.

Despite his skill, she had detected the hint of underlying hurt in his voice. It wasn't necessarily hurt. That was the wrong word. And no, he wasn't offended. She'd never once seen Ryder Creed get offended.

She still felt the kick to her gut. It was worse than him being hurt or offended. Slight as it was, she felt like she had disappointed him.

Was it a character flaw that she cared about him? Didn't want him hurt? Mauled by a dog?

She shook the entire notion out of her mind. She needed to concentrate. If she gave herself too many options, she'd fail at the task at hand. Be steady, calm. She'd take her lead from this man she cared about and respected. And yes, trusted.

The dog hadn't taken his eyes off of Ryder except to shake the flies off of him. He was vaguely aware of Maggie. He gave her quick glances, sometimes emitting a low growl. But the closer they got, even the growls were ending in guttural notes that sounded more like a whine or a cry than a warning.

The whole time, Ryder talked to him with that soothing reassurance that Maggie found could be hypnotizing.

He called him "a good boy," guessing he was male by the blue collar. Every word rang sincere and genuine. He told him everything would be okay.

He *promised* him.

And Maggie knew he meant it. Would he be crushed when the dog lunged at him again? Would he defend himself if the massive jaws came down on that thin, black sleeve? What if the dog didn't let go? What if he gave the arm a shake until bone snapped?

She needed to stop. To clear those images out of her mind.

It didn't help that Ryder's hands stayed at his sides. She understood that he didn't want the dog to feel threatened. No sudden moves. Nothing swinging his way.

The thought made her glance around for branches big enough to act as a club if she needed to get the dog off of Ryder.

And yet, Ryder didn't seem to think of any of this. Instead, he continued toward the dog, one foot in front of the other, steady and calm like a tightrope walker. His pace was shorter and slower than his normal gait. If there was such a thing as a dog whisperer, Maggie imagined this was exactly what he looked and sounded like.

Now they were within four feet then three. This is where they were before when the dog lunged at him. But instead of Ryder bracing his sleeved forearm in front of him to prepare, he did something that automatically made Maggie's stomach sink to her knees. He reached his hand out to the dog, palm down. His right hand! The arm that wasn't protected.

"You're okay, buddy. We're not gonna hurt you. You're a good boy, aren't you?"

And then the dog did something that shocked Maggie.

He let out a long, low whine, more sadness than pain. He readjusted himself, stiff and awkward. Maggie felt her entire body tense up. It took concentrated effort to keep her hand from going to her holster.

"You're okay, buddy," Ryder encouraged him. "Can you walk? We just want to help you."

The dog pulled himself up. It was difficult for him to step over the tangle of brush that he had made his hiding place. He was completely tan except for his black muzzle and the bloodstain that covered his chest and shoulder. He was weak and wobbly, but he limped his way forward. Even hurt and injured, his stocky, muscular body made him look dangerous. His dark eyes, short ears, broad head and square muzzle contributed to the perception. Enough so, that Maggie couldn't believe it when he lowered his head and limped his way to Ryder.

"Good boy! What a good boy you are, Hank!"

The name was the clincher, now visible, embroidered on the back of his collar.

That's when the dog's tail lifted slightly from between his legs. Hank wagged. Ryder squatted down and opened his hand, keeping it low so as not to intimidate the dog. Maggie found herself holding her breath. The dog could jump at him and knock him over.

Hank slinked his way closer, big eyes settled on Ryder's face. He stopped just inches from Ryder's fingers, and he dropped his head. Ryder petted him gently and scratched behind his ear, and the big dog wagged ever so slightly, again.

Chapter 30

Creed left a voice message for Dr. Avelyn Parker. It was long past office hours at her Milton Veterinary Clinic, but she returned his call in less than ten minutes.

Years ago Creed and Hannah had convinced the young veterinarian to be the exclusive caregiver for their kennel. Creed designed a facility to her specifications on their property, and in some cases, he provided more advanced equipment than Dr. Avelyn and her two partners had in their own clinic. So instead of constantly driving dogs to the vet, Dr. Avelyn spent a portion of her weekly schedule at their facility.

He tried not to take advantage of their agreement, but at times like this, he was grateful that her knee-jerk reaction was to start giving him instructions on what to do.

"It'll probably take me thirty to forty minutes to get there," she told him before she hung up.

They were closer to Creed's property than they were to Maggie's rental car. He was relieved when she insisted they go back. And even more relieved when he offered to have Jason drive her to Pensacola, she didn't argue with him.

The ride back was quiet. Creed figured the stress and exhaustion of the day had caught up with both of them. The adrenaline drain left him too tired to talk about what had just happened. He still couldn't believe the big dog had made it so easy on him.

The back of Creed's shirt stuck to the leather seat. He glanced in the rearview mirror to check on Hank. He was breathing hard, but his head was down. Then he got a glimpse of his own face. His bristled jaw and forehead glistened with sweat.

"It was amazing watching you," Maggie said after a long silence. "You got him to trust you."

He didn't mention that it was easier to get Hank to trust him than it was to get her. Instead he said, "I think he was just glad to have someone help him."

"How long do you think he's been out there?"

"I don't know. Looks like the bullet is still in him, which might have kept him from bleeding to death."

Maggie's cell phone chimed. She pulled it out and tapped it a couple of times.

"When you were talking to Dr. Avelyn I texted Vickie," Maggie said. "Sheriff Norwich is in critical but stable condition."

Creed couldn't believe he'd forgotten about her. It felt like days ago, not hours.

"Was it a heart attack?"

Maggie tapped in a message. Within seconds came a response.

"Yes," she said.

She and the medical examiner exchanged several more texts.

He realized he still didn't know how Maggie had gotten involved in this case. From what he understood, she made the trip because of an auctioned off storage unit and some grisly finds.

When she finally slid her cell phone back into her pocket, Creed said, "You certainly got more than you bargained for this time."

She hugged him before she climbed into Jason's SUV, and told him she'd see him tomorrow. He watched the taillights weave between the trees.

When he opened the Jeep's back door to get Grace, the big dog looked up at him. Hopefully the air conditioner made him more comfortable. At least he didn't have to worry about the flies anymore. Creed didn't like to think how much time the dog had spent at the edge of the woods, scared and in pain and hungry. He wouldn't be able to feed him or give him water just yet. He'd wait for Dr. Avelyn's instructions.

"You're a good boy, Hank. Just a little bit longer."

He took Grace in to stay with Hannah. Jason had already filled her in, and she met him at the back door with a mug of freshly brewed coffee. Hannah had already checked on Sheriff Norwich, too.

"They won't know more for twenty-four hours," she told him. "Lord have mercy, this has been some kind of day."

"How's Brodie?"

"She and Kitten went up to bed after dinner. She mentioned something about helping collect evidence?"

"Yeah. She's full of surprises," Creed said, wiping a hand over his face and hoping to remove the exhaustion.

With all that had happened he hadn't had time to worry about Brodie. He took a sip of coffee while his eyes watched out the window for Dr. Avelyn's headlights.

Suddenly, Hannah laughed, and he cocked an eyebrow at her.

She shook her head and said, "Abandoned and wounded dogs just keep on finding you, don't they? It's like you have some kind of radar."

"It's like I have a steak in my pocket." He smiled. "Wait until you see this guy. He actually scared the hell out of me."

Headlights turned in at the end of the driveway. Creed gulped down the rest of the coffee and was out the door. He drove over to their clinic, unlocked the back door and started switching on lights, all the way to the surgery suite.

He turned around just as Dr. Avelyn came in. He almost didn't recognize the woman in the sleek, black dress and high heels.

"Wow! I'm really sorry. It looks like I dragged you away from something important." What was wrong with him? In all these years why hadn't he considered the veterinarian actually had a life?

"No big deal," she said, kicking off the heels. She opened a locker and pulled out shoes and scrubs. When she noticed him still staring at her she stopped. "What?" she asked.

"Nothing," he said quickly and a little embarrassed. It wasn't like he could tell her she had nice legs. Really nice legs.

"I'll go get Hank," he told her instead.

Chapter 31

It had been a while since Creed had scrubbed in on a surgery. He would have felt better if he had taken a shower. He ended up washing down his entire torso, the back of his neck and face before he started scrubbing his hands and forearms.

Dr. Avelyn could do the surgery on her own, but he was glad she let him stay. And grateful she allowed him to help.

The big dog was sedated by the time Creed returned. Dr. Avelyn waved a handheld device over the back of his neck.

"He's been chipped," she said. "Should be able to find the owner."

"If the owner did this, I'm not giving him back."

She continued prepping but stopped and pointed to one of Hank's paws. "He recently had his nails trimmed and filed down." She waved her hand over the rest of the dog. "He doesn't look like he's been abused. Other than the gunshot wound, he looks like he's in good shape. I suspect the owner didn't do this."

"I don't have any experience with pit bulls. I really thought he might bite me."

"All the bully breeds get a bad rap. Most of them are actually good-natured and affectionate. But this guy isn't a pit bull."

"No?"

"American Staffordshire Bull terrier. And he really is a beautiful one. They get a bad rap, too. They're friendly, intelligent. Love to please their people. But lots of energy. I tell my clients, expect to walk and run them. They like to keep busy."

"Sounds like the perfect scent dog."

She glanced up at him. "In your mind you're already keeping him, aren't you?"

"He came to me. He was scared. I was scared, and he came to me anyway. He trusted me." Creed shrugged like he hadn't given it much thought beyond that, but yes, in his mind he wasn't going to let anyone hurt this dog ever again.

"The breed is very loyal. There's a good chance he was protecting his owner."

Creed hadn't thought of that.

She was cleaning Hank's chest and shoulder. Creed handed her fresh sterile pads, one after another. They could finally see the wound much better without all the dried blood and caked mud.

"He was definitely facing the shooter. Looks like the bullet is lodged in his chest muscle just above his right shoulder."

She started working. Creed watched, hyper-alert for anything she asked him to hand to her or to hold. He stayed focused on her fingers, but looked up every once in a while, to check her eyes, searching for any indication of how bad it was. Only now did he notice she was wearing makeup. He really had pulled her away from something special.

Creed was used to a life where he dropped anything and everything for the sake of a dog. Or Hannah. Or Brodie. But he realized he shouldn't expect that from others.

"I really am sorry I ruined your evening," he told her.

"Actually you did me a favor," she said without looking up at him. "I hate blind dates. I don't know why I let friends talk me into them."

A date! That was all Creed heard, and now he did feel bad.

"Don't worry about it," she added. "I'd do the same thing for any of my other clients."

"But you have two other partners who cover for you."

"Are you saying you want to hire another vet for here?"

He recognized a hint of hurt in her voice.

"No, that's not at all what I'm saying. I'm just trying to apologize for being an inconsiderate jerk. I don't want you to ever feel like I'm taking advantage of you."

He could tell from her eyes that she was smiling underneath her mask.

"We're good. Seriously, don't worry about it," she told him.

"Well, I owe you one."

"Okay. Yes, you owe me one."

Then she held up her forceps to show him the bullet.

Chapter 32

Pensacola, Florida

Jason had offered to follow Maggie from the medical examiner's offices to her hotel on Pensacola Beach. She had been unusually quiet during the drive. She thanked him for his offer and said it wasn't necessary.

He didn't know the woman well, but he knew Ryder was crazy about her, despite the fact that he refused to talk about it. Maybe they were just exhausted, but still, Jason wondered if something had happened between Maggie and Ryder. Something more than finding an injured dog.

Jason drove by the Segway House and noticed one of his friend's vehicles parked in the far corner of the lot next to a shiny, black Mercedes. Not one of the handicapped slots close to the door. He shook his head and smiled. This place had been a home to him when he got back from Afghanistan. After all the hospitals. After all the frickin' rehab. It was one of the few places that didn't make him feel like a freak, because so many of the other guys had it worse.

Like Benny. Both of his legs were amputated above the kneecaps. And yet the guy didn't want to take up a handicapped parking. Instead, he parked in the far corner of the lot.

"I've got this down," Benny told them. "Someone else might need it more than me."

Though he used a motorized wheelchair, his vehicle was specially rigged with a hydraulic ramp.

The Segway House wasn't just for veterans. It was a safe haven for teenage runaways, domestic violence victims, and other lost souls. It was one of the first places he could talk about what he'd experienced. He certainly hadn't been able to talk to his family.

From the very beginning, they'd made it clear they didn't want to hear about it. They wanted to pretend his arm hadn't been amputated. That he was the same ole Jason even as they gave him their best pity looks. His mom told him it was too sad to talk about. His father hadn't even come to the hospital. Said it was too hard to see his son all broken and in pain.

Too hard.

His mom wanted him to stay with them, but Jason knew he would suffocate from their expectations.

But at the Segway House, he met veterans in worse shape than himself. They could joke about it. Trade war stories.

It was also where he'd met Hannah Washington. Almost two years ago she offered him a job as an apprentice dog trainer. It came with a doublewide and a kennel-full of daily chores. He didn't recognize it at the time, but what she really offered him was a lifeline.

Still, he was drowning, and he didn't know it until Ryder handed him a second lifeline. He let Jason choose a puppy of his own to raise and train. The offer came with a catch though. Jason had to promise to stick around and not abandon the dog. From the day they met Ryder had seen and recognized what others had not. Jason's death wish, his Option B.

Jason made his way through the lobby, waving to the receptionist who recognized him. Everyone remembered him. Mostly they remembered his black mechanical hand. Hannah's boys called him the Terminator man or Transformer guy. They thought his prosthetic made him a superhero.

He found his friends in their regular spots around a poker table: Benny, Colfax, Doc and a new guy named Theo who was temporarily replacing their friend, Eric. As soon as Jason came into the room, Benny and Colfax called out his name like this was the local watering hole. No alcohol or smoking was allowed in the Segway House, but the atmosphere was sort of like a neighborhood pub.

Jason slipped into his regular chair that had been left empty and ready for him.

"Looks like a high-stakes game," he nodded at the piles of plastic chips in the center of the table.

"Doc keeps upping the ante," Benny said.

They weren't allowed to play for money. They tallied the points for the week in a notebook. The losers chipped in and bought the winner dinner or drinks at their other hangout: Walter's Canteen on Pensacola Beach.

Doc was the misfit. Older than the rest of them, he was what Jason had heard described as classically handsome, cleft chin and thick wavy hair. He looked and talked like a celebrity. He was an Army surgeon; whose own PTSD came from patching up guys like those around the table.

"Doc, it's kind of late," Jason said. "I thought your wife liked you to be home for dinner."

"Yeah, how is your beautiful, young wife?" Colfax emphasized "young."

Doc often complained about keeping up with his new trophy wife, even as he bragged about her. She was wife #3, and they'd all heard stories about the ex's, and how hard Doc had to work to pay for all of them. But it was in jest. The man obviously did okay. He drove a Mercedes and dressed in clothes that even Jason recognized as designer stuff.

"Deal you in?" Colfax asked.

"No, I can't stay," Jason told him. "Just stopped in to say, hey."

"What, you got a big date or something?" Doc asked.

"Right, cause I'm such a stud."

Benny and Colfax laughed. Doc didn't. And Theo, who didn't know any of them well enough, stared at his cards.

"No," Jason added. "Have to be up early to work a scene."

But he stayed and talked until he realized he, Benny, and Colfax were the only ones left. Theo got tired of losing. Doc got a text and had to go. They ribbed him about the young wife, but Jason thought the text might be a patient because Doc looked too serious.

Just when Jason was getting ready to leave, a woman walked into their room. Tall, blond and gorgeous and so far out of his league he had to tell himself to close his jaw and stop staring.

"Sorry, guys," she told them. "I was just looking for someone."

"You mean like a few good men?" Jason couldn't believe his boldness. "You found us!"

"Cute," she said, but with a smile that wasn't at all condescending or even annoyed. Instead, it was…hell, it was sexy, especially the way she looked him in the eyes.

"I'm Jason," he managed over the butterflies forming in his gut. "This is Colfax and Benny. Why don't you join us? We're just playing some poker."

"I can't. Sorry guys," and she said it to all three of them like she genuinely appreciated the offer. "Rain check?"

"Absolutely."

She started back out the door but turned and said, "By the way, I'm Taylor."

And then she was gone.

The three of them stared after her until Benny broke the trance and said, "Wow." Then to Jason he added, "Way to go. You are a stud. Who knew?"

Jason just shook his head, but he couldn't shake the smile off his face even as he said, "She is so far out of our league."

Chapter 33

Margaritaville Beach Hotel
Pensacola Beach, Florida

Maggie paced while she listened to Gwen Patterson tell her she was being ridiculous. Gwen was her friend, mentor, nagging mother figure, and Doctor of Psychology. Mostly in that order.

"I don't know," Maggie said. "I've never seen him look at me that way before. He didn't just look pissed off. He looked…he looked disappointed."

"I'm sure you'll be able to talk it out. He was worried about the dog. You were worried about him."

Maggie stood on the balcony of her sixth-floor hotel room. The view of the Gulf was breathtaking even in the dark. It wasn't right to complain about such trivial things instead of enjoying this view.

"I'm sure you're right," she finally told her friend.

"What I want to know is why are you in a hotel room?"

"Excuse me?" Maggie asked.

"Why aren't you staying with Ryder and Hannah? I thought they had all kinds of room in that huge house."

"It's complicated."

"We've talked about this before. You make things too complicated."

Of course Gwen was right. Maggie could handle tracking serial killers and confronting them easier than she could handle personal relationships. After her father died, Maggie's mother started drinking and bringing home strange men to spend the night. Some of the men thought her twelve-year-old daughter should be part of the deal.

In her mother's defense, the woman was usually passed out when the fondling and inappropriate touching occurred. But for Maggie it had destroyed her ability to trust anyone close to her. Especially men.

"But hey," Gwen said when Maggie took too long to respond. "I'm all for staying on the beach, ordering room service and sinking your toes in the sand. If I know you, I'm guessing you won't even do that."

"You don't know that," Maggie countered. "I'm getting ready to order some room service."

Her cell phone beeped, letting her know she had another call coming in. She glanced at the ID.

"The medical examiner is calling me," Maggie told her friend. "Thanks for listening. I better take this."

"Okay, but don't come back without sinking your toes in the sand."

Maggie smiled. If Gwen could only see the view she was looking at right now.

"Hello, Dr. Kammerer."

"Hey, how long did you plan to spend down here?" Vickie asked.

"Maybe through the end of the week. Why?"

"With Sheriff Norwich sidelined, we're going to need some help. I looked you up. This stuff is your specialty." She sounded surprised.

"I told you that," Maggie said.

"Sure, but you didn't mention that you're the head of a special serial crime unit. A whole unit with digital forensics and crime lab services. This case definitely meets the requirements, and don't tell me you have a waiting list. You're already down here."

"Dr. Kammerer, are you requesting my assistance?" Maggie couldn't keep the smile from her voice.

She had spent a long, hard day with the woman, and had already decided early on that she liked her, even liked working with her. That wasn't always the case when she worked with local coroners or medical examiners.

"Yes, I am requesting," Vickie said. "And I just realized I'm doing a piss-poor job of it."

Day 2

Chapter 34

K9 CrimeScents
Florida Panhandle
Tuesday, June 16

Brodie worried that they might not allow her back at the crime scene. After all, she wasn't an official anything. She was a helpful guide yesterday, and her freakishly long arms had come in handy. Today she might just be in the way. But she was anxious and excited to work along side Vickie and Maggie again.

It didn't matter that her sleep had been filled with maggot-riddled bodies. When she woke up, she marched to her bathroom and spent a good ten minutes washing her hands. When that wasn't enough, she stood under the showerhead welcoming the powerful stream of water even though she had taken a shower last night.

It was difficult to explain. She didn't mind getting dirty and sweaty, but she knew her obsession with washing—especially her hands—was a side effect from days, weeks, months of sleeping in her own filth. She was glad no one questioned her. Except for Isaac and Thomas. But that was only because they didn't want their mom making them wash their hands as much as Brodie washed hers.

At breakfast, Hannah told them Sherriff Norwich's condition remained unchanged. She was responsive and being monitored.

"Was it a heart attack?" Jason asked.

"Yes, it was, and she has you to thank for knowing what to do."

"Nice to know the hand works," he said flexing the black mechanical fingers.

Both Isaac and Thomas threw up their arms and shouted, "Transformer Guy!"

Jason smiled at them then caught Brodie's eyes and did an eyeroll that the boys couldn't see.

"Maggie and Vickie are coming back here. They're going to take Brodie's trail back in," Hannah told them. "Sheriff department's men are coming up Coldwater Creek."

"They using the launch site Ryder found?" Jason asked.

Hannah nodded.

"Where is Ryder?" Brodie craned her neck to look out the kitchen window. Usually he and Jason came in together after kennel chores. She realized he must not be with Maggie if she was coming with Vickie. Their romantic dinner must have gotten cancelled completely.

"He and Grace spent the night in the clinic," Hannah said.

"Is Grace okay?"

"Oh sure she is. A bit worn out. Which by the way, Jason, Ryder said you and Scout will need to continue the search. He might join y'all later."

Then Hannah told Brodie about the dog Ryder and Maggie had found. How Dr. Avelyn had performed surgery last night to remove a bullet. Brodie listened quietly. She knew Hannah was making it not as scary because of Isaac and Thomas being there at the table, though both boys listened intently. Brodie would ask for details later. She wondered whether it was the same man who killed those people in the forest.

There was a time when Brodie wouldn't have a problem with shooting a dog. She wondered if that was still true. Once upon a time, Iris Malone had sent a big, frightening hound after her when Brodie tried to run away. The dog clamped its huge jaw around her ankle. It felt like his teeth sank all the way down to the bone. The scar was an ugly reminder. But Jason had helped her get over her fear of dogs.

She looked up now and found him watching her.

"You okay?" he asked.

She nodded. Everybody was always asking her if she was okay. It was annoying. But she liked when Jason asked. She liked it a lot.

He glanced at his phone that he had left beside his plate. Then he pointed to her plate.

"Finish up. Maggie and the medical examiner are almost here. We need to be ready to go."

"Really?" She slipped. And it was too late to hide it. She could feel the surprise register on her face before she could hold it back.

Jason simply put his head down and pretended to concentrate on forking up another piece of pancake and sausage, but Brodie saw the uptick of a smile at the corner on his mouth before he took a bite.

Chapter 35

Blackwater River State Forest

Brodie watched Vickie assessing the crime scene, turning until she made a full circle. The big tarps held in place but were now sunken in the middle with pools of water, twigs and leaves. Fallen branches had blocked their path in a couple of places, but here in the clearing the puddles appeared to be the only nuisance.

And the mosquitoes…and flies. Even Hannah's magic concoction might not meet the challenge.

"Could it be any more humid?" Vickie said, and today Brodie recognized her deadpan humor. Or sarcasm. Okay, she still didn't understand the difference, but she enjoyed when Vickie did it.

A pile of old clothes was where Vickie wanted to start this morning. The medical examiner had already told them what she wanted to collect. She'd asked Jason and Scout to search the portion of the woods directly behind this victim.

She kept calling the abandoned clothes a victim, but even as Brodie helped lift up the tarp, she couldn't see anything more than a limp, dirty shirt that was once striped and canvas pants.

Vickie pulled out a white sheet from her backpack. As she unfolded it, she handed two corners to Brodie, gesturing for them to stretch it out and lay it alongside the mess.

"I would love to scoop her up and put her into a body bag, so I could peel her apart on one of my tables. But that might not happen so easily, ladies."

"What makes you think it's a her?" Brodie wanted to know. She thought the clothes were too dirty to tell.

"Good question. Maggie, get a couple of evidence bags ready. I don't want some of the smaller pieces to go to the sheet. Just the big, messy stuff."

Vickie squatted down. She tugged her latex gloves up high over her wristwatch. She brushed her fingertips across the top until they could see the fabric. Faded red, yellow and blue stripes on gray. Or probably white, not gray.

Not satisfied with her fingertips, she reached over to her backpack's outer pocket and removed a brush. Then she started running the bristles carefully over the rest of the clothes. Within minutes Brodie could see the outline taking form. Sleeves down by the sides, pant legs straight out.

For a minute Brodie thought it looked exactly like someone would display an outfit on the bed to see if the pieces went together. She remembered her mother doing the same thing years ago.

Then the realization hit her.

This was just like the man they'd found yesterday, the one who looked like he had simply gone to sleep in the grass.

Knowing that didn't make it any less shocking when the medical examiner started peeling apart the top of the shirt.

"She's still gooey," Vickie announced. "Fair warning. I've seen this kind of stuff flip the cookies of some of the toughest cops I know."

It was too late for Brodie. She couldn't take her eyes away. She could see bones as the medical examiner collected them one by one. Some still had tissue attached. Vickie lifted them up, and Maggie met her halfway with an evidence bag.

"Mark it scapula and clavicle."

Her fingers went back in but this time she pulled on the shirt's tag and it easily separated, coming free into her hand.

"You asked how I could tell the victim was a female," Vickie said to Brodie. "When we don't have much left, we look at what we do have."

She stood and held up the tag.

"This woman was short, perhaps a bit overweight and she shopped at JC Penney's."

"Now you're just showing off," Maggie said.

"You can tell all that because of the shirt she's wearing?" Brodie asked.

"Yup. It was a size 16 petite. And St. John's Bay is an exclusive brand for JC Penney's. Or it used to be."

"No shoes. No socks," Maggie said. "Is it possible he took her from her home?"

"Very good," Vickie rewarded her with a grin. "Or it could just mean that her shoes were interesting enough for a predator to grab. I'm thinking that might be what happened to her head."

Chapter 36

Blackwater River State Forest
Coldwater Creek

Creed trailered his boat to the isolated launch site where he and Maggie had found Hank. Earlier he had texted Mark Hadley with the GPS coordinates. He parked next to the Sheriff's Department SUV and trailer. The men were about an hour ahead of Creed. From Hadley's texts, it sounded like the trip up the creek was quiet and uneventful.

Creed was still thinking about Hank. Dr. Avelyn had him resting comfortably. She had gone home shortly after midnight, promising to stop back after breakfast and insisting Creed do the same. After she left, he pulled the mattress from the office's foldout sofa. He brought it in and placed it about ten feet from Hank's kennel. It was close enough that he could hear if the dog was distressed. But Hank slept, not even noticing Creed or Grace.

Hannah promised she'd check on the dog, and she reminded Creed that one of his many security cameras allowed her *and* him to see the dog in his hospital kennel no matter where they were. As long as he had cellular reception.

By the time he put the boat in the water he'd already peeked in on the dog several times. He'd also called Hank's owner and left a voice message. Dr. Avelyn had been able to access the owner's contact information because of the microchip. The address listed was in Virginia. Hank was definitely a long way from home.

Now that Creed and Grace made their way up the creek, he felt his muscles relaxing, his mind clearing. He tilted and twisted his neck and rolled his shoulders, trying to release the tension from the last twenty-four hours. He needed only one hand on the trolling motor to steer as he let the boat glide, sometimes squeezing along the high banks and zigzagging around debris.

Grace sat across from him. Ears flapping back in the draft. It was early enough that the breeze brought some refreshing coolness off the surface of the water. Spring-fed, Coldwater Creek stayed surprisingly cool all year.

He'd forgotten how the view from a boat presented an entirely different experience of the forest. White and pink crepe myrtles grew at the edge of the woods, their colors brilliant against the evergreens. Bluffs eroded by the wind showed off layers of red sandstone. The clear tea-colored water allowed a glimpse of the sandy bottom and creatures scuttling across it.

Up above, a blue heron glided along with them following the line of the creek. Once in a while Grace's head swiveled at the sound of something splashing into the water.

"We need to do this more often," he told the little dog.

She adjusted herself and set her head back to catch the breeze again, as if in agreement.

He kept track of the GPS coordinates and realized he was almost to the site. This was definitely a quicker and easier way in than trekking through the woods.

He was bringing the boat to the crime scene in case they needed it to help carry remains. Creed also wanted to survey the banks along the way. So far, he hadn't seen any areas with skid marks or worn-out patches of grass where a boat had been dragged ashore. But anyone could easily anchor a boat and climb up without much trouble.

In Creed's mind, Hank was proof that the killer had been using the same boat launch. He wished he'd thought of that before he drove his Jeep in last night. They could have staked out the place and waited.

The guy would be furious that they had found it. But Creed was certain he'd easily find a new way to gain access. Gut instinct told him this killer wouldn't stop just because he lost his boat launch.

Chapter 37

Maggie watched Norwich's men wrap the sheet carefully and put the victim inside the second body bag. In the first one, they had already deposited as much of the woman victim as possible, including the pieces of clothing that clung to tissue and bone. It was obvious that scavengers had made off with some pieces that might never be found.

Brodie and Vickie had another white sheet laid out and ready alongside the dead man Brodie had tripped over yesterday morning. Maggie took several last photos then waited for CSU tech Hadley and Deputy Danvers to roll the body over and onto the sheet.

His eyes were still open.

Unlike the other male corpse, the maggots hadn't been able to gain access to this man's nose, mouth or eyes. The wet mud had preserved his last look: panic, anguish, or simply pain. Take your pick. Whatever his last feelings, none of them were pleasant or peaceful.

But there was another surprise.

"Looks like he's been shot or stabbed," Vickie said as she started taking photos. When she finished, she squatted down close to get a better look.

Maggie could see the bloody wound was caked with mud, but it had already stained his shirt down around his abdomen.

"Let's wrap him up," Vickie said, gesturing for help.

Brodie and Maggie stood back and let the experts do their job. Maggie put a hand on Brodie's arm but the young woman continued to watch.

"You okay?" Maggie asked.

Without looking over at her, Brodie said in a calm and steady voice, "I swear if one more person asks me if I'm okay I'm going to scream."

Despite the calm tone, the words stopped everyone. Glances were exchanged, but Brodie silently stared straight ahead at the dead man. No one said a word and went back to work.

Hadley and Danvers carried the body bags one at a time, down through the short stretch of woods to the water's edge. Maggie had never seen a young man sweat as much as Deputy Danvers. She watched him closely, not wanting another heart attack or heatstroke.

Vickie asked Brodie if she'd get them some water, and Maggie thought the medical examiner was worried about Danvers, too. But Vickie was unwrapping something from out of an evidence bag.

"I don't want to alarm everyone," Vickie said. "Especially when I'm still speculating." She brought out a couple of bones and held them out in her gloved fingers for Maggie to examine. "These fell just inside the woman's collar. Can you see the striations along the edge?"

Maggie didn't have her gloves on, so she bent to examine them without touching the bones.

"That doesn't look like an animal's teeth marks," Maggie said. Unfortunately, she did have some experience recognizing cut-marks. These gashes and grooves were most likely man-made.

"Again, I'm only speculating at this point," Vickie told her, "But I'm guessing a serrated knife with this pattern of dips and points. A hacksaw makes a fine irregular line. And a butcher knife leaves a straight, smooth cut."

"Why dismember her if you're going to dump her in an isolated part of the forest?"

"That's your job," Vickie said.

"He may have still wanted to remove her identity."

"But no one was supposed to find her."

"I think we're going to discover that she's different," Maggie said. "She might be someone he knew."

Now, Vickie looked over Maggie's shoulder and said, "Thanks, Brodie." She slipped the bones back inside the evidence bag. "You're a lifesaver." She took one of the water bottles from Brodie, opened it and started gulping.

Maggie was about to do the same when Scout came zigzagging out of the forest to greet her. She'd almost forgotten about Jason and Scout. The Labrador's tongue was hanging out of his mouth and to the side. Drool dripped down.

There was too much saliva.

Maggie went to pet him, and he shook his head, sending ropes of saliva flying over his shoulders. She tried to calm him, putting her hands on each side of his head, but he shook her off. And he seemed to shake himself off balance, wobbling then swaying from side to side. That's when she noticed his eyes blinking like she'd never seen a dog blink before.

"Something's wrong with Scout!" she shouted.

Again, she tried to hold his head to see if he was injured, but now he staggered, suddenly too weak to stand.

"Scout!" Jason came racing from the woods.

As he weaved between trees, Maggie could see him struggling to pull off his daypack.

"Hold him," Jason yelled. "Don't let him run off!"

That wasn't a problem. Just as Maggie grabbed the handle on the dog's vest he collapsed to the ground.

"What's happening?" Brodie yelled. She dropped to her knees and put her arms around Scout's neck.

Maggie kneeled to hold him from the other side.

"A trash dump," Jason said. "He found a two-liter soda bottle."

He fell in place beside them, out of breath, his face slick with sweat. He was still fumbling with the pack, unzipping and digging.

"I think it was a shake-and-bake bottle," he told them. "It was capped, but there was other stuff. Patches, eye droppers, nasal spray containers."

"Shake-and-bake?" Brodie asked.

Jason found what he needed. He ripped open the pouch.

"Brodie keep holding him," he told her. "Don't let him go. Maggie, can you tilt his head up and facing me."

The dog wasn't responding, but his eyes were open. She clamped her hands on each side and lifted his head in Jason's direction.

Jason grabbed the dog's big snout, wrapping his black, mechanical fingers around it to close Scout's mouth but not so tight that the drool couldn't still spill out.

Maggie watched Scout's eyes. No more blinking. Now they were wide and watching his handler. They were the only part of him that seemed to be working.

"You're gonna be okay, buddy," Jason told him using a calm tone. To the rest of them, he said, "I didn't even realize what he'd found until it was too late. I'm pretty sure he already inhaled some of it."

This time Maggie could hear the panic in Jason's voice.

Maggie and Brodie tightened their grips.

He continued to hold the dog's snout. With his other hand, Jason took what looked like a nasal spray with an injector. He adjusted it between his forefinger and thumb then placed the tip inside one of Scout's nostrils. Keeping steady, he pushed the plunger in one even motion.

When he finished, he tossed the empty container into his pack and pulled out a basket muzzle. He slipped it on without Scout making a fuss.

Then Jason dragged a sleeve over his sweaty forehead. His hands came up under Maggie's, relieving her. He held his dog's head in his big hands, caressing the temples and rubbing his ears. The whole time, Jason kept watching the dog's eyes.

"You're such a good boy," Jason said, his voice a bit steadier now, but still on edge.

Scout wasn't moving. Brodie scooted around so that the dog's body leaned against her. Now with her hands free, Maggie moved one under the dog's chest until she could feel a heartbeat. It seemed a bit slow. So did his breathing.

"Maybe he needs another dose," Jason said quietly, but Maggie could hear the hitch in his voice. "I've never done this before. Just watched training videos."

"You're using naloxone?" It was Vickie, standing above them.

"Yes. Naracon naloxone. The intranasal spray."

"Do you have another dose?" she asked. "From what I remember there's no downside to using more."

"We always carry two doses. One for our dog, one for ourselves." But now, Jason didn't hesitate. He plucked up the pouch and pulled out another container. He removed the basket muzzle and administered the second dose, then replaced the muzzle.

Maggie kept an eye on her watch. With her hand still flat against Scout's chest, she started counting heartbeats. Thirty seconds went by then sixty. It felt like an excruciatingly long time. She couldn't bear to look at Jason, so she focused on Scout.

Seventy-five seconds…ninety.

A slight increase in beats.

One hundred seconds…one hundred twenty.

Scout groaned softly. He started to sit up. His big head swiveled around to look at all of them. His tail thumped against the ground once then began a slow wag. He twisted his head to see something behind Jason. The tail wagged more.

Grace pushed her way into the circle, and the Labrador tried to get to his feet then changed his mind.

"What's going on?" Ryder called out.

Then Maggie could hear his footsteps quicken as he raced across the scrub grass.

"What happened?"

"A trash dump," Jason explained. "I think there were fentanyl patches. Other stuff. I didn't even recognize what it was until I saw a shake-and-bake bottle. I gave him one dose of naloxone and he didn't respond. I just gave him another about two minutes ago."

"Do you know if he inhaled the meth, too?" Ryder asked

Maggie knew shake-and-bake was a homemade method for making methamphetamine. Drug users put the necessary ingredients into a regular two-liter soda bottle, replaced the cap and shook it until the desired chemical reaction occurred.

She understood it was probably dangerous for dogs to inhale, but it wasn't an opioid like fentanyl. Most likely Ryder was asking because it might require something different than the dosage of naloxone.

Ryder had his cell phone out and was already keying in a message.

"The cap was still tight on the bottle," Jason said. "I double checked."

Ryder's head jerked up. "You touched it?"

"I didn't know what the hell any of the stuff was."

"How are you feeling?"

"I'm okay."

"We need to get you checked, too." Ryder told him. "We'll take the boat. It's faster. Dr. Avelyn's already at our place. We need to get Scout in quick."

"He seems to be doing okay," Vickie said.

"Treat and transport," Ryder told her. "The in-field dosage is enough to block the effect of the opioid. Depending on how much he inhaled, he might need an intramuscular injection of naloxone."

Maggie recognized that Ryder was using the same gentle tone he used with his dogs, but she could sense his underlying panic.

They all helped get Scout to his feet. Ryder started lifting the dog, when Jason stopped him.

"Thanks, but I can carry my own dog," Jason told him.

"The effects of the drugs might not have hit you, yet," Ryder said. "You might start feeling it in the next several minutes. Let's just get you guys out of here."

Jason nodded. He didn't look offended, but he didn't look happy. Ryder lifted Scout into his arms then up over his head and across his shoulders with Scout's legs dangling over each side of Ryder's chest. Maggie had seen photos of soldiers carrying their K9s this way, but she'd never seen it personally. Scout had to weigh sixty or seventy pounds.

Maggie and Brodie went ahead of them, following Grace to the water while they pushed low hanging branches out of the way. After Jason, Scout and Grace were safely in the boat, Maggie caught Ryder's arm.

"You must be exhausted," she said to him. He looked like he hadn't slept. "I can come along and drive."

"Thanks. I'll be fine."

It sounded a bit dismissive, but when she met his eyes, she found something entirely different. He brought the palm of his hand and caressed her cheek. She caught herself leaning into it, and suddenly realized how much she had needed the reassurance, not just that he was okay, but that they were okay.

Chapter 38

Blackwater River State Forest

Udie wanted to shout and laugh, but instead, he stayed where he was. He pressed the length of his body against the huge branch in the live oak. Its thick canopy made it difficult to see everything, but it also kept him hidden. This time he wore his green work trousers to make sure he blended in.

He waited for all of them to leave and help get the black dog through the woods to one of the boats. When the last of them disappeared between the trees, Udie slid out of the tree and headed in the opposite direction.

He knew there had to be a way to get these dogs out of here. He just didn't realize it would be so easy. The trash bag full of drug garbage was one of his more brilliant ideas.

Instinctively, he rubbed at the rash on his neck. Those stupid patches were the worst. If they did this to his skin, he figured they'd probably affect the dogs or maybe one of the people collecting the stuff.

That it knocked that big dog off his feet was a huge score for Udie. A few more "accidents" like that, and maybe they would stay the hell away from here.

After the thunderstorm had chased everyone out of the forest yesterday, Udie waited it out. He planted several trail cams in the trees overlooking the clearing and then a few more along the creek. They were wireless and cellular. They activated by motion and were able to transmit real-time alerts to his new iPhone.

Electronic gadgets were always something he had a knack for. And hiding cameras in a variety of places used to provide a natural high for him. That was until he started getting the stream of easy and cheap drugs.

The wilderness cams were less predictable than the ones he hid in buildings. Weather affected them, of course. And the live video feed wasn't perfect, but it had been good enough to tell him when the sheriff's department's men had arrived on the water. It alerted him a second time when the tall man and little dog launched his boat.

Late last night when he saw the fresh tire tracks at his favorite launch site he realized he had to use another. For years he'd been using that place, but finding another route wasn't hard at all. He knew Coldwater Creek and all the tributaries that forked in and out. There just weren't many areas to park and launch a boat. It meant a longer walk, so he needed to leave. Unfortunately, he needed to get back and get to work. But hopefully, this little incident would delay things.

He scratched at his neck, again. Swatted a couple of mosquitoes away. Then he pulled at his shirt, stretching it away from his skin to get a look at his shoulder.

Damn it!

The rash was growing and turning into tiny, little blisters.

Chapter 39

Baptist Hospital
Pensacola, Florida

Jason felt fine, except for the sick feeling in his gut. He couldn't stop worrying about Scout. And he couldn't stop blaming himself.

The ER doctor had checked him out and said he was good to go. Ryder had already texted him a couple of photos. Said Scout was doing really well. He wasn't showing any more symptoms, but Dr. Avelyn wanted to keep him in the clinic for observation. By bedtime Scout would be able to return to Jason's doublewide.

All of that should have made Jason feel better. Instead, he kept playing it over in his mind, finding that bag of trash. He should have seen it sooner. Dogs relied primarily on their noses to process information. Humans used their eyes, and Jason certainly had a higher vantage point than Scout. How did he miss it? And why didn't they stumble across it yesterday?

The black, plastic bag had been left open, tossed into the grass with some of the contents spilling out. Jason was pretty sure animals hadn't ripped it open.

He left the ER and found a hallway that led into the main hospital. It was almost lunchtime, and Benny wouldn't be here for another hour to pick him up and give him a ride home. Jason had insisted that Ryder drop him off. He appreciated Ryder's offer to stay, but he didn't need a babysitter. If he couldn't be with Scout, he wanted Ryder to be there.

Even before they got to the hospital Jason knew he was okay. He knew what it felt like to have opioids in his system. In the early days, right after the IED went off and took half his arm with it, he'd been on a regiment of pain pills.

After the amputation and during rehab, doctors offered him pill after another pill without Jason asking. If he mentioned he couldn't sleep, he was handed a script for sleeping pills. None of them really helped, and he hated the side effects, but he never refused any of them. Instead, he had collected a treasure trove for what he called in his mind—never out loud—his Option B.

On the boat, Ryder reminder Jason that he had two doses of naloxone in his own daypack, so they had enough for Scout and one for Jason. Neither dog nor handler needed it. They took Scout to their clinic and left him with Dr. Avelyn. When Jason said he was fine, Ryder waved him back to the Jeep.

"Better safe than sorry," Ryder told him. Then he added, "We need to make sure you're okay. Scout will need someone to watch him for the next twenty-four hours."

Jason didn't argue. Ryder was a smart guy. He knew Jason might be lax in taking care of himself, but he'd do anything to take care of this dog. Ryder knew that was true even before Jason knew it himself. It was exactly how he'd gotten Jason to give up his Option B.

He took a detour making his way around to the front of the hospital. He wanted to check on Sheriff Norwich at the information desk. Maybe they were allowing visitors. They were not. He knew better than to ask how she was doing.

When he arrived at the cafeteria it was crowded. He contemplated the process and which line he wanted. There were several, and people seemed to know their way through the maze. He felt a nudge from behind and realized he was probably in the way.

"Hey, it's one of those few good men."

"Excuse me?" But when he turned, he immediately recognized the woman, despite her blond hair in a ponytail and despite the nurse's uniform.

"Jason, right?"

"That's right."

He couldn't believe she was standing directly in front of him. She was almost as tall as him, and this close, her eyes were strikingly blue with a hint of green.

"And you're Taylor," he said without breaking eye contact to look at her name badge. And he did it all without stumbling over his tongue.

"So are your guys with you?"

"My guys?"

"The poker players?" She was looking around, but he knew she wasn't looking for Benny or Colfax. She had stopped to say hello and was now looking for an exit strategy. Or she was meeting someone. Either way, he was familiar with this part.

"No, only me. I just got out of the ER."

"ER?" And suddenly, he had her full attention.

"No big deal. I'm fine. I'm a K9 handler. My dog found a trash bag full of drug paraphernalia. We both had to be checked out."

"Is your dog okay?"

"I think so. I hope so," Jason said and was surprised at the emotion still in his voice. He was a little embarrassed by it and looked away, pretending to check out the progress of the cafeteria lines. "I was just going to grab a bite. Any recommendations?"

"Stay away from anything pre-packaged. I usually do the salad bar, but I've heard some of the grill's specials are decent."

She looked over her shoulder. The place was filling up, and he knew she probably had a short lunch break. He was getting ready to excuse himself and make it easy on her. Then she gestured to a table on the other side of the room.

"How bout you grab that table, and I'll get us some lunch. If you don't mind trusting me."

That wasn't at all what Jason expected.

"Um…let me give you some cash."

"We can figure that out later."

And she was gone, swallowed up into the crowd of likewise scrubs and lab coats. He stared after her then realized he needed to pick his jaw up off the floor and go grab that table.

Ryder had ribbed him once about using his dog to pick up women, but he never thought it might actually work.

Chapter 40

Jason devoured the pulled pork sandwich and was working on the French fries when he noticed Taylor watching him. He wiped a hand over his mouth, thinking he must have something on his face, which only made her smile then look away. Her eyes darted around the cafeteria like she was waiting for someone, again.

"One thing I learned," she said, "from living with a group of guys, you don't mess with their food."

"You lived with a group of guys?"

"Northern Afghanistan. I was with an Army FFST."

"That's sort of like a mobile medical unit?"

"Fast-Forward Surgical Teams. We moved with the troops or set up close to the fighting forces. My unit had two surgeons, an anesthetist, an operating room nurse and a critical care nurse. I was the only woman. Our main goal was hemorrhage control within that golden hour. We patched you guys up and prepared you for medical evacuation. But we never got to see the end results."

She pointed at his arm with her fork, and said, "Impressive hardware."

"The best of DARPA."

"DARPA?"

"Yeah, I'm experimental."

"I bet you are."

Jason felt the back of his neck go hot. Was she flirting with him?

"So that explains the Segway House," he said, searching to get a grip, before she completely threw him off balance. "You're a veteran."

"I just moved here from Virginia three weeks ago. I don't know too many people."

"Well, you really are welcome to play poker with us. Benny and Colfax are there most nights."

"But not you?"

"I work pretty long hours." And he suddenly remembered Scout. He hadn't checked on him in almost an hour. He resisted the urge to slip his cell phone out. "I owe you for lunch."

"A whopping six dollars. Buy me a drink sometime," she waved him off, but unfortunately, she took it as an opportunity to end their lunch. "Speaking of work. I need to get back to it." She stood up and he followed suit, both gathering up their discarded napkins and silverware.

"How about dinner to go along with that drink?" Jason offered. *Too much, too soon.* God, he really was not good at this.

When she hesitated, he jumped in to rescue her before she turned him down. "It's okay," he told her. He had already checked for rings, but he knew that might mean nothing with healthcare providers who were constantly pulling on gloves and washing their hands. "I understand. You're probably seeing someone."

"Actually, I just broke up with someone."

"That's great." He heard himself say it before he could stop it from falling out of his mouth. He shook his head. What was wrong with him? "That's not what I meant."

But she was smiling at him now.

"I don't think I'm ready just yet," she said.

"Okay. Then just a drink? Or coffee. Sometimes it's nice to have someone to talk to."

He saw she was thinking about it, even as her eyes continued to roam around the cafeteria. Groups were leaving, only to be replaced by new ones.

"You know Walter's Canteen on the beach?" she finally asked.

"Yeah, I do."

"I get off around seven."

"That sounds great." Then he wanted to slap himself. "Wait, I can't tonight. I'm sorry. Scout. My dog. He's supposed to be under observation for twenty-four hours."

"Sure, no problem."

But Jason could see that it was a problem. She'd put herself out there, and he turned her down. After he'd prodded and convinced her to give him a chance.

"What about another time?" he asked carefully, not wanting to push.

"Sure. Some other time. I really need to get back upstairs. You know where to find me."

She turned and was gone. Weaving and blending in until she was out the door.

That's when he realized he didn't know where to find her. He was pretty sure that was her way of saying, "Oh, hell no."

Chapter 41

Margaritaville Beach Hotel
Pensacola Beach, Florida

Maggie stood back two feet from the sliding glass door to her hotel room's balcony. It was still a magnificent view of the Gulf despite rain and wind pelting the glass. Flashes of lightning illuminated the dark clouds. The waves rolled and crashed.

She was grateful that today she wasn't out in the middle of the storm. They had called it quits early. Two new deputies had boated to the scene, scheduled to secure the area until the recovery efforts began again the next day. They had brought with them duffel bags of gear, but she couldn't imagine spending the night out there.

Ryder had texted several updates about Scout and Jason. But he'd also sent her the following message:

> I DON'T THINK THAT TRASH BAG WAS
> THERE YESTERDAY.

Ryder and Grace had spent a good deal of time at the crime scene before any of the rest of them had arrived. Maggie remembered all of the surveyor flags planted across the area. But Jason and Scout had gone deeper into the woods. She suspected Ryder was thinking Grace would have alerted to the bag. Unlike Scout, Grace was a multi-task dog. She was also trained to find and alert to drugs and explosives. Last fall the little dog had tried to tell them about a booby-trapped bomb when they thought they were digging up a grave.

Maggie wanted to tell Ryder that Grace might not have gotten to the trash bag. There was so much decomp, and that's what Ryder had asked her to find. Instead, Maggie let it go for now. The tarps they had left to cover the bodies hadn't been touched. If the killer had come back, he'd want to destroy evidence, not add more. It didn't make sense.

But Maggie had to admit this guy was a puzzle. For most serial killers, the killing was the gratifying part. And yet, this killer had left one of his victims alive.

She hoped the victims would tell them more about the killer than his handiwork.

So far, they had recovered three bodies: the man Brodie had tripped over (who they labeled John Doe #1); the second man they'd found lying in the grass (John Doe #2); and the presumed woman or whatever was left of her. But they knew from Grace and Scout that there were more victims.

The medical examiner seemed anxious to start the autopsies. The gunshot wound in John Doe #1 brought new insight and evidence. Originally, because of the wound on the back of his head, they believed the man had been bludgeoned and left for dead.

She remembered the dirt and grass under his fingernails, the scratch marks that indicated he might have crawled his way out of the shallow grave. Maggie had witnessed some horrendous murders over her tenure as an FBI profiler, but in her mind, the worst were those killers who inflicted the most pain. Those who enjoyed hearing the screams, encouraged the begging, and waited for the final whimpers of resignation.

Those guys were the most dangerous.

Their level of depravity left no room for bargaining or negotiating. Their victims were as good as dead from the moment they were targeted.

But this killer...what category did he fit into? Gut instinct was telling her the killer had left believing John Doe #1 was dead. And the shallow grave was intentional. Just like he'd left the other bodies out in the open. He expected nature to clean up his mess, to hide his secrets.

But why did he kill them?

That was the question bugging her. And there was something else.

She grabbed her cell phone off the bedside table. She'd taken plenty of photos, but there was one that stuck with her now. She swiped until she found the first shots she'd taken after they rolled the man onto his back. Stomach wounds tended to bleed a lot. The bottom of his shirt was caked with blood. A large oblong stain soaked the fabric. It stretched from across his belly.

She pinched the phone's screen to enlarge the area of the wound. Then she could see what had caught her attention and hadn't let go. There was a paper towel drenched with blood, so much so, that it blended in as part of the shirt. She had to look closely to see the edges of the faint pattern.

Actually, now she could see that it was a couple squares as if someone had torn them from a roll and pressed them to the wound. But the paper towels weren't wadded up like you'd expect to do, if you were trying to staunch the bleeding. No, these were simply laid across the shirt perhaps in a way to make sure the bleeding didn't stain anything else.

Maggie shook her head. She was grasping at straws, or in this case, paper towels.

She checked her wristwatch. She had enough time to shower, grab something to eat and still be there in time for the first autopsy.

Chapter 42

Medical Examiner's Office
Pensacola, Florida

Traffic delayed Maggie. That was one thing about this area. She noticed that she couldn't go far without driving over a bridge, each of them two-to-three miles long with gorgeous views of water. There wasn't a quick route anywhere, especially from Pensacola Beach to Pensacola. Thirty-five and forty-five mile per hour zones slowed to a crawl through business districts and over two separate bridges. This time of year, traffic seemed to be crazy in both directions.

So Maggie was late.

She texted Vickie and told her to go ahead, but the medical examiner had already started. By the time Maggie arrived, made it through security and gowned-up, John Doe #1 was cleaned up, splayed out and had an organ or two weighed and set aside.

"He didn't die from the gunshot," Vickie announced as Maggie came across the pristine autopsy suite.

She gestured to the bullet, now on a tray. There were other trays lined up on the counter with other interesting pieces. The medical examiner had been busy. She must have started as soon as she got back from the forest.

Maggie came in closer to examine the bullet.

"Small caliber," Maggie said. "It didn't kill him, but it made him bleed…a lot."

"I'm still speculating," Vickie said, "but I think he got shot first. And I don't think it happened in the forest."

Vickie stopped what she was doing, pulled off her latex gloves and sorted through a stack of photos that had already been printed out.

"There wasn't enough blood underneath him," she told Maggie.

"Couldn't it have soaked into the ground?"

Vickie pulled out several of the photos and put them down, one at a time, side by side on an empty spot of the counter.

"Take a look," she said. "Lots of fallen leaves and pine needles. It was pretty thick. The magnolia leaves are large."

She pointed to the third photo from the left. Maggie could see where the medical examiner or Hadley, the CSU tech, had raked up a patch of the leaves and needles and put them in an evidence bag.

She was right. Blood hadn't made it to the ground.

"So he was shot somewhere else and brought to the forest to be buried," Maggie said.

"Except he wasn't dead. And I'm betting our bad guy was surprised at that."

"Because he didn't have his gun along, or he would have shot him again."

"Hadley bagged a dead tree branch," Vickie told her, pointing to another counter at the other end of the room. "About three feet long. Lots of blood. Bark's gone. I'm crossing my fingers we might be able to pull a print."

"Why do you have all the evidence?" Maggie asked. "Doesn't Hadley and the sheriff's department have a crime lab?"

"Ours is better," Vickie said. "My district covers a lot of territory."

Maggie raised an eyebrow at her, and Vickie stepped back from the counter. She could see the medical examiner contemplate what she was about to say.

Finally, she put her hands up in surrender and said, "Sheriff Norwich is great, okay? But with her in the hospital...let's just say there are several of us who don't trust Chief Deputy Glenn. Don't get me wrong, I'm sure he's a nice man, but he also loves the media's attention."

"Hadley is one of the several who agrees?"

"Actually, it was Hadley's idea. And besides that, I'm hoping I have access to the FBI's crime lab." She waited a beat and added, "I'm hoping I *still* have access?"

"Of course," Maggie told her. This was far from the first time she'd dealt with local law enforcement juggling around each other.

Relieved, the medical examiner went back to the counter and picked up an evidence bag. She put it in front of Maggie.

"I think the contents of that crumpled fast food sack might pay off," Vickie said.

Inside the evidence bag was a half-eaten cheeseburger. Another bag had about a dozen French fries. The actual brown paper sack was in its own evidence bag.

Maggie could remember at least one incident where Keith Ganza at the FBI's crime lab had been able to come up with DNA from a half-eaten sandwich. The murderer had taken several bites and left the sandwich on his victim's kitchen table.

Instead of agreeing or being pleased with the possibility of identifying this killer, Maggie said, "I can't believe how sloppy he is."

"I thought you FBI profilers called it disorganized."

"Have you ever been to a crime scene where the victims were just left out in the open? Simply tossed and left for nature to finish the work?" Maggie asked.

The medical examiner put hands to hips and gave it some thought. "Not with multiple victims. I do remember a guy in northern Minnesota who drilled a hole in the ice to drop his victim into a lake. He only prolonged the inevitable. Come spring thaw, the body eventually popped right up. But no, I haven't seen anything like this. You know, though, his sloppiness is our treasure trove."

She wagged a finger for Maggie to come take a look at one of the other trays. Laid out on a sterile cloth were short tan-colored hairs. Each was about an inch long, a few a little longer. Vickie already had one mounted on a slide and under a microscope.

"Dog hair," she told Maggie. "Enough of it that we might be able to determine the breed."

Maggie folded her arms across her chest and caught her lower lip between her teeth.

"What?" Vickie asked.

"Ryder and I found a tan-colored dog last night. We were checking out the area for a boat launch."

"There are a lot of tan-colored dogs."

"Yes," Maggie admitted. "But this one had a gunshot wound."

Vickie threw her hands into the air and said, "Well, this just gets better and better."

Chapter 43

The medical examiner invited Maggie upstairs to her office, so she could feed her little dog. She also needed to grab the necessary forms and labels. Maggie wanted to overnight the pieces of evidence to Keith Ganza at the FBI lab. Vickie had already packaged everything appropriately and told Maggie where she could drop them off. All that was left, were the labels.

"I've called ahead," she told Maggie. "You'll be fine for overnight delivery as long as you get there by seven tonight. Ask for Carol if you have any problems."

On the elevator ride up, she instructed Maggie about the hair sample she'd need from the rescued dog.

"If the veterinarian retrieved a bullet, bring that along, too."

Maggie was convinced the dog was connected to John Doe #1. If not his owner, then he might be someone who had handled the dog.

"This is Sugar," Vickie announced when the dog greeted them at the door.

Sugar returned to what was obviously her place at the window. The big, comfy chair had a colorful quit thrown over the back. It looked like the prize spot in the room.

Maggie wasn't surprised to find Vickie's office as meticulous as her autopsy suites. However, she was impressed to find it cozy, almost like a studio apartment without a kitchen. Her desk, by comparison, was small but quite beautiful: a slab of repurposed wood on a simple metal frame.

"Can I get you coffee? Tea? I have an assortment next door."

"Any chance you have a Diet Pepsi?"

"I will check."

While she was gone, Maggie made small talk with Sugar. All of these dogs were making her miss her two, big guys: Harvey and Jake. She had called her brother, Patrick after she got out of the shower.

She worried more and more about Harvey. He was starting to slow down with age. In the last several months she had made her two-story, Tudor home more senior friendly for him, adding steps to the bed and ramps to his favorite place on the sofa.

Jake was a whole different story. It was only in the last year that he'd decided to stay put and not run away. Her huge corner lot backed to a stream and woods on the other side. Maybe Jake believed those Virginia woods would somehow lead him back to the Sandhills of Nebraska where her friend, Lucy Coy had found him. Maggie tried not to take Jake's urge to roam personally.

"Found one," Vickie said, smiling and holding up a can of Diet Pepsi.

"I hope you didn't have to go far."

"Just the convenient store at the end of the block." Before Maggie could gasp, Vickie added, "Kidding. Vending machine on the ground floor."

"Well, thanks."

Vickie had gotten herself an iced tea, freshly brewed. The aroma filled the office.

"So how long have you and Ryder been together?"

Maggie almost choked on her sip of soda.

"Actually, we're not together," she managed to say.

"Really? Why not?"

"He's here. I'm in Virginia." Even in her head, Maggie thought the excuse sounded lame.

A dinging sound from next door saved her. Both Vickie and the little dog jumped up and were headed out the door.

"Excuse me," she told Maggie. "Sugar's pancakes are ready."

Chapter 44

Blackwater River State Forest

Udie dragged his boat from its hiding place in the bushes. His new cell phone buzzed in his back pocket.

He yanked it out already angry before he read the new message. All hell was breaking lose. Whatever small victory he'd claimed earlier in the day had evaporated.

He punched in a phone number and waited.

"What are you doing with his phone?" the voice said in place of a greeting.

"Oh hey, you recognize this number," Udie told him.

"You're supposed to get rid of everything. I'm starting to believe you're not very good at this anymore, Udie, my man."

He still made the cross words sound like a good-humored jab. The kind of thing Udie had seen him exchange with his friends. And Udie so wanted to be one of his friends. But the situation in the forest was spiraling out of control. He'd need to take some serious measures to make it go away.

"Udie, are you listening to me?"

"It's a brand-new phone. One of the newest versions," Udie said in defense.

"They can track you, dude. You know that, right?"

"Not if they don't know who the guy is." But Udie suspected they might figure it out soon. How much longer could he keep it a secret? Could he patch it all up before then?

He tried to change the subject. Deflect. A handy trick he'd learned from his mother.

"So the guy you shot had a dog?" Udie threw it out like a fishing line, laying the hook right there to be grabbed and swallowed.

"How do you know that?"

"Somebody found him."

"What are you talking about, Udie?"

"The dog. A guy named Ryder Creed said he found him."

"Creed? I shot that dog. It's dead."

"No, not dead."

"The dog's still alive?"

"Apparently. You're not very good with a gun." He tried to mimic the guy's own words.

"Son of a bitch!"

Udie grinned so wide his mouth hurt. A couple of his teeth were bothering him. No big deal. The stupid rash was driving him crazy. He resisted the urge to dig his fingernails into his shoulder.

"Want me to take care of it?" Udie offered, enjoying the temporary control. Just as well get whatever he could before all hell broke lose.

"You think you can do that? That would be great."

"No worries." He let the man relax then he added, "Can you get me more pills? Those patches are crap. They made me break out in a rash."

That had to be what it was, although Udie knew he hadn't used a patch for weeks. Maybe a month. He still had a stash of them.

"For you, my friend, I can certainly get some. I'll leave them in the regular place. I've got to go."

He clicked off without nagging Udie about the illicit cell phone. Deflect and distract. His mother had taught him some decent tips. It was times like this that he sort of missed her. *Sort of.*

The black magic, the superstitions, all the strange stuff she'd started bringing home gave him the willies. But when she found out how much it bothered him, she found another place to store the stuff. He did appreciate that. Still, it was too little, too late.

Toward the end, she grated on his nerves so bad he could barely listen to her. The drugs helped him tune her out for a while. He could go somewhere else inside his mind. Anything she said sounded like a hum, a mumble, hardly registering with him. Except that last scream. The one that sounded like a screech owl.

No one was surprised to hear that she had suddenly picked up and left town without a word. Anyone who knew her seemed to suspect she had problems. They all felt sorry for Udie.

He learned quickly what people were willing to do when they felt sorry for you, or maybe a bit guilty, because they might have contributed to your circumstances.

Whatever the reasons, Udie suddenly had more people taking care of him than he could imagine. Neighbors offered to paint the little, old house that his mother had neglected. His house now. Those first months they brought him casseroles, sometimes a fresh baked pie and lots of cookies.

He was only nineteen at the time. They were impressed that he'd picked up and started running her cleaning business all by himself.

Clients kept him on. They trusted him, because as strange as Udie thought his mother was, people did trust her in an illogical, emotional way.

They listened to her mumbo-jumbo like it was a religious sermon. She had that effect on people when she started talking about souls and auras and karma. As a little boy, he'd watched her and was fascinated by the way she could mesmerize—almost hypnotize—people with her ability to tell them things about themselves or their loved ones who had passed away. Things that made their eyes go wide and their jaws actually drop open.

She claimed she could hold a person's hand and see the last ten seconds before their death.

Some people wanted to know. Others were simply curious. Udie hated it.

She took his hand one morning...one of her last mornings. Instantly, her face went pale and her mouth formed a perfect O, but no sound came out of her. She stared straight at him, not a single blink. The fear and horror he saw in her dark, brown eyes could still send shivers down his back.

"So much fire," she finally whispered.

That was enough for him.

She was a crazy woman!

She could see things so clearly; things that weren't real. Yet, she couldn't tell him who his father was. Wouldn't tell him.

"We were both so young," she'd say, following it with something equally ridiculous like, "It was a summer of love."

It was her strange and twisted effort to ensure him that he was conceived out of love.

It wasn't until he was a teenager that he suspected who his father was. His mother spent a lot of time around the man. Not *with* him. But in close proximity. She acted like a silly schoolgirl whenever he was anywhere near her. It was easy to see she still cared for him.

And that's when Udie's anger began to build. He tried easing the anger with a little shake-and-bake that took the edge off. Until it wasn't enough. He began experimenting with stuff that came with cool names like Dance Fever, Goodfellas, and Murder 8.

The more he learned, the more the anger festered. Because the man was married. He had a wife and beautiful life. And Udie and his mother had nothing but a little, old house and a back-breaking cleaning business.

It wasn't until recently that Udie realized the guy probably had no idea Udie was his son. That made it hard to blame the guy. So it was Udie's mother's fault. She'd chosen to not tell him. Let him off the hook. Allow them to collect trash and mop floors while the guy had a huge swimming pool in his backyard.

But Udie had managed to direct his anger entirely at his mother even after she was gone. He started getting to know the man, respecting him. Wanting to be like him. A few carefully stolen items from the man's personal trash, and Udie was able to confirm that the guy was, indeed, his father.

He was waiting for the right time to tell him. After, of course, Udie earned the man's respect and his rightful place as his business partner.

Looking back, he knew he'd never forgive his mother for not telling him. For depriving him of a father. Instead of sharing it with him she bitched and nagged at Udie. Constantly.

Life was so much better without her.

Now, he did what he wanted to do. He was comfortable with his little house and his little business. He liked that people didn't notice him or pay any attention to him. If they did, it was only because they were reminded of how sad it was that his mother had left him, and how remarkable it was that he had made a life for himself.

If only he could stop hearing his mother's voice in his head. That screech! That scream. He wished he could turn it off. None of the drugs could flip that frickin' switch.

Other than that, his life was good. Or at least it had been before that man and woman and their stupid, little dog invaded his sanctuary.

He refused to let them turn his life upside down.

Chapter 45

Creed had finished all the kennel chores. He had just checked on Scout when Jason came through the clinic door. The handler looked worse than his dog.

"How's he doing?" Jason asked.

"Good. His heartbeat and blood pressure are back to normal. Pupils look good. Dr. Avelyn left a little bit ago. She'll be back in the morning, but she said you could take him home for the night. Said to call if you notice anything out of the ordinary."

"Can I see him?"

"I'm sure he already smells and hears you. He's in the big kennel in back.

While Jason was with Scout, Creed pulled out his cell phone. There was still no message from Hank's owner.

Dr. Avelyn believed the dog might have been protecting his owner when he was shot. Hank must have been facing his assailant to get hit in his upper chest. The bullet was lodged in the tissue right above his shoulder when Dr. Avelyn extracted it. She seemed pleased and cautiously optimistic that it hadn't done too much damage.

Creed wasn't convinced about her theory on the owner. As part of a Marine K9 unit in Afghanistan, he had been trained to do anything and everything to protect his partner. Dogs were even given a higher rank than their handler. Creed knew without hesitation that if someone tried to shoot his dog, he would do whatever was necessary to prevent that. Including taking the bullet himself.

But from experience, he also knew some dogs would do the same for their owners. One of his dogs, a Rhodesian ridgeback named Bolo, had taken down to the ground more than a few men he believed were a threat to Creed. Bolo was a talented scent dog, but his tendency to be overprotective of Creed was one of the reasons Creed had to be careful when and where he used the dog.

"He's hungry," Jason said coming from down the hallway. "So that's a good sign."

"He's always hungry."

"True. Did Dr. Avelyn say if I can give him dinner tonight?"

"You should probably check with her."

Jason already had his cell phone out and was tapping in the message.

"So the ER doc said you're okay?" Creed asked. He didn't want to come right out and tell Jason that he looked like hell.

"Yeah, I'm fine." He glanced up from the phone and rubbed the back of his neck. He must have noticed that Creed wasn't satisfied, because he added, "Just a bit worn out."

Jason leaned against the wall and crossed his arms. Creed noticed something was clearly bugging him. Usually Creed left the emotional prodding to Hannah.

"I just don't understand women, you know?" Jason said. Before Creed could tell him that he was the absolute wrong guy to help him, Jason continued. "I met a gorgeous woman. Really smart, too. A nurse at the hospital. She was an Army nurse in Afghanistan."

Creed sat back and listened.

Jason shook his head and forced a smile as he said, "So completely out of my league."

"Why do you say that?"

"Did you not hear me? She's gorgeous and smart."

"You met her in the ER?"

"Hospital cafeteria."

"Oh, sounds romantic."

"Actually it was. She bought me lunch," Jason told him.

"Maybe she didn't get the memo about you being out of her league."

"I know, right?" But this time Jason said it with a real grin, before going serious again. "She probably felt sorry for me. I mentioned about being in the ER. You know, what happened with me and Scout. She probably felt bad for my dog."

"Yeah, gorgeous, smart women do that a lot. Buy lunch for guys when they feel sorry for them. Especially when they know they're out of their league."

Creed waited to hear more. When none came, he asked, "So how did you manage to screw it up?"

"I offered to buy her a drink or dinner. She actually agreed. Told me she gets off at seven and asked if I knew Walter's Canteen. Then I remembered Scout."

Creed glanced at his wristwatch. "I can take care of Scout."

"No, I already blew it. And you know what, if she doesn't get it…you know, about Scout being a priority then maybe I'm not missing out.

"I've never been good at figuring out women," Jason continued, "Whenever I went somewhere with Tony, women flocked to him. I was his wingman. If a girl wanted Tony, she usually brought along a friend for me."

Creed knew Jason still missed his friend.

"Sounds like a sweet deal. But then you never get to choose or fight for the woman you really want to be with," Creed told him.

"Says the guy who sits back and lets his gorgeous, smart woman keep coming to him whenever and wherever she chooses."

It felt like a sucker-punch, but Creed knew the kid didn't mean it that way. Actually, Creed didn't realize it was that apparent to anyone else. Instead of offering an excuse, he said, "True. But my gorgeous, smart woman scares easily."

"I get the feeling Taylor does, too. So what do you do?"

"I let her call the shots."

"And it gets you the kind of relationship you want?" Jason asked.

"Not at all."

"I'm confused."

"That makes two of us. I honestly can't tell you what kind of a relationship Maggie and I have. But I get the feeling it's all she can offer right now."

"And if it's not enough for you?'

Creed shrugged. "Hannah says things happen for a reason."

"And Hannah is a very smart woman," Maggie said, coming in the door and startling them both.

Chapter 46

Creed had gotten used to Grace giving him a heads up. Her tail would have been wagging before Maggie had gotten out of her rental vehicle. But Grace was with Brodie and Hannah.

If Maggie heard his and Jason's conversation, she didn't let on. Jason, however, flushed red, told her "hello," and went to get Scout. Seconds later he was leading the big dog out the door.

"Scout looks good," Maggie said. "Is he okay?"

"They're both doing good."

"And Hank?" she asked, looking around as if she expected to see him to emerge, too.

"He's still pretty groggy."

She took the chair directly opposite of Creed in the room that was part office, part lounge. It was small, so they were almost knee-to-knee. He and Hannah had spared no expense for the surgical suite, the recovery kennels and other equipment. Whatever Dr. Avelyn had asked for or recommended, he bought without question. But Creed didn't expect any of them to spend much time in an office. It was really for Dr. Avelyn if she needed to work remotely, handling business for her Milton clinic while she was here. Still, the sofa folded out into a bed. But Creed and Grace had dragged its thin mattress to Hank's room. Creed planned on spending his nights here until Hank was well enough to be moved.

"Sorry, I didn't let you know I was coming," Maggie said.

Maybe she had heard some of the conversation.

"Not a problem," he told her. "You know you're welcome any time."

"Dr. Kammerer finished the autopsy of John Doe #1. I offered the FBI's crime lab to process some of the evidence."

"Anything interesting?" He asked when he really wanted to ask why she was still on this case. Did it have anything to do with the storage unit in Pensacola? It was the original reason for her trip down.

When she called him last week, it sounded like she barely had time for them to get together for dinner one night before she headed back. Now she was working a crime scene in the forest, helping bag remains and offering the FBI's crime lab.

Maybe Jason had hit a nerve. Maybe he wasn't content with where things were with him and Maggie or letting her call all the shots.

"Actually, there is a lot of stuff to process. I can't believe how sloppy this guy is."

"I can't believe he's been dumping dead bodies so close. I thought the forest was safe except for a black bear now and then."

"Vickie did find something interesting. Dog hair on the victim's clothing."

She paused as if she expected him to make a connection without further explanation. Then she finally added, "Short, tan-colored dog hair."

"You think it might be Hank's?"

"I think there's a good possibility. Vickie can have her lab techs check. They'll be able to tell if it is his."

"But she needs a sample," he said.

"Yes."

"Plucked?"

"If possible. Was there a bullet?"

"Yes. Small caliber," Creed told her. "It hit him just above the shoulder. We're hoping it didn't cause any damage." But she wasn't asking about the dog. Only the bullet.

"Can I take that back with me?"

"I guess so."

Being a dog handler had trained Creed to hide his immediate reactions, even his emotions. Dogs sensed their handler's moods. He kept himself aware that emotions ran down the leash and could affect his scent dog's performance. He was careful about not telegraphing his alarm or anxiety or, in this case, his disappointment. He was able to tuck away the sting without Maggie seeing it.

She hadn't come to see him. Or check up on Hank. She had come for the hair sample and the bullet.

"I've been leaving messages for his owner," he told her, steering his mind clear of his disappointment.

"License tag?" she asked.

"Microchip. Dr. Avelyn scanned it and was able to get contact information."

"Did you get a hold of the owner?"

"Not yet. He hasn't called back."

"Can you give me his contact information?"

"Sure."

Then she glanced around, suddenly uncomfortable as if she had just realized something.

"What is it?" Creed asked.

"I think his owner is the victim Brodie stumbled over. I think he might be John Doe #1."

Chapter 47

K9 CrimeScents
Florida Panhandle

Brodie jerked awake. A flash of light streaked across her bedroom window. She pushed herself up and waited for the thunder. None came.

Her bedsheet was damp with sweat and tangled around her legs. She searched for Kitten while she pinched herself hard on her forearm.

It hurt!

That was a good thing. It meant she wasn't dreaming.

The trick had worked in the past. But it didn't help to wake her if she was in the middle of a nightmare. Sometimes the Charlottes came to her. Just last week, one had been standing right next to her bed. Brodie pretended to be asleep, but she could feel the girl's presence. She remembered digging her fingernails into her skin and feeling nothing, but she could still feel those unblinking eyes watching over her.

Iris Malone had called all of them Charlotte including Brodie. She snatched little girls with long, dark hair who resembled her daughter. The daughter had died years before. With each one, Iris hoped to replace

Charlotte until the new girl dared to disobey, or worse, try to escape like Brodie had done.

The light flashed across her window, again, just as she heard something move behind her. Brodie twisted around expecting to see one of the Charlottes. But it was only Kitten snuggling down in the pillows.

"We need a guard dog," she told the cat.

His response was to stretch out and bury his face under his front paws. Ryder had offered her a dog to sleep on the floor beside her bed. She wasn't sure she was ready for the responsibility that came with a dog. She didn't think it was fair to ask a dog to take care of her if she couldn't return the favor.

Brodie checked the digital clock on her nightstand. It was a few minutes before midnight.

Sometimes the security lights came on in the middle of the night. Ryder had them installed on all of the buildings. They had motion sensors that could be triggered by animals or other intruders. Or when Jason came home late. But she knew he was in his trailer tonight with Scout. And Ryder was at the animal hospital with Hank.

Maybe Ryder and Grace had decided to go to their own bed. Ryder's loft was the second story of the kennel. A walk from the hospital to there would certainly trigger several of the lights.

She slipped out of bed and went to the window. But she stayed at the side where she could peek out without being seen from down below.

All the lights were off right now. The moon lit the grounds, so she didn't need the security lights. There was no one. Or perhaps Ryder had already made it from the hospital to his apartment.

She could see his windows from here. They were all dark. There was a dim glow in the kennel's windows. Ryder never left it dark. A few of the dogs panicked if the place went black. Generators were prepared to switch on at a moment's notice if the electricity got knocked out.

She found herself thinking about Jason. How brave he was with Scout. He was steady and calm using his artificial hand like it was a natural part of him. Brodie wondered if the others had heard the hint of fear in his voice.

When she first arrived, Jason had taken time out to tell her stories about the dogs in their kennel. All of them had been abandoned in some way. Chance's owner chose her abusive boyfriend over her dog. Molly and her family were found in a vehicle buried under a mudslide. Molly was the only survivor. They were sad stories, but Jason made them sound like triumphant adventures with happy endings.

She liked Jason…a lot. She liked to be around him. They talked about the books they were reading, exchanging favorites. He pointed out different birds and taught her how to imitate them by holding her tongue a certain way or whistling through her teeth. He said a dog could hear a whistle from farther away than a person calling out.

She shared with him her fascination of the night sky: stars and planets and constellations. She taught him how to tell directions in the dark as long as he could see the sky.

The light streamed across her window again.

It came from the corner of the fieldhouse. Not the hospital. Not the kennel. Maybe Ryder had decided on a late-night swim.

Then she saw the man. He was only a shadow plastered against the outside wall of the building. He was so still she wasn't sure what she was seeing. But the security light blinked dark again, and he began to move.

He slid along the wall toward the back of the building. Just before he reached another corner he dropped to the ground behind some bushes. No other lights flicked on. About twenty feet on that side of the fieldhouse, the woods began.

She waited and watched, holding her breath. Her heart throbbed against her chest. Brodie pinched herself, again.

It hurt!

This wasn't one of her dreams. She needed to go wake up Hannah.

Chapter 48

Creed pulled only his jeans on. He didn't take the extra minutes for boots. As soon as he got Hannah's alert that someone was sneaking around their property he was in tactical mode, despite waking up suddenly. His muscles tensed. He took careful steps while his eyes began to focus in the dark.

He told Grace to stay then he slipped down the dark hallway. He stopped at the office to take a quick glance out the window. It looked out at the fieldhouse, but not the back end. He didn't keep a weapon anywhere in the animal clinic. He grabbed the metal desk lamp, ripped off the shade and wrapped the cord tight around the base. It felt heavy and was long enough to swing.

Satisfied, he went back into the hallway and punched the app on his cell phone that brought up the security cameras. He tapped one that had a decent angle of that area. The whole time he tapped and glanced, he moved. The camera wasn't capturing any movement.

He shoved the phone in his back pocket and slipped out the front. Instead of heading directly to the fieldhouse next door, Creed eased along the clinic's outside wall, weaving his way to the other side.

All of these buildings backed to the forest. They had cleared trees each time they added to their facility, but only as many as necessary. Both Creed and Hannah liked the idea of being nestled in the woods. They saw it as a protective barrier. Until something like this happened. Until someone took advantage and used the woods for camouflage.

His eyes adjusted quickly to the moonlight and the shadows it created. He knew his property intimately. Every shrub and path, but he rarely ventured out barefoot. Everything was still wet from the afternoon rains. It softened the leaves from crunching. Nothing stopped the caps of acorns from stabbing his soles.

The humidity had already started to make his skin slick with sweat. He ignored the rivulets running down his bare chest. He tightened his sweaty grip on the lamp as he peeked around the corner. Shadows danced across the back of the fieldhouse. Most of them were branches bowing and swaying in the breeze.

The hum of the air conditioning units made it difficult to listen. His eyes searched the ground then moved to tree trunks and even skimmed up into the trees. He made his way toward the corner where Brodie had last seen the man. The whole time he watched the shrubs that led back into the forest.

With his back to the wall Creed shot a look around the corner.

There was no one.

But even in the moonlight he could see fresh footprints along the length of the building and disappearing into the shrubs. He followed as far as his bare feet allowed, pulled out his phone and snapped several photos of the best impressions in the damp clay.

Then he backtracked to the clinic, leaving muddy prints from the door all the way down the hall.

"Everything's okay, Grace," he reassured her. She was panting but wagging. Hank slept soundly, thankfully not noticing Grace's anxiety.

Creed sent a couple of quick texts to Hannah. Told her that he and Grace would be there in a few minutes. Then he found the phone number for Mark Hadley. With Sheriff Norwich still in the hospital Creed wasn't sure who he should call. He knew he'd be waking up the CSU tech.

"Hello?"

"Mark, it's Ryder Creed. Sorry to wake you. The deputies assigned to the crime scene in the forest, you need to contact them. Someone was sneaking around my property, and he headed back into the forest."

"You think it's the killer?"

"I don't know. But I suspect it's the same guy who chased Brodie."

"Could you tell if he's armed?"

"No."

"Okay. I'll let them know. Thanks for the heads up."

"Sure."

Creed thought about letting Jason know about the intruder, but his doublewide was on the other side of the property close to the dog kennel and Creed's loft apartment. There was nothing else that could be done right now. He remembered how exhausted Jason looked and Scout definitely needed the rest. He decided to let them sleep.

When Creed and Grace walked in the back door to the big house, he almost ran into Hannah in the dark.

"Lord have mercy, you took forever."

"I texted you. He's gone."

He flipped on the kitchen lights to find her holding a shotgun. Hannah's husband, Isaac, had taught her how to shoot before he left to die in Iraq. Hannah did many things well, but she wasn't a marksman. Fact was, she hated touching a gun and didn't like them around her boys. But she said the shotgun allowed her half a chance to hit an intruder. It was unsettling to see it grasped in her hands. It revealed how frightened she was.

Brodie sat at the counter with Kitten in her arms. Hunter and Lady were at her feet.

"Are you sure he's gone?" Brodie asked in a voice that reminded him of a little girl, not the full-grown woman in front of him.

Standing in the middle of the two of them, he realized he'd failed miserably. His top priority was supposed to be keeping them safe.

And yet, Brodie surprised him when she said, "It's my fault. I led him here."

"It's not your fault," he told her. "Don't you dare think that." He must have slipped and let his frustration show, because both women jerked their heads to look at him. Even Grace sat staring up.

"I think he's been in the woods the entire time we've been at the crime scene." He saw Hannah's eyes go wide, and he was surprised she hadn't thought of it sooner than he did.

"We've been going back and forth from here for two days," Creed continued, now returning to a calm and steady tone. "He would have followed us at some point. So it's not your fault, Brodie. That very first day he had to see the helicopter come down for Sheriff Norwich."

"But coming here in the middle of the night. What does it mean?" Brodie asked. "Do you think he came to hurt us?"

Creed wished he could reassure her. He looked to Hannah for help, but she was waiting for his answer, too.

"I don't know," Creed finally admitted.

One of the first things Brodie had asked of him when she came to live with him and Hannah, was that he always told her the truth. For sixteen years Iris Malone had brainwashed her into believing that Brodie's parents didn't want her back even pretending to talk to them on the phone.

"But I promise," Creed added, "that he won't hurt you. Or Hannah and the boys. Or the dogs. I won't let that happen."

He saw her shoulders relax just a little, and he was relieved that she didn't hear any doubt in his voice. Because honestly, he had no idea if he could keep that promise.

Day 3

Chapter 49

Creed waited until after eight o'clock to leave a message for the medical examiner. Yesterday, Maggie had mentioned that Dr. Kammerer had been working late into the evening, so he was surprised when she answered the phone.

They barely got through their greetings, and Vickie launched into details about what she'd found.

"I sent the bullets over to ballistics. Both were small caliber. Interesting, to say the least. And I have someone comparing the dog hair. Maggie's checking on the dog's owner."

"Actually, none of that is why I'm calling," he told her.

"Oh. Okay."

"I know you collected some items that are being processed for fingerprints and DNA. Do you have anything that the killer might have worn, or maybe an item he held onto for a period?"

Creed was thinking about the footprints. Two days ago Grace had been able to pick up the lingering scent and identify it enough to lead him and Norwich to the edge of the creek where the killer had docked his boat. But after all the rains he might need something else.

"Are you asking if we have anything with the killer's scent?"

"Yes. Exactly."

"How long does scent stay on an item?" she asked.

"Depends on the item. If it's a piece of clothing that's been recently worn and not laundered, there are usually skin rafts caught in the fabric. When we're tracking a missing person, a piece of clothing is what works best. Shoes are great because very few people wash them.

"We use a person's saliva or breath when we're training for a particular illness or disease, but I've never used it to track an individual. Scent preservation kits use a pad that's swiped under the arm or across the back of the neck."

"Scent preservation kit?"

"We just started doing those." He didn't want to get into a lengthy discussion, but when the medical examiner remained silent, he figured he owed her that much. After all, what he was asking from her was for a piece of evidence from an open case.

"Mostly, they're being used for elderly people with early dementia. They collect their own scent, or a family member does it. The kit has a scent collection pad, a jar or specimen cup with a tamper-proof seal and ID label. If we provide the kit, Hannah prefers we store them. Families sometime forget where they put it. And nursing facilities don't always want the responsibility of storing them. They do need to be kept out of heat and sunlight. Our contact information is in their files to call us if the person walks off and gets lost."

"That's interesting," she said.

The entire time he was talking he heard papers rustling.

"We did retrieve a fast food bag with his leftovers," she told him. "I'm hoping there might be enough for a DNA sample. But Maggie just sent all that off to the FBI's crime lab."

Creed knew what he was asking to do was a long shot. He wasn't even sure it would work.

"What are you hoping to accomplish?" Vickie asked. "Are you thinking your dog can sniff out the killer?"

"I know it sounds crazy, but I think he's still hanging around the crime scene."

"And if she finds him?"

He hadn't thought it all out yet, but he didn't want to tell her that. All Creed knew, was the guy had started coming out of the forest and onto his property. A killer—a serial killer—was taking a risk to observe and scrutinize where Hannah and Brodie and Jason and Grace and all their dogs lived.

At the crime scene, Creed had seen what the man was capable of doing. The fact that he was taking such a risk told Creed it wouldn't be long before he targeted one of them. Before he hurt one of them.

"Grace will be attached to me," he told the medical examiner. Then he added, "And hopefully, there will be plenty of law enforcement officers there who can apprehend him."

He added this last part only because he knew it was what she wanted to hear. But Creed didn't expect the guy to stick around if the woods were crawling with sheriff's deputies.

"Hold on and let me look at Hadley's list. He found and bagged some items that I haven't seen yet."

Creed wondered if he might be able to talk Maggie into getting back that fast food bag. If the guy had carried it, curled his fingers around to crumple it, maybe the bag would still have some of his scent? Maybe there was even a napkin inside?

"You might be in luck," Vickie came back on. "Although, I have to tell you we have no way of knowing whether this belonged to one of the victims or the killer. But Hadley noted it wasn't found with or near the bodies we recovered."

"What is it?"

"A black ball cap. Tampa Bay Buccaneers."

Chapter 50

Pensacola Beach

Taylor heard the whop-whop of the helicopter's rotors. She needed to get up and prepare for a fresh set of casualties. She could feel the hot air blowing in on her. But she didn't smell the blood. Or the dust.

There was so much dust.

They could never keep it out.

Dust and blood.

Both stuck to her sweat-drenched body. She always scrubbed and scrubbed, but the scent stayed in her nostrils.

She waited for it to come to her now, riding on the hot air that washed over her body. But it wasn't blood or dust that she smelled. It was salty and wet and refreshing.

Refreshing?

She startled awake and sat up in bed. It took her a moment to realize where she was. The patio door was open a few inches, just enough to billow the sheer curtains. She could hear the waves. No helicopters. She glanced at the bedside clock and started to jump out of bed then remembered it was her day off.

She hadn't had one in a long stretch, preferring to work and to keep her from counting the days until she could see William. She stretched out on the bed and wished she hadn't told John Lockett to go home. If Derrick was going to take forever to get her a meeting with William's grandparents, maybe she could use a little distraction.

And not for the first time since yesterday's lunch, she thought about the young soldier named Jason. She'd almost allowed him to become her latest distraction. It was a good thing he couldn't meet her for a drink last night, or he might be here waking up with her.

Derrick, the devil, was right about her. She did have a bad habit that needed to be broken if she intended to have her son back in her life. She thought she had a good chance with Lockett to start something healthy. Something safe.

Who was she fooling? She had no idea how to do relationships.

None of that, however, kept her from thinking about Jason. He was much younger than Lockett. And shorter, but she liked that Jason stood eye to eye with her. He seemed sweet and genuine, but one look at his prosthetic, and she knew he had seen and experienced things that could have destroyed him. And that made her even more curious.

At the Segway House, she remembered finding his clumsy flirting charming. He obviously wasn't used to doing it, but she liked that it didn't stop him.

She had avoided dating military men, but the more time that separated her from her deployment, the more she felt the desire to talk about it. And it certainly wasn't conversation for civilians. Howard had reminded her that only another veteran, who still had the stink in their nostrils and those sounds in their heads, could understand.

When she saw Jason and the other two guys around the poker table, she had been so tempted to join them. She knew they had invited her because of how she looked. Would they still be interested if they discovered she had scars, too?

She turned onto her side and watched the water beyond the big boats. A whole day to herself. What the hell was she going to do? It was too early for drinks at Walter's Canteen and probably too early for poker at the Segway House.

She pushed herself out of bed and decided to make a protein shake then go for a run. She turned on the small television that faced the kitchen. Sometimes she needed voices in her apartment to stop her mind from looping over and over the same ole stuff.

As she pulled out the ingredients, she watched the local news waiting for the weather forecast. It was something she did on a daily basis in Virginia. Here in the Florida Panhandle it didn't matter. Sunny, hot, humid and a chance of an afternoon thunderstorm. But before the weather came on, the news anchor started talking about the body of a man found in Blackwater River State Forest.

For some reason it sent a chill down Taylor's back. She grabbed the remote and punched up the volume.

From the map in the corner, she could see the forest was just over the I-10 Bridge and in Santa Rosa County.

"No details on the identity of the man have been released. The sheriff's department has confirmed that they are investigating the death as a homicide. There are other unconfirmed reports that there might be more bodies buried at this site. We'll have more on this story tonight."

Taylor told herself that it had nothing to do with Lockett.

Of course, it didn't. You're being ridiculous.

She said it out loud as if that would convince her.

Chapter 51

K9 CrimeScents

Creed was at the end of his long driveway, about to make the quick trip to Pensacola to pick up the ball cap. When his cell phone started ringing, he wanted to ignore it. He saw the caller's ID and tapped the Jeep's touchscreen to receive it.

"Good morning," he said.

"Hey, I'm glad I got you," Maggie said with a hint of urgency.

Creed immediately caught himself holding back a sigh. Was she calling only because they needed something else from him to process?

Then she surprised him when she added, "I owe you an apology."

"An apology? What for?"

"You're being polite. I've been acting too much like an FBI agent."

"It's a big part of who you are. Nothing wrong with that. I tend to act like a dog handler about 110 percent of the time."

"And it's one of the things I love about you. But mine involves killers and crawling inside their minds. It's not always healthy."

He felt an uptick of his pulse. She just said it was something she "loved about him." Then just as quickly he dismissed it. It wasn't the same thing as saying she loved him. People said stuff like that all the time. Of course, people did.

But not Maggie O' Dell.

Neither one of them had used the word "love," even the one night they'd spent together making love. Actually, Creed appreciated that they didn't throw the word around. He'd slept with lots of women and never once uttered the word. He didn't expect it from Maggie, and he certainly wasn't looking for it.

So why was any of this bothering him?

She'd called to apologize. That was huge. Accept it and move on.

"Don't worry about it," he said. "You shouldn't apologize for loving your job."

"Well, I called to see if you could have dinner with me tonight on the beach."

He knew she was staying at Margaritaville. *On the beach.* They could have dinner anywhere. Was she inviting to the beach as a prelude for an overnight stay?

"I can't. I'm sorry." He shook his head and wanted to kick himself. Before she could respond, he said, "We had a visitor on our property last night."

"What do you mean a visitor?"

"Brodie was the only one who saw him. Hannah's checking the video feeds from our security cameras to see if any of them caught a glimpse of him."

"Did she recognize him?"

"It was dark. He was creeping around in the shadows. Tripped one of the motion-sensor floodlights. That's what woke her up. But she thinks it's the same guy who chased her in the forest."

"I don't like this. He's starting to take bigger risks."

"And becoming more dangerous."

When she didn't answer immediately, he continued, "He's got to be pissed that we found his hiding place, right? I mean the guy dragged those bodies into a part of the forest where no one else goes. He felt comfortable enough to leave them to melt into the landscape. Then all of sudden, Brodie and I come along and ruin it all."

"You think he's targeting you?"

"I'm worried he's targeting Brodie."

He waited out her silence. The longer it lasted, the more it confirmed his suspicion.

Finally she said, "He may have left us something that will identify him. There's a good chance we have his fingerprints. Maybe his DNA."

"No offense, but how long will that take? In the meantime, he's free to sneak in and out of the forest. I think he's getting more desperate. He's definitely getting bolder coming onto my property."

"What about having the sheriff's department assign a deputy?" she asked.

"To patrol my property?" He let out a frustrated laugh. "I'll take care of my own property."

Another phone call started coming in. He could see on the display that it was Mark Hadley, the CSU tech.

"I've got a call coming in from Hadley," he told her.

"Ryder, just be careful, okay?"

"I'll talk to you later," he said and ended the call to pick up Hadley's. "Hi Mark."

"I'm on my way back out to the forest, but I wanted to update you. McLane and Gallagher didn't see anybody else in the forest last night."

"He must have taken a different path."

"Oh, they didn't see him, but he was definitely there. He took their boat."

"You're kidding."

"At the break of daylight when Danvers and Sullivan came up the creek to relieve them, they found the night shift's boat about two miles down. It was tilted against the bank, left on display for them to find. Has a hole in it about the size of a basketball."

"What kind of crazy game is he playing?"

"There's something else," Hadley said. "Local media knows there were bodies found in the forest. Not just one."

"Chief Deputy Glenn?"

"You didn't hear that from me."

"How's Sheriff Norwich doing?" Creed asked.

"She's out of intensive care but still in the hospital. There's talk she might not be back for a while. I heard Dr. Kammerer asked that FBI agent for official help on the case. I hope that's true because this could get messy and dangerous."

"I'm pretty sure she already is on the case," Creed told him. "Hadley, be careful out there."

Chapter 52

Pensacola, Florida

Maggie checked for messages then jammed her cell phone into the back pocket of her jeans. She didn't like any of this. Ryder was right about the killer. But if she admitted that to him, he'd see it as justification to take things into his own hands.

She already heard the urgency in his voice. There was a slight hint of panic, too. She couldn't blame him. She knew before she suggested it that he wouldn't trust the local law enforcement officials. This was something she actually understood.

There were few people Maggie trusted, and on several occasions that lack of trust had resulted in her going rogue without any backup. Rarely did the consequences matter to her, whether they were reprimands from her boss or physical injury to herself or even the psychological scars. She did want she believed was right, what was necessary. And most of the time, she'd do it all again.

That was something she and Ryder shared. Call it stubborn. Call it pig-headedness. It was dangerous and nobody understood it as clearly as she did.

She left the rental vehicle down the lane and walked back to Storage Unit B12. She unlocked the padlock, slid the bolt, and pulled up the garage door. Then she took a couple of steps back. It still smelled awful, but after several days of ripe decomp in the forest, putting up with this would be a breeze.

Vickie had given her the key. Two days ago the medical examiner wasn't comfortable leaving Maggie alone to sort through the contents. Now, she didn't hesitate to give her the key. Funny how murder and a serial killer could bring people together. How it could win mutual trust.

She thought about Ryder, again. She didn't blame him for being impatient with local law enforcement. But she detected his impatience with her, too.

Why hadn't she been able to narrow down who this guy might be? He was sneaking around the forest, coming and going in broad daylight as well as at night, and yet no one had a clue as to who he was. Other than Brodie, no one had even caught a glimpse of him. How was that possible?

She was hoping her crew back at Quantico would provide some answers. Agent Antonio Alonzo had all the contact information for Hank's owner. Maggie was guessing that Hank's owner was the man Brodie stumbled over in the forest. The man they were referring to as John Doe #1.

But it wasn't just the fact that the man probably had Hank's dog hair on his clothing, which Vickie's lab would be able to determine. No, Maggie had a gut feeling the bullets would show that both man and dog were shot by the same gun. As she tried to piece things together, she wondered if perhaps the killer didn't know about the dog until Hank came at him to protect his owner. He probably believed the dog ran off and died. But how did he not realize the man he shot was not dead? He would have had to transport his body from where he shot him to the forest.

The boat launch.

It only now occurred to her. The place where Hank was shot. That had to be where his owner was shot, too. How many afternoon thundershowers had washed away evidence?

She checked her wristwatch. She wondered if she could remember how to find it on her own. But first, she needed to take a better look at the contents of this storage unit. She had another gut feeling about something inside.

She made her way through the mess, high stepping over and weaving through the obstacle course. There appeared to be no rhyme or reason for how things were stacked or arranged. It was so disorganized, with so little forethought, that simple pathways weren't left to maneuver through the space.

Maggie suspected the items at the back had been placed there first. Containers, trash bags, specimen cups and buckets were added as they were acquired, simply put down in whatever empty spot remained and filling the unit from back to front until there wasn't any space left.

Toward the back she found more sturdy plastic containers with faded labels. She pulled out her cell phone and took a few photos. Using the flashlight on her phone, she squatted closer to try and read the labels. A blue and yellow logo at the top read UnitedBIO. Underneath in small type it read, The Living Bank.

The containers may have been transparent at one time but were now milky white. It was impossible to see what was inside. But these were placed one on top of another. There were different sizes and of course, the largest weren't at the bottom. It looked like a sloppy tower that could topple over with a simple touch.

Next to these containers were the cleaning supplies she remembered seeing the first day. And the stack of paper towels. Although they were packaged separately, it looked like they all had the same pink and yellow pattern.

Again, she took photos. Then she grabbed one of the rolls and tucked it under her arm.

She took more photos as she crisscrossed through the maze. Almost back to the door she stopped in front of a five-gallon bucket. It was one of at least a dozen scattered among the rubble. But this one was labeled: TISSUE SAMPLES.

Maggie put down the roll of paper towels and pocketed her phone. She dug out gloves from her pocket and grabbed the lid. It was on tight. She glanced around and found a metal bar that may have belonged to a shelf at one time. The screws were still attached. It fit perfectly between the lid and bucket. She pried one side then the other. A third time and the lid popped.

The smell of formaldehyde hit her like a fist. She jerked back almost losing her balance and catching herself before she tumbled into a couple of garbage bags.

Unlike some of the other containers, this bucket had no punctures that Maggie could see. So whatever was inside, had most likely been preserved.

She joggled the lid until it came completely free. Then she held her breath and lifted it up.

Maggie was prepared to see tissue samples. Or maybe another body organ. She was not prepared to see the woman's head facing directly up at her.

Chapter 53

Maggie waited in her rental vehicle for Vickie and Escambia County Sheriff Clayton. Storage Unit B12 was now a possible crime scene.

She had placed the lid back on the bucket, tucked the roll of paper towels under her arm and carefully made her way out, closing the garage door behind her. Now she sat with the air conditioning blasting on her, hoping the smell of formaldehyde would leave her nostrils. She wanted to think of anything other than the woman's last look of horror; eyes wide open.

She pulled out her cell phone and called Agent Alonzo. The package of paper towels sat on the passenger seat.

"Hey Maggie," he answered in a singsong greeting. "Good timing."

"I hope that means you have something for me."

"Hold on. I'm texting you the driver's license photo of Hank's owner."

Her phone pinged and she brought up the image. Sometimes driver's license photos were old or quirky and difficult to use for any identification purposes. She enlarged the image, and though it was grainy, there was no doubt in her mind that this was John Doe #1. This was Hank's owner, John Lockett from Richmond, Virginia.

"That's our victim," she told Alonzo.

"I'm getting his vehicle information, and I'll put out a BOLO for it. Maybe we'll get lucky and the killer is cocky enough to be driving it. By this afternoon I should be able to tell you any credit card activity. It might tell us what hotel he stayed at or any restaurants he visited. You didn't find a cell phone?"

"No. It's possible it's still lost in the forest somewhere or maybe where he was shot."

"His phone number was with his contact information," Alonzo said. "That's all I need. I'll see if it's still on. Could be still in his car."

"Can you tell me anything about him? Why he was here? Does he have family or friends in the area?"

"Seems like a pretty ordinary guy. I haven't found much. No arrests. No warrants. Not even a parking ticket. He was a bartender for a classy place that makes them wear shirts and ties. I got that from his Facebook page. He doesn't have much on there, but I've downloaded a few recent photos. He has two of him with his dog and a blond woman. Someone named Taylor. I'll text those to you in a little bit."

"A bartender from Richmond, Virginia," Maggie said. "How did he end up getting murdered almost a thousand miles away by a serial killer?"

"You said the dog survived?"

"So far, yes."

"If only he could tell you what happened. It would make it so much easier."

Maggie thought about that. Ryder certainly believed in his dogs more than he did investigators. Was there a way that Hank could tell them who killed his owner?

"So did you find anything at all in that storage unit?" Alonzo asked. "You know the actual reason you went down to Pensacola? Has Joe Black struck again?"

"Someone definitely started a strange collection. See if you can find out anything about a company called UnitedBio. One word with a capital B on bio. I'm guessing it provides tissue samples and assorted organs for research. I'll send you over a photo of a label I found on one of the containers. Have you been able to find out anything more about the original lessee of this unit?"

"You'd think it would be simple, but this storage company's been sold and bought in the last several years. The previous owners weren't exactly organized. Current owner told me they found rental agreements stacked in bank boxes. Some of them had water damage from a leaky roof. Nothing was stored on computer. The new owner basically started digital files and contacts from scratch.

"Unit B12 began as a month-to-month rental paid in cash. It doesn't look like there was any written contract. Just a phone number to contact. At some point the person paid cash in advance for two years. The phone number has been out of service for almost that long."

"You can't track it?"

"Oh, I did. It used to be a housekeeping number connected to a place called Recovery Gardens. Looks like it's a drug addiction rehab facility located between Pensacola and Panama City."

"Drug rehab?"

"Place looks upscale. The rooms look like hotel suites. Fancy grounds. Lots of gardens. Imagine that."

"For the rich and famous?" she asked.

"No, they have some programs available for the less famous. Especially for veterans."

"This doesn't make sense. I haven't seen anything in this storage unit that looks like it came from a drug rehab facility. Or any drug related items."

"So what is in there?" Alonzo asked.

"Specimen jars, containers of all shapes and sizes. A few are laboratory grade. Most of them are plastic household stuff that you'd use to store leftovers. And there's a bunch of takeout containers. Even a couple of disposable drink cups. The supersize."

"The cups have stuff in them?"

"Yes, globs that I'm happy to let the medical examiner identify. Of course, the formaldehyde ate through the bottoms and leaked out."

"Are you sure all the tissue samples and globs are human?"

"Good question. The heart in the Tupperware container was human. But at one time it was in formaldehyde, too. That's why I'm starting to think this mess could be leftovers from a research lab."

"If someone hoped to start his own collection, he certainly wasn't taking care of it," Alonzo said. "Hey, I remember reading about a guy up in Connecticut who kept his collection in Mason jars."

"I worked that case," Maggie said, and she did not want to remember it.

"Oh, sorry. I sometimes forget that you're like...old...er."

Maggie smiled. "Speaking of old. I do have one other thing," she said, glancing at the paper towels. "Can you track down whether a product is still being sold or if it's been discontinued?"

"Fun trivia," he said. "That is definitely in my wheelhouse."

"I'll send you a couple of photos." Maggie watched in the rearview mirror as Vickie pulled up behind her. "Antonio, I've got to go. The medical examiner just arrived. Oh, and I forgot to tell you, I did find something interesting that wasn't just a glob of dried up tissue or a pickled organ."

"Good for you. What was it?"

"I found a woman's head in a five-gallon bucket."

"Of course, you did," Alonzo told her, and she could almost hear his big, wide grin. "I'll catch you later."

Chapter 54

K9 CrimeScents
Florida Panhandle

Brodie was happy to help Jason with the kennel chores. Sometimes it still surprised her that just months ago she had been afraid to set foot inside a building with so many dogs.

The place was light and airy. Sunlight flooded in through the windows set high above the dogs' sightline and stretched to the ceiling of the warehouse-sized facility. On one end was an open concept kitchen with cabinets, counters and appliances, that made it look like it belonged in a custom designed house. Hannah told Brodie that Ryder wanted to create a building that not only kept the dogs safe, but comfortable and well fed.

There were crates of various sizes along one wall for dogs that wanted the safety of their own dens. Sprawled out on the other side were dog beds of different shapes and sizes. Recently, Ryder had added a couple of sofas and some soft chairs. Brodie wondered if the additions were more for Jason and Ryder. She had found one or the other on different occasions sleeping with the dogs.

It made her smile. The two men looked so different, but they were very much alike when it came to taking care of their dogs.

Jason continued to bring in supplies while Brodie loaded the dishwasher. A row of monitors lined the wall, and she glanced at each of them. They showed black-and-white views from the security cameras mounted around the kennel and the exercise yards.

She started to look away when one of the last screens caught her attention. Two of the larger dogs had something cornered against the fence. Something black. Something that didn't belong in the yard.

"Jason," she yelled. "Jason, hurry!"

He dropped the bag he was carrying through the back door.

"What's wrong?"

She pointed to the screen.

He took one look and raced out the door to the yard. Brodie ran close behind.

"Chance! Winnie! Stop!" He shouted at the top of his lungs without slowing down. The dogs immediately obeyed.

The huge German shepherd named Chance had a piece of the black plastic in his mouth. Jason pulled it out and grabbed the dog's jaw, opening it to look then sticking the fingers of his real hand into the dog's mouth. Chance allowed it, but his eyes were wide.

"Check Winnie's mouth," Jason told Brodie.

Winnie was a gentle, yellow Lab, but she was a food thief. Brodie knew most of these dogs had at one time lived on their own, abandoned, fending for themselves. It was one of the first things she felt she had in common with them.

"She doesn't have anything," she said.

"Are you sure, Brodie? You've got to be sure."

She pried the dog's mouth open again, and Jason did the same with Chance.

"Nothing," she told him.

The black, plastic bag looked like an ordinary garbage bag that someone had thrown over the fence. Other than the piece Chance had bit off, it looked intact.

Jason poked the bag with his prosthetic hand. He looked back at both dogs.

"Take them to the front yard," he instructed her, "and shut the gate so the others don't come over."

"What do you think it is?" Brodie asked as she gathered her fingers under each dog's collar.

"I don't know," he admitted, and she heard a hint of panic in his voice. "Take them back."

"You think it might explode?"

"Brodie, please! Just take them back. Okay?"

"Okay."

She'd never heard Jason yell before. Even the dogs were anxious now. But they didn't put up a fuss when she guided them. Some of the other dogs had noticed the commotion and started to go through the gate.

"Stay," she told them.

Chance and Winnie pushed through the entrance, and Brodie shut and fastened the gate. But she stayed in the outer yard. She turned around and leaned her back against the fence to watch Jason.

He had waited until he knew that she and the dogs were safe. She watched him pick up a long branch from under one of the trees. Using its full length, he snagged the bag through the opening Chance had made. Carefully, he lifted it. Then as if he were casting a fishing line, he raised his arm and flung the bag as far outside the yard as he could. At the same time, he turned his back and crouched down. Brodie did the same.

Nothing happened.

There was no explosion.

She looked up, and Jason was already heading for the back gate to check out the bag again. Brodie followed. This time he didn't send her away. The two of them stood over the garbage bag staring at the contents that had come out when it hit the ground.

"What is that?" Brodie asked. It looked like slabs of meat but with blue-green powder all over it.

Jason had pulled out his phone and was tapping out a message. He took a photo and sent it, too.

"Jason, what's going on?"

"I think someone tried to poison our dogs with a couple of raw steaks."

Chapter 55

K9 CrimeScents
Florida Panhandle

It was easier for Udie to maneuver around the property during the day without all those motion-sensor lights flipping on. You'd think they were protecting a bank full of gold bars instead of a kennel filled with mutts. They didn't even look like high-priced pedigree dogs. Just a bunch of mutts.

He didn't waste his time waiting to see the results. Maybe they'd take his warning and stay the hell out of the forest, or he'd need to do something more drastic.

Now, he needed to concentrate on those deputies.

He hiked back to his boat. He popped a couple pills and washed them down with warm cola. The new drugs were making him feel in command.

Back on the water, he felt invincible. He knew it would calm him, if he gave it a chance. The gentle slosh against the boat was soothing. Sweat trickled down inside his shirt and dripped from his face. He pulled off a couple of paper towels from the roll at his feet and wiped the back of his neck. He stopped short of where the rash began.

Last night he had rummaged through his mother's medicine cabinet and found a bunch of tins and tubes and bottles. Despite all her homemade cures and potions, he was pleased to find she kept some basic drugstore medicines.

Udie had found one for rashes and smeared the pink stuff on until it dried and caked up. It helped with the itch, but it didn't seem to reduce the bumps and blisters. Some of those were starting to ooze. And his sweat kept washing away the lotion.

He squirted it on his hands now and applied more to his neck. The boat was drifting downstream. He guided it through the narrow tributary until it spilled out into the wider creek. He was so obsessed with his rash that he didn't anticipate running into the boat coming up the creek.

He didn't even see that damned thing!

He maneuvered around the overgrown bend, and suddenly, there it was.

A sheriff's boat.

One man. Not in uniform, but he wore a black ball cap with the sheriff department logo on it. Udie recognized him. He'd seen him with the women collecting pieces of stuff and putting them in evidence bags.

"Hey there." The man waved to him.

"Hey." Udie lifted his chin and kept the hand stained with pink lotion out of sight.

"Catch anything?" the man asked as their boats came closer to pass by.

Of course, why else would he be out here?

"Large mouth bass," Udie lied.

"Yeah? What are you using for bait?"

Now Udie remembered. He'd heard them calling this man, Hadley. He was some kind of crime scene tech.

"Live crawfish, beetle spinners." Man, he was so good at this. Of course, the pills helped.

"Nice. Well, good luck," he said and motored on his way.

They had come within ten feet of each other. Not close enough, Udie decided for the man to see that he didn't have a single piece of fishing gear in his boat. He'd need to remedy that, and that's when it occurred to him that fishing line could come in handy for a few other things.

He was feeling pretty good about things until his phone rang. While he was in the woods, he was basically unreachable. But the guy must be desperate, Udie noticed. He was calling the dead guy's phone number.

"I'm a little busy," Udie answered as the boat glided by one of his favorite spots.

"What the hell's going on?"

Mr. Charisma had morphed into Mr. Angry. He'd let him rant and rave. By now, Udie was feeling too good to be rattled.

"I just heard on the radio that they found bodies in the forest. Those better not be our bodies, Udie."

He wanted to say: *Don't you mean your bodies, asshole?* But he wasn't stupid.

"I have everything under control," Udie told him. In his head he was already making a list of everything he'd need. The drug didn't just relax him, it made him brave and brilliant.

"Sounds to me that you don't have anything under control. Listen to me, Udie. We have a good thing going. If you want to be a partner like your mother was before she ran off, we need to handle this."

"What's that?" Udie said, pretending he couldn't hear him. "You're breaking up. I must be losing you." Udie pulled the phone away from his ear. He ended the call then turned the phone off.

That'll teach the bastard not to mention his mother

Chapter 56

Medical Examiner's Office
Pensacola, Florida

Creed waited for Vickie in the small lounge down the hallway from the autopsy suites. Her assistant had led him to the windowless room and offered coffee or tea, assuring him that the medical examiner would be back shortly. She told him she was called away to pick up something but wouldn't be long.

All he wanted to do was grab the ball cap and head back home. If it belonged to the killer, Creed would be able to train Grace to track the man down. He hadn't figured out the rest. Of course, he realized the cap might belong to one of the dead, and all the time and training might lead to a grave instead.

His phone pinged.

It was a text message from Jason asking him to call as soon as possible.

Creed hoped it didn't have anything to do with Hank. When he checked on him before he left, the dog was awake but groggy. He glanced at his wristwatch. Dr. Avelyn should be there about now.

He scrolled and tapped Jason's number. The kid picked up immediately as if he were waiting for the call.

"What's going on?" Creed asked.

"Everything's okay," Jason said only making Creed stand up and pace. "Someone tossed a garbage bag over the fence in the outer yard."

"Someone? What the hell was in it?"

"A couple of T-bone steaks rolled in some kind of blue powder. Dr. Avelyn thinks it's a cleaning product."

"Which dogs found it? Did they eat any of it?"

"Chance and Winnie, but we don't think either of them ate it. She's giving them charcoal tablets just in case, and we've got both of them in the clinic for observation."

Creed released a long sigh and rubbed his hand over his bristled jaw. Less than twenty-four hours.

"This is getting ridiculous," he said as he paced the length of the small room. "That bag wasn't there this morning. I always walk the yard. Now he's sneaking around during the day. I'm really glad you noticed the bag."

"It wasn't me. It was Brodie. She noticed on the livestream monitors. She thought the dogs had something cornered. We both thought it was an animal."

"She's certainly getting a wicked initiation into our business, isn't she?"

Creed heard some ruffling sounds. When Jason answered this time his voice was lower. Brodie must have been within earshot.

"She seems to think it's her fault."

"I told her not to do that." Creed winced and shook his head. "I need to stop this guy."

"*We* need to stop this guy," Jason corrected him. "What do you have in mind? Because I have some ideas of my own."

"You think Benny and Colfax would have time to meet with us today?"

"If we buy them lunch and drinks at Walter's Canteen, I think they'll make time."

Creed checked his watch again and said, "Make it a late lunch, around one or two o'clock. I'll meet you guys there."

"Got it."

Just as he slipped his phone back into his pocket, Creed heard voices in the hallway. He stepped out to find Vickie with her hands full of brown evidence bags. Maggie followed carrying a white five-gallon bucket and had what looked like a roll of paper towels tucked under her arm.

"Have you two been out fishing?" he joked.

"Oh, we just keep finding all kinds of treats," Vickie said. "It's frickin' Christmas in June."

Chapter 57

Recovery Gardens

Kayla Hudson had allowed Luke a play date at his friend's house. She didn't particularly like the friend. Owen was a nerdy, know-it-all, but he and Luke enjoyed the same brainteaser games. And besides, what mattered most to Kayla was that Owen's mother had been a nurse before she became a stay-at-home mom. She was one of the few mothers in Luke's group of friends that knew anything about type 1 diabetes.

Traffic was so hectic she could hardly enjoy the scenery along US-98. It didn't help that Eric's panicked phone calls and voice messages had made her more tense and anxious than usual. He had that luxury suite, a swimming pool and those lovely pathways surrounded by beautiful gardens. There was 24/7 access to cafés and a coffee shop. What more could he want? How could he not relax and enjoy any of that?

She knew it was the drug withdrawals that caused his paranoia and the hysterics. It had to be. Suddenly, he cared about some guy named Simon. She wondered if Eric was pissed that Simon looked like he was worse off than Eric, but Simon got to go home.

No one would tell her anything over the phone. Confidentiality. They didn't care that Kayla was his wife. For some reason she wasn't listed on his admission documents as a contact, and so it didn't matter that she was his wife. She sat right next to him as he filled out those papers. Why in the world wouldn't he have put her name down?

They had very strict rules, she was told. That her name wasn't listed, disqualified her as a visitor.

"I'm certain all of the rules were explicitly explained to your husband when he checked in," the woman in the Family Guidance office told her. Seriously, they had an office called "family guidance" that offered no guidance other than, "Those are the rules."

She tried to talk to Eric by phone, only to be informed that he was allowed just one phone call per week while he went through Phase 1. And he'd already made his phone call for the week. That seemed a bit harsh. And again, she realized how little she had paid attention to his admission into this program.

Truthfully, she had been flabbergasted by the extravagance of the place. And although she hated to admit it, she had felt a little jealous. No, that wasn't true. She felt a lot jealous. That was the reason she hadn't paid any attention to the rules or even thought to ask. It looked like a five-star vacation to her, and she found herself wishing she could trade places with Eric.

Also, a small part of her didn't believe Eric would follow through. He had only agreed because he suddenly felt like he was making some major contribution to Luke's welfare by ordering up this magic dog. He wanted to be there for the training part like it gave him some purpose in life.

Deep down, Kayla already figured she'd be alone even this fall when the dog was supposed to be ready. By then, Eric would probably be back to using. Back to his zombie self. She couldn't even remember what he was like before he went off to Afghanistan. Before Luke's diabetes.

No, Kayla didn't expect her life to get any better any time soon.

But Eric's last voice message had affected her so much she couldn't shake the feeling that something awful was going to happen.

Unlike his other messages, he sounded almost calm. The panic was gone. His tone had an eerie acceptance to it.

"No matter what, I love you Kayla," he said, his voice clear and stronger than it had been in weeks. "Please tell Luke I love him. I know you don't believe it, but you two are my everything."

She swatted at the unexpected tears.

Whether this was only part of a drug withdrawal disillusion, the finality of it sounded convincing. He truly believed he wasn't going to see her or Luke ever again.

She pulled into the long service road that looped around the luscious grounds of the facility. They refused to answer her questions over the phone, but in person, she would demand to see her husband.

Chapter 58

Creed wasn't sure he heard correctly.

"You think this storage unit has something to do with the crime scene in the forest?" As he asked the question he looked from Vickie to Maggie and back to Vickie.

"Our resident FBI agent believes that," Vickie said. "She still needs to explain it to me."

"When you cleaned John Lockett's body do you remember removing a paper towel?" Maggie asked.

"Wait a minute." Creed stopped them. "The dead guy in the forest was actually Hank's owner? You know for sure he's John Lockett?"

The expression on Maggie's face softened. "I should have texted you," she said. "Yes, we made a visual ID about an hour ago. We're still trying to check fingerprints to confirm."

"And if his fingerprints have never been processed before," Vickie added, "we'll see if there are dental records to confirm."

At one point, Creed thought Hank's owner might be the one responsible for the dog's gunshot wound. Now, that he knew that wasn't the case, he realized Dr. Avelyn may have been right about Hank trying to protect his owner. Creed felt a sudden gut-punch, grasping the full extent of the dog's loss.

"I have Agent Alonzo digging for more information about Lockett," Maggie said.

He was grateful she didn't verbally acknowledge his dismay even as he could feel her eyes do exactly that.

"Was he married? Did he live with someone? Kids?" Creed wanted to know.

He could tell that Maggie knew what he was really asking. He wondered if there was anyone else Hank had in his day-to-day life. He needed to find out if the dog had other connections or relationships Creed might be ripping him away from if he kept him.

"Alonzo will find out." Maggie reassured him.

Vickie was offloading the evidence bags onto counters and paid little attention to their conversation.

"There was a paper towel stuck to his shirt," the medical examiner said finally answering Maggie's question. "It looked like someone just put it there. It certainly wasn't going to stop the bleeding."

"Do you still have it?" Maggie asked.

"The paper towel?"

Vickie furrowed her brow like she didn't have time for inane details. But then she grabbed a pair of latex gloves, yanking them on as she walked to the counter at the far end of the room. She found the evidence bag she wanted and brought it back. She wrote on the label and broke the seal of red tape.

"There are two squares," she said as she pulled the shirt out. "I left them stuck to the shirt."

As Vickie carefully unfolded the fabric, Maggie gently pried open the package of paper towels she had been carrying. She set the wrapper to the side. Then she unrolled two sheets and separated them from the roll. She placed the sheets across the top of the shirt arranging its edge next to the blood-stained paper towels.

The tiny yellow ducks and pinks flowers lined up almost perfectly to the bloodstained ducks and flowers. There was no question, the patterns matched exactly.

"So the paper towels were bought at the same store," Vickie said. "A strange but insignificant coincidence."

"Not a coincidence," Maggie said. She picked up the package she had carefully removed from the paper towels. She found what she wanted on one side and handed it to Vickie. "It's an advertisement for garden seeds. Check out the expiration date."

"August 21, 1999?"

"I had Agent Alonzo do some checking while I waited for you and Sheriff Clayton," Maggie explained. "This pattern was discontinued in 2001. The company was sold to a larger corporation, so the brand doesn't even exist anymore. What are the odds that two unrelated people in Pensacola would just happen to have the same twenty-year-old rolls of paper towels laying around in their garage…or storage unit?"

"Interesting," Vickie said. "So because of the matching paper towels, you think the killer had access to Unit B12?"

"Yes."

"And you think it matters because…?" Vickie still sounded skeptical.

Creed watched the two women waiting for a good time to interrupt their forensic gamesmanship. All he wanted was the black ball cap and to be on his way. But he was curious why Maggie thought it mattered.

"Because we recovered a woman's body in the forest," Maggie explained. "But we didn't recover her head."

"What about the skull I found?" Creed asked.

"I've checked. It was a male's," Vickie told him without taking her eyes from Maggie's.

The medical examiner seemed to understand the connection Maggie had made to the storage unit, but Creed was still lost.

Vickie looked at him, pointed to the five-gallon bucket and said, "Maggie may have found the poor woman's head."

Chapter 59

"You're okay giving him a piece of evidence?" Maggie asked Vickie. She wasn't pleased, but she'd waited until the exchange was over, and Creed had left.

"I pulled a couple hair samples from it. Those are more important than the actual cap. Besides, he'll bring it back." Vickie stopped what she was doing to look over at Maggie then added, "You're not gonna rat me out?"

"No, of course not. It's just that I know what he wants it for."

"He thinks the long arm of the law moves too slowly," Vickie said. "It's not like he's going to run off into the woods to capture the guy by himself."

Maggie folded her arms over her chest and released a frustrated sigh. "He's a former Marine. That's exactly what he has in mind."

"Too bad you two *aren't* in a relationship, or you'd be able to tell him not to do that."

"Very funny."

"I'm just saying you might want to reconsider upgrading your status."

Maggie tried to roll the tension from her shoulders. She was worried about Ryder. She saw the urgency in his eyes, but she wasn't going to discuss it with the medical examiner. She already had too much insight on the subject. Time to move on.

"You'll be able to check DNA samples," Maggie said. "From the body in the forest against DNA from the head."

"Sure."

"I'd like to send samples to the FBI lab, too. They might be able to identify her." Then Maggie asked, "Were you able to confirm the woman in the forest was beheaded intentionally?"

Vickie had found bones inside the woman's collar with cut-marks.

"It looks that way. I'll take a look to see if the head has similar marks. I have to tell you," Vickie said, "I'm not seeing much continuity with this killer. He shoots one guy but doesn't kill him. But he decapitates a second victim, which seems like overkill."

"What about John Doe #2?"

"Well, this is where it gets even more interesting," the medical examiner told her. "I know you'll find this compelling because it has to do with maggots."

Vickie rubbed her hands together like she was excited to share. "He had no bullet wound. There was no trauma to the head or any part of his body. Don't serial killers usually keep to the same modus operandi?"

"Sometimes it's part of their ritual," Maggie said. "They try to get better using the same tactics. But there can be a level of experimentation. This guy is so clumsy, so disorganized, I can't imagine him taking the time to perfect or experiment. How do you think John Doe #2 was murdered?"

"Remember the maggots I removed from him? I told you I thought they were uncharacteristically small and sluggish. I sent toxicology some of his hair and tissue."

"Did they find anything?" Maggie asked.

"I haven't heard back yet. But I hate waiting, and those pesky maggots kept nagging on my mind. Chances are, anything they ate might still be in their crop. So I had one of my assistants grind some of them up."

Maggie winced at the thought, and her discomfort only made Vickie grin.

"Opioids," the medical examiner told her.

"You were able to tell?"

"Yup. But I'll wait to see if I can confirm with the toxicology report. I suspect he died of a drug overdose."

"Were there any drugs in John Lockett?" Maggie asked.

"I'm still waiting. But I should have his back tomorrow."

"How difficult would it be to intentionally kill someone with an opioid? I mean is that what you're speculating? That the killer may have given a drug load that purposely caused an overdose? Does the victim have to somehow be a willing participant?"

"Illegally made opioids, like some of the fentanyl we're seeing, can be very dangerous. Sometimes it's mixed with other drugs like heroin, cocaine or methamphetamines. Addicts use a powder version or a liquid that's put in eyedroppers or nasal sprays. So it's not like they're measuring out the same dosage.

"Unfortunately, overdosing is not difficult. But here's something to consider," Vickie said, and she pulled out a couple of photos from one of her stacks.

Maggie recognized the garbage bag Scout had found in the woods. One of the photos showed the contents lined up. The paraphernalia included the two-litter soda bottle, some nasal spray containers, blotter paper and several empty boxes of Fentanyl transdermal patches along with discarded wrappers.

"We thought the killer might have a drug problem," Vickie said. "But what if this was the stash he used to overdose his victims?'

"Why would he show us?" Maggie asked as something in the back of her mind started to nag at her. Something she had seen or heard. What was it? Alonzo had brought up something about a drug rehab center.

"These patches," Vickie told her, as she pointed to the empty boxes. "I'm no expert in the illegal drug business, but those are pharmaceutical grade and doctor prescribed."

"Is it a slow or painful death?" she asked.

"Breathing slows down. So does the heart. There's a decrease of oxygen to the brain. The person becomes unresponsive. Maybe slips into a coma. I suppose it's possible to not even notice what's happening until it's too late."

"I've tracked serial killers who tortured and raped their victims. A couple extracted body parts or dismembered their victims. Some eagerly admitted there was a certain gratification they'd get from seeing the fear and pain in their victims' eyes. They liked the control over another human being's life. They liked to see them grovel. But I haven't seen anything quite like this."

"Well, I have one other thing that might cheer you up," Vickie said. She walked over to a desk in the corner and picked up a file folder. She came back and handed it to Maggie.

"What is this?"

"John Doe #2," Vickie told her. "We were able to identify him from his fingerprints. He was arrested about three months ago. Case was dismissed. All that's in the file. Turns out he was a veteran named Simon Perry."

Chapter 60

Walter's Canteen
Pensacola Beach, Florida

At the last minute, Jason invited Brodie to go with him. Ryder wouldn't be happy about including her. Not because he didn't think women shouldn't be included. The man surrounded himself with and depended on women every day.

Jason knew Ryder was overprotective of Brodie. He still saw her as a vulnerable little sister. Jason wasn't sure what it would take for Ryder to see Brodie for who she was: a strong woman with incredible instincts and survivor skills that they'd only gotten a glimpse of.

"I'm meeting Ryder and the guys for lunch on the beach," he'd told her. "Why don't you come along?"

It chewed him up inside to watch her eyes consider it like a brand new and exciting adventure then go off in that sad, faraway stare. He'd seen it before, so it didn't surprise him, but he hated seeing it. He wished there was some way he could convince her to come see a piece of the rest of the world. He wished she would trust him to keep her safe.

And he knew this was how Ryder felt. Seeing that look in her eyes, Jason found himself wanting to do whatever it took to keep her from feeling scared or abandoned ever again.

"Maybe another time," she'd told him when her eyes finally came back. "I'll stay and watch Hank and Chance and Winnie." She looked down for a second or two, and Jason thought she might be reconsidering. When she looked up, she added, "I remember really liking the beach."

"Maybe we could go when it's not so busy," he said. "We could take Scout with us. They have outdoor seating."

Looking back now Jason realized he sounded too eager. He didn't want her doing something she was uncomfortable with just to please him.

He was the first to arrive at Walter's Canteen. The lunch crowd was thinning, but every stool at the bar's counter was full. The owner—a barrel-chested, gray-haired man named Walter Bailey—greeted Jason. He waved off the hostess. Then he escorted Jason to a primo table back in the corner next to a window with the best view of the Gulf.

"My favorite Army Ranger, Seaver, how are you, young man?" Walter's rich, baritone voice made every guest he greeted feel special.

"I'm well. How are you, Commander, Sir?"

"It's another beautiful day. I can't complain. Are your boys joining you?"

"Yes. There'll be four of us."

Walter waved at the hostess again and held up four fingers. Then suddenly, the man leaned down close to Jason's ear and whispered, "Don't look up, but there's a pretty, little filly at the bar that hasn't taken her eyes off you since you came in."

Jason's back was to the bar's counter, so he couldn't twist around without being noticed. Still, he told the man, "Sir, I think you're pulling my leg."

"No, no, she's been here before. I never forget a pretty face. Orders a shrimp salad and a bottle of Sam Adams. She's always alone. Never left with a bloke either. And now, here she comes." He raised his bushy eyebrows at Jason then winked.

Walter pretended he didn't notice her making her way across the room. Jason knew there were plenty of tables set close together that she would need to weave around. He wanted to turn and catch a glimpse, but Walter gave a slight shake of his head.

"How about I send over a pitcher? Get you started then I'll check back when your boys arrive," Walter told him, patted him on the back and left in the other direction.

"You and your boys playing poker here today?" Taylor asked.

Jason's mouth went dry. He stood up, bumping the table and almost sent his chair tumbling backwards.

"No poker today. Just a late lunch. How are you?" He managed over a tongue that suddenly seemed too big for his mouth. He pointed to the chair across from him. "You have time for a drink?"

"Aren't you meeting your guys?"

"I'm a little early."

She hesitated.

"Unless you're in a hurry," he said, once again giving her an easy out. Why did he keep doing that?

"I guess I have a few minutes," she said. "Just until your guys get here."

She sat down. And Jason sat down.

"How's Scout doing?"

He was stunned that she remembered then a bit flustered that she noticed he was stunned. She seemed to notice everything.

"He's doing pretty good."

Just then a waitress brought a pitcher of beer and a tray with five glasses surrounding a platter of peel-n-eat shrimp. Before Jason could tell her he hadn't ordered the platter, she said, "Boss said the first pitcher and the shrimp are on the house."

She set the glasses down followed by small plates and silverware at each chair.

"I'm Rita. I'll check back when your other friends get here. Give me a holler if you need anything before then."

"Thanks Rita."

"You know the owner," Taylor said with a one-sided smile that told him she was impressed.

"For a Navy guy he's okay." Jason poured two glasses full and set one in front of her without asking whether or not she wanted it.

"Lots of vets around here."

"This area is very military," he said. "It has the Naval Air Station here and Whiting Field. Lots of advanced training programs for Marines and Navy pilots. It's home to the Blue Angels. There's also Eglin Air Force Base. And it seems to be a great place to come back to and retire."

"Did you grow up here?"

She picked a shrimp off the platter, and he was pleased to see her peel it like a pro.

"Not Pensacola, but close by." He didn't like to be reminded that his family was only two hours away and that he rarely visited. "What about you? Is Virginia home?"

"Good memory. No, it was just a convenient place to be for a while."

"And Pensacola?"

"My husband's from here."

"Oh," he said sipping his beer and making sure he didn't say something stupid, but keenly aware that she had said "husband" not "ex-husband."

"And no, he's not in my life anymore." But that was all she offered.

She popped the shrimp into her mouth and started peeling another. Jason now understood Walter's wisdom. Somehow the man had noticed that Taylor might still be hungry. What was it he said? She usually had a shrimp salad and a bottle of Sam Adams.

"So why *did* you move here?" he asked.

"To be closer to my son."

He could feel her watching him now, scrutinizing his reaction to this piece of information. He caught himself measuring his sips. Keeping them from turning into gulps, which was what he really wanted.

"What's his name?" he finally asked.

The simple question warranted another one-sided smile, and he felt like he had cleared some invisible hurdle.

"William."

Chapter 61

Recovery Gardens

"I'm not leaving," Kayla told the receptionist. "Not without seeing my husband."

"Ma'am, as I said before, your husband is not allowed visitors during this phase of his recovery. It's important to respect the process."

"I just need to make sure he's okay."

Finally the woman seemed to give in. It had been almost thirty minutes of back and forth with too many interruptions of buzzing doors and ringing phones. She pushed her chair back and turned to the computer to her right. She tapped at the keyboard. Without looking at Kayla, she said, "I don't see your name as a contact, ma'am. Just his doctor."

"I was with him when he checked in."

"Even if he was allowed visitors, you'd need to be on his contact list."

"That's ridiculous. I'm his wife!"

"I don't make the rules."

"Can I talk to his doctor?" Kayla asked, trying to tamp down the anger and frustration. Although being calm had gotten her nowhere.

"Dr. Winslow isn't in today. I'm sure you could call his office." She started tapping more keys. "Give me a minute. I can give you that phone number."

The door buzzed and one of the visitors Kayla had seen going in a half hour ago was now coming back out. Before it closed Kayla grabbed the door and darted through.

"Ma'am, you're not allowed to go in there."

But the receptionist was sectioned off from the hallway that led to the rooms. Instead of hurrying down the hall, Kayla immediately ducked into a restroom. She leaned against the door and listened. Sure enough, footsteps ran by.

Surprisingly, there were no alarms going off.

Of course not. That would send the patients into a panic.

Then Kayla heard someone clear his throat behind her. A deep, distinctly male someone.

"You realize this is the men's restroom?"

She turned to find a man washing his hands at the sink. He had feathery, silver hair and glasses at the tip of a bulbous nose. He was wearing green scrubs.

She figured she was busted. That certainly didn't take long. She was never much of a rebel.

"Are you a doctor?" she asked.

"Are you a patient?" he countered.

"They won't let me see my husband." She could hear the desperation in her voice, and for once, it was genuine and not manufactured.

"Who's his doctor?"

"Dr. Winslow."

The man snorted and said, "It figures." He finished drying his hands like her presence hadn't interrupted him.

Finally he turned to face her and asked, "What's your husband's name?"

"Eric. Eric Hudson."

"Do you know his room number?"

"No."

He frowned at her.

"They said I'm not on his contact list." The hiccup of emotion in her voice scared her now. "I brought him here. I sat right next to him when he filled out the papers."

"Did they happen to mention who is on his contact list?"

"Only Dr. Winslow."

This time the man let out a long sigh. He was obviously irritated.

"Come with me," he said, and he took her elbow, but in a gentle manner.

Still, Kayla thought of it as leading the sheep to its slaughter. The bastard was going to turn her in. But instead of turning back toward the reception area, he gestured for her to go with him down the hallway. They came to an office, and he pointed for her to go in and take the chair in the corner. Then he slid behind the messy desk.

Kayla searched the room as he pushed up his glasses and swiveled to the computer. The nameplate on the office door was Dr. Albert Phillips. Amongst the clutter were several photos of him with a woman. Some of the photos included three handsome grown men.

"What did you say your husband's name is?"

"Eric Hudson. He checked in early last week."

Dr. Phillips chicken-pecked the keyboard with his index fingers.

Kayla scooted the chair closer to the desk. She couldn't see the computer screen, so she watched his eyes. Only now, did she realize she was breathing heavy. Her heart pounded against her chest so hard she was sure it would leave a bruise. It sounded ridiculous, but that was what it felt like.

His forehead furrowed as his eyes darted back and forth over the screen. He wiped a hand over his jaw. Then tapped some more. When he finished he sat back in his chair. He crossed his arms over his chest. He was frowning again.

"Your husband had a relapse."

"A relapse? What do you mean? How can he relapse in here?"

Dr. Phillips sat forward. He leaned in, placed his elbows on the desktop and tented his fingers over his lips.

"They found him unresponsive. He may have overdosed."

"What are you talking about?" And now Kayla didn't recognize her own voice. "How could that happen?"

"Sometimes they find a way to sneak in drugs no matter how careful we are."

"Are you serious? They wouldn't even let me in. You can't possibly be talking about my husband." But she remembered his panic, the paranoia, and now she felt sick to her stomach. If he were scared and desperate would he take something, anything to feel better?

Dr. Phillips was quiet now, staring not at the computer screen but somewhere down toward his shoes. When his eyes came back up to hers, the look was painfully unnerving. It was sad and apologetic.

All the anger and frustration seemed to drain from her. She felt a sudden chill. Her skin was clammy, and her stomach churned.

When he said nothing, Kayla asked in almost a whisper, "Is he...dead?"

Chapter 62

Walter's Canteen
Pensacola Beach, Florida

Jason poured the last of the beer and lifted the pitcher when he caught Rita's eye. He pointed to the empty platter, too, and she nodded. He did all this without interrupting Taylor. Without interrupting, but not without her noticing. Her eyes always noticed, and between her eyes and that one-sided smile, Jason could tell he was scoring points.

"He lives with his grandparents." She was talking about William. The subject—and the beer—seemed to open her up. "My in-laws. Mike and I met in Afghanistan. I was two months pregnant by the time I got back to the states. I'm not even sure how it happened. I was always so careful. It's amazing how vodka makes you feel safe and invincible from everything."

She looked out the window as if searching for answers. Jason stayed quiet. Waited. Hoped Benny and Colfax would be late.

"Mike still had a year left. We did the quick justice of the peace thing to make it legal when he was home on leave. He went back and two months later he was dead. He never even got to meet William."

Jason reached across the table with his real hand, hesitated then put it over hers. She let him.

"I went back to work after William was born. I had all this experience, right? One of the Army surgeons I was deployed with started a surgical center in Panama City."

She ran her fingers through her hair but kept her other hand safely tucked under Jason's. "I knew he was bad news. He's a lot older than me, so I was always turning him down when we were in Afghanistan. But we actually made a good surgical team. He kept offering me a job. Big money. More than enough for me to take care of William. So we packed up and moved.

"He was doing mostly reconstructive and cosmetic surgery. You'd think that would be sort of therapeutic, right? Restoring lives after spending so much time just stopping the hemorrhaging."

"It didn't work out?" Jason asked.

"There was a lot wrong with it. Including the part that he was married."

He could feel her searching his eyes as if looking for judgment. If she saw anything, Jason figured it would be that he wanted to pound the guy.

Evidently satisfied, she continued. "You know the biggest problem? For some reason I thought we'd be helping, you know, veterans who were disfigured or kids born with deformities. But it was liposuction and collagen injections, tummy tucks and boob jobs. Cutting into perfectly healthy tissue just to look better."

"What did you end up doing?"

Now, she pulled her hand away. He kept his in the same place pretending not to notice.

"I was so completely lost back then." She sat up straight, her entire body language going from her relaxed and humble confession to anxious and uncomfortable. "William started spending time with his grandparents in Pensacola. I started spending my spare time hating myself."

She didn't even meet Jason's eyes now, and he wondered if the married surgeon had been the one occupying that spare time. He really wanted to pound the guy now.

"When William's grandparents offered to take him for a longer while, I was…I'm embarrassed to admit this, but I was relieved. I thought it would be the best thing for him. God knows, I needed to leave."

She paused and her fingers started folding her napkin. Then she continued. "So I left him with his grandparents, and I went back to Virginia. I figured I would get settled, work through some of my demons then bring William up. I got a job working in trauma. I thought that would help. But I went back to coping the way we all did in Afghanistan."

She shrugged and found his eyes, again. "You know, vodka, whiskey, whatever someone managed to find. Isn't that what you guys did? How did you manage?"

She gestured to his prosthetic. Jason realized she was looking for a break.

"It couldn't have been easy," she added.

"For a while I had what I called Option B." He sat back then pulled his hand from the middle of the table and wrapped his fingers around the beer glass.

"I was being very smart and cagey," he allowed a slow grin to mask any other emotions that might show up on his face.

"I saved up all the different prescriptions the doctors handed out," he told her. "They gave me a lot. It was sort of like pills were their way of putting a bandage on everything. Can't sleep? Here you go. Pain still bad? Try these. You feeling depressed? This will help.

"I had them sorted by color and size. I knew exactly which ones to take first then second. It's best to have a plan, because if you take the wrong ones first they might just make you too sleepy to finish the job."

She was looking at him, but not with the requisite look of pity that he expected. There was something else. Something more disturbing than pity. It looked like admiration.

"I was always too much of a coward," she admitted.

"There's nothing brave about it," and he let his distaste come through. "I've lost too many friends who decided offing themselves was easier."

"So what happened with you? Did some girl come along?"

"A dog came along."

"Really?"

"Ryder Creed gave me a puppy. Offered to train me as a K9 handler. But if I wasn't going to stick around, I needed to give the puppy back. Because dogs get attached. And by then, I realized I was already attached to Scout, too. But Ryder didn't just give me a dog, he gave me a purpose."

"Wow! And you did it all without alcohol."

"Oh, my friend, Tony and I did our share of drinking over there. Mostly we were homesick. We'd talk about all of the things we wanted to do when we got home. But when I really needed to escape…now, promise you won't laugh. I read a lot."

"Read? Like books?'

"Yes, like books. It was the way I escaped ever since I was a kid. *Mutiny on the Bounty, Robinson Crusoe.* My mom sent me my favorite authors when their latest novel came out in paperback."

She was smiling at him. Not the subtle, one-sided, flirty one, but a full smile.

"I know, it's lame, right?" he asked.

"Not at all. I think it's sweet."

He groaned.

"Noble," she said attempting to fix it.

"Oh God, no."

"What's wrong with noble?"

"Girls don't want noble. They don't want sweet. They want the bad boys."

She shook her head at him but was still smiling. When her eyes met this time, they were serious. She told him, "I think sweet and noble would be a very welcomed change."

And that's when Benny and Colfax decided to show up.

Chapter 63

Creed felt like he was interrupting a party when he arrived at Walter's Canteen. He needed them sober and serious. From the sounds of their raucous merriment, he realized he might be too late. He found himself smiling at them instead of being disappointed.

Creed couldn't remember seeing Colfax laugh…ever. One side of the man's face looked like it had melted. Scar tissue ran from his temple down his cheekbone. It seemed to move and come to life with his laughter.

Benny had shoved his wheelchair away from the table and was slapping his thigh, sending the empty pant legs below both knees waving a bit where they weren't tacked down.

Creed saw the gray-haired owner and figured Walter was telling one of his stories, but even his head bobbed with laughter.

No, the person responsible for regaling all four men and putting them in stitches was a pretty blond sitting next to Jason.

It was Jason who noticed Creed first. He stood before Creed crossed the room and pulled a chair from an empty table close by.

Walter looked up at him then glanced down around Creed's feet and said, "No Grace?"

"Not today."

"Ryder Creed," Jason gestured toward the young woman, "This is Taylor."

He reached over the table to shake her outstretched hand.

"Donahey," she told him. "Taylor Donahey."

"I didn't realize," Walter said. "An Irish lass."

"Careful," Creed told her. "Commander Bailey has more charm than all of us guys put together."

"Oh, I'm already aware of that," Taylor said. "Actually, he promised me a *real* drink out on the patio while you men do…" She stood and looked around the table then waved her hands and said, "Whatever it is that you do."

"That's right." Walter used the edge of the table to help him stand. "Good thing my knees have a bit of arthritis or you boys wouldn't have a chance."

"You two don't need to leave on my account," Creed told them. He didn't want to end their fun.

"No, no. We'll be back," Walter said.

"You will be back, right?" Jason asked Taylor.

Creed realized the kid had it bad. He glanced at Benny who rolled his eyes. Colfax, however, seemed equally enamored and anxious for her return. But the look on Jason's face was enough to convince Creed he wouldn't let the kid come with him to track the killer. It wasn't worth the risk.

As if on cue, a waitress replaced the empty pitcher in the middle of the table with a full one. She set a glass in front of Creed.

"Get you something to eat?" she asked him.

He glanced at the platter with empty shrimp shells.

"Some more of these. And a pile of fries."

"You got it."

"Oh, and bring the whole bottle of ketchup," Jason told her.

Benny maneuvered his chair closer to the table so he could pour himself another glass of beer. He held up the pitcher and looked to Creed, motioning for his glass. Creed slid it over. When Benny handed the full glass back to him, he looked sober and serious and ready to give Creed his complete attention.

"Jason filled us in about this asshole in the forest," Benny said. "Tell us what you need."

"I was able to get my hands on a ball cap that the investigators found, but they're not sure it's his," Creed told them.

"What kind of cap?" Benny wanted to know.

Creed wasn't sure why it mattered. "Sports cap. Wide bill. Black with a skull and crossed swords. Football in the middle. It's the Tampa Bay Buccaneers."

"That's definitely the killer's," Colfax said.

They all stared at him, waiting for his explanation. He gulped his beer and wiped his crooked mouth before he noticed.

"What?" he said. "Nobody in their right mind wears a Buccaneers' cap."

They all laughed again, and Creed told himself that he really needed to spend more time with these guys.

"So you're thinking Grace can get his scent off the cap," Jason said. "But what if it really isn't his cap?"

"Then she leads me to another grave," Creed told him. "But also I wondered about using some other technology. I have night vision goggles."

Benny waved a hand at him to dismiss that idea. "Not gonna help much at night in the forest. Night vision devices still need some light. Plus, you can't see if he's behind a bush or a tree."

"What about heat-detecting equipment?"

"Yeah, exactly," Colfax said. "That's what you need."

"But I need something that's not big and clunky," Creed said.

"*We* need something," Jason corrected him.

"I got a couple of thermal imaging cameras," Benny said. "These are the coolest devices. They're about eight ounces with a six-inch microbolometer. They're made to be handheld, but you can easily use a mini-rail and attach it to a helmet."

"How does it work?" Creed wanted to know. "I get that it detects heat signatures, but what do you actually see?"

"I haven't had a chance to try these new ones out yet. But it's not going to give you a clear picture. It distinguishes an object that's giving off warmer temperatures."

"So I might not be able to tell if it's a person or an animal?" Creed asked.

"No, no," Benny insisted. "You'll be able to tell it's a figure walking upright. You can see him and his movements. Just not clear enough for facial identity."

"How soon can I borrow those?" Creed asked.

"I brought them in my pickup," Benny said, sitting up proud of himself. "We brought a few other things, too. I know you like all the security cameras and those gadgets, but dude, for this, you need some serious stuff."

"Hey," Jason elbowed Creed. "Did you invite Maggie or tell her about any of this?"

"No. And I don't want her to know."

"Well, she's here."

"Hi guys," she said as she approached their table. "Benny and Colfax, right?"

Creed watched the two men, all gaga again in the presence of a beautiful woman. Colfax stood and pulled out a chair for her. Benny was already waving down the waitress for another glass.

"I'm staying next door," Maggie said. "At Margaritaville and saw Benny's pickup."

"It's pretty cool, isn't it?" He smiled at her.

"I didn't mean to interrupt. I was just stopping by to say hello."

"We always welcome a pretty woman at our table," Colfax told her, helping push her chair in like a gentleman.

Creed could feel her glance at him. She had asked him to have dinner with her on the beach, and he never mentioned that he was already having lunch on the beach. But that wasn't what she'd be upset about.

Although she hadn't said anything back at the medical examiner's office, he could tell she knew exactly what he wanted the black ball cap for. And he could tell she wasn't happy about it.

Chapter 64

Blackwater River State Forest

Udie transferred all the gear and new equipment he'd bought at the hardware store from his truck to the boat. He wondered if two five-gallon cans were enough, but he didn't have room in the boat for more. He had already stacked things that probably shouldn't be stacked on top of each other, but he wasn't going far. He wanted to offload everything before sunset.

For once the afternoon thunderstorms held off. Luck was on his side. But there was a small timeframe before the storms rolled in later in the evening. By then, Udie hoped to be finished. If things went as planned, he'd be in bed before the downpours came.

Udie pulled out the dead man's cell phone. He'd added the wildlife cams because the apps loaded quicker than they did on his old phone. He tapped the first one and saw nothing out of the ordinary. He brought up the second camera, and low and behold, he had a birds-eye view of a sheriff's deputy. Yesterday he caught one of them taking a piss, and he wanted so badly to turn on the audio and scare the hell out of him. But then it would be all over.

On closer inspection, he realized this wasn't one of the regular deputies. This was the guy he met in the boat, the evidence collector. The women hadn't come back, but this guy kept digging up stuff. Udie wished he'd been able to put up the cameras earlier. He had no idea what they'd taken so far. But he was going to make sure they didn't take anything else.

The cell phone vibrated with another text message. His partner had already left a string of them along with a half dozen voice messages. The guy sounded like he was becoming unhinged.

He figured the guy would be amazed and proud when he saw that Udie had taken care of everything. So he ignored the messages. After tonight, neither one of them would need to worry about this dumping ground ever again.

Chapter 65

Walter's Canteen
Pensacola Beach

Taylor had forgotten what this kind of camaraderie could feel like. After baring her soul to Jason, she thought she'd want to slink away. But being around these guys was a quick reminder that they all had scars and regrets and stories that few others would find funny. It was one of the things she actually missed about Afghanistan. She was having a great time, and she wasn't even drunk. Well, not drunk by her standards. She definitely had a pleasant buzz going.

There was only one problem. When she and Walter came back to the table, Taylor immediately felt the scrutiny of the latest guest. A woman. An attractive woman.

Jason introduced her as an FBI agent. She obviously knew all of the others including Walter, although there was some mention of her staying at the hotel next door. So this woman—Maggie—was not a regular part of the guys' group. And yet, she seemed to fit in so easily.

Taylor tried to relax. She convinced herself that she was simply disappointed because she enjoyed being the only woman and having all the attention. Definitely a flaw she needed to work on. She had very few women friends. Okay, she had no women friends at the moment. She quickly admonished herself. None of that had anything to do with why she was having such a good time earlier.

But just when she started to settle in again, she noticed Maggie look up at her from across the table. She had her cell phone out and in seconds her eyes returned to the screen.

Taylor ignored feeling intimidated again. It couldn't be personal. The woman didn't even know her. She was being ridiculous.

Walter excused himself to greet new guests. A few minutes later Ryder checked his watch and said he needed to get back to work. Taylor watched him exchange a look with Maggie, but the FBI agent didn't appear compelled to leave her seat at the table.

"I'll talk to you later," Maggie said.

Taylor thought she noticed that Ryder was a bit surprised. Earlier she thought the two might be a couple, but now she dismissed it.

"I need to steal the guys for a few minutes," Ryder said.

"All of them?" Taylor laughed and hoped it wasn't too obvious how much she *did not* want to be left with this woman.

"We just need to help Benny unload some things," Jason told her. "We'll be right back."

She watched them leave. Maggie did not. She was still occupied with her phone. Taylor pulled the pitcher over and filled her glass though she really didn't want any more beer. She wanted to leave with the guys. She watched other people. Looked for the waitress. Thought about going to the bathroom.

"Sorry," Maggie suddenly said, surprising Taylor. "I didn't mean to be rude." She held up her cell phone. "I'm working a case that just keeps getting more puzzling. You might have heard about it on the news. A couple of bodies were found in the forest."

"I did hear something about that. Are Jason and Ryder working on that case, too?"

"Yes. They and their dogs are amazing."

Taylor didn't know their dogs, only that Scout had come in contact with the same drug paraphernalia that had sent Jason to the ER. She figured it must be a drug case. Dogs were used to sniff out illegal contraband. It made sense that the feds would be involved.

Another awkward silence, only Taylor noticed that Maggie didn't look uncomfortable at all.

"Have you known them long?" Taylor asked looking for some common ground.

"The first case Ryder and I worked on was about two and half years ago. How about you?"

"I met Jason, Benny and Colfax a few days ago," Taylor said. Had it only been a few days? She sipped the beer.

And then as if it were simply a normal part of their conversation, Maggie asked, "So how long have you known John Lockett?"

Chapter 66

Maggie watched for her reaction as Taylor almost spit out her beer.

"Excuse me, what did…what was it you just asked?"

Maggie tapped her cell phone, swiped the screen then held it out, up and over the table. It was one of the photos Agent Alonzo had sent her earlier in the day. One from John Lockett's Facebook page. From the minute the young woman sat down, Maggie knew she recognized her. It just took a while to remember where she had seen her.

The woman looked surprised then confused. Maggie wasn't sure what she had expected. But Taylor's reaction certainly didn't amount to culpability in a murder.

And as realization seemed to wash over the woman, Maggie watched the look of shock transform into grief and sadness.

"Oh my God. Is John…" She sat back and gulped in a deep breath. "You found him in the forest?"

Maggie glanced back at the door, glad that the guys were taking a long time. She had been torn about whether to follow them out and talk to Ryder. He and Jason were plotting to do something. She felt like she was teetering on a tightrope, because she knew if she offered her help or advice, it would be seen as interference.

Besides, if she could identify the killer soon, they wouldn't need to run off into the forest and try to catch the guy. And right now, she had something better than any of the bagged evidence the medical examiner had. Maggie may have just stumbled on the reason John Lockett had left his home in Virginia to travel down to Pensacola, Florida. And that reason was sitting in front of her.

She picked up her glass, stood and moved around the table to take a seat next to Taylor. She poured herself another beer trying to keep up a casual appearance, so if anyone else noticed Taylor's distraught face, they might discount it as two friends in conversation and not as an interrogation of a witness.

"We haven't publically identified him yet," Maggie said. "But yes."

Taylor sat still while her eyes darted around the room. Maggie tried to track where she was looking, and finally wondered if the woman was simply watching for Jason's return.

"How?" she asked. "How did he end up in the forest? He didn't…"

She was struggling now. Maggie couldn't determine if it was guilt. Maybe she did know more.

Finally, Taylor asked, "He didn't commit suicide, did he?"

"Because you rejected him?"

There was a quivering sigh. Her hand shot up to rub her forehead. She pushed her hair behind her ear.

"Yes," she said and then came her confession. "He came all this way because he wanted us to be together. I told him I couldn't. Not now. I tried to be gentle. But I told him he needed to go home."

"Taylor," Maggie said calmly and waited for her eyes. "He didn't commit suicide." She waited a beat before she added, "He was murdered."

Maggie watched again, measuring the reaction. She could swear the woman was less surprised by this outcome.

"He had his dog with him," Taylor said, and now her eyes searched Maggie's. "Is Hank dead, too?"

That she was concerned about the dog, moved Maggie to ease up on her. She didn't think Taylor had anything to do with Lockett's murder. But she suspected the woman might know the man who was responsible.

"We think Hank's okay, but he was shot, too."

"Shot?"

And now, Maggie wondered why that part was a surprise. She was about to ask when out of the corner of her eye she saw Jason maneuvering his way through the guests at the entrance waiting to be seated.

"I need you to talk to me about this," she told Taylor in a low voice. "But not in front of the guys, okay?"

"Yes, of course."

Taylor glanced up, and in a matter of seconds Maggie saw that the woman was very good at tucking away her emotions.

"Taylor, Maggie, I'm really sorry," Jason said, his expression serious and his tone urgent. "We just found out one of our buddies is being air-lifted to the hospital."

"Baptist?" Taylor asked.

"Yeah."

"Would you like us to come along?" Maggie asked before Taylor decided it would be a good excuse to just get up and go with him.

"No. Thanks though. You two stay. Ryder already took care of things with Walter, so please stay. Have some dinner. Or dessert. I'll text you both as soon as I know something."

He started to leave then turned back. "Actually, I'll text Maggie," he said directly to Taylor. "But Maggie, you mind giving Taylor my number?"

"Sure," Maggie said, and she was trying to decide whether to be impressed or suspicious that Taylor hadn't given him her phone number yet.

Chapter 67

Florida Panhandle

Creed was halfway home when he got the call from Jason. It'd been a long time since he'd stopped in at the Segway House and played poker with the guys. Benny and Colfax were like family, but he hardly knew Eric and Doc and the handful of other guys who sat in once in a while.

This would be tough for Jason. He liked Eric Hudson enough to offer one of Scout's siblings to the man's little boy. Jason and Hannah had spent a good deal of the last six months learning how to train a diabetic alert dog. Scout's sister, Sarge, was doing remarkably well, and even Creed thought she would be ready for the job come fall.

Over the years Creed and Hannah had trained dogs to detect a variety of scents other than the dead and missing. It didn't take Hannah long to insist they include other scents when she recognized how much of a toll it took on Creed to work too many search and recovery cases. They added drugs and explosives. But they also started training dogs to detect C. diff, a bacterial strain that could be deadly if diagnosed too late.

Then the Department of Homeland Security asked for their help to sniff out the bird flu. And although they hadn't trained a medical alert dog before, Creed figured between the three of them, they could train a dog to detect just about anything. He was hoping that was true tonight, and he could add serial killer to the list.

He hated to admit he was a bit relieved that he'd now be able to implement his plan and not need to lie in order to exclude Jason. Chances are, the kid would be at the hospital well into the night.

He found Brodie in the clinic. He heard her before he found her. She had dragged the mattress closer to Hank's kennel, and she was reading to him. Grace and Scout were with her. All of them looked up at Creed like they didn't appreciate him interrupting the story.

"Don't stop on my account," he told her.

"No, that's okay. It's almost dinner time."

"Have you had any luck getting him to eat?" Creed asked.

The dog had refused everything Creed had offered. Last night Creed had begged, even tried to hand-feed him, and the dog still broke his heart.

"He ate almost a cup of chicken and rice." She smiled up at him, knowing it would make him happy. "We all ate together. He watched Grace and Scout enjoying theirs, and he finally decided to join in."

"That was a great idea."

He should have thought of that, that the dog might like some company. He slung his daypack off his shoulder. He didn't realize he'd left the zipper open. The black ball cap dropped to the floor.

"I brought this for Grace," he said, but as Creed went to grab it off the floor, Hank braced up against the grate of his kennel. His teeth were bared and he was growling. Growling viciously at the ball cap.

"Hank, it's okay, buddy."

"Wow! I haven't seen him do anything like that." Brodie had jumped to her feet.

"I'm putting it away," he showed the dog as he scooped it up and shoved it into the pack. Then he took the daypack out of the room, down the hallway and left it in the office.

Hank had just confirmed that the ball cap belonged to someone he didn't like. It had to be the killers.

Creed came back to the room, and Brodie was talking to the dog. He'd settled down but his eyes rolled to check out Ryder in the doorway.

"Brodie, would you do me another big favor and check in on him tonight?"

"Sure. You and Maggie finally going on that date?"

"No, but Grace and I have something we need to do."

He couldn't lie to her. It was the one thing she'd asked of him. But he also wouldn't tell her his plans.

"Is Jason back yet?" she asked.

"No. He might be late. A friend of his is in the hospital."

"Okay. I'll take Scout back to the house with me."

Jason was right. Brodie was certainly getting an initiation into their business and their lives. He hoped it wasn't too much for her. He kept reminding himself that PTSD could rear its ugly head with little warning. He sure hoped he wasn't missing a warning.

"Hey, Ryder. If we end up keeping Hank can he sleep in my room?"

He realized he hadn't told any of them what he'd learned about Hank's owner. "Sure," he said. "I'm curious. You can have any dog in the kennel, why Hank?"

"Did you see how scary he looked and sounded? Nobody's going to sneak into my room if he's there."

Creed felt his jaw clench, reminding him how important it was to catch this guy.

Then Brodie added, "Besides, he really seems to like when I read to him. I think we're going to be good friends."

Chapter 68

Pensacola Beach

Taylor didn't expect him to answer, let alone on the second ring.

"I'm a little busy here," Derrick told her.

"You bastard," she didn't even try to restrain her anger.

"What exactly has your panties in a twist?" he laughed.

She was sitting next to the balcony's sliding glass door high above the crowded beach. Storm clouds were in the distance threatening to snuff out the setting sun. Instead of letting the emerald green waves soothe her, Taylor focused on the storm clouds.

"Why didn't you just let him go home to Virginia?"

"Ahh…the persistent Mr. Lockett. I know his type. He would have come back eventually."

She wanted to adjust the earbud but settled for pushing back a lock of hair. Her fingers were trembling. It took a concentrated effort to keep her breathing from becoming a gasp for air.

"So you had to kill him?"

She was surprised when Maggie told her Lockett had been shot. She remembered in Afghanistan how bad of a shot Derrick was. He didn't think he should have to carry a gun. His surgical fingers were too valuable to be pulling triggers. Others were expected to protect him.

"Didn't I tell you that you needed to keep your mind on getting your son back? Wait a minute."

Taylor heard his tone change, and her entire body tensed.

"Where the hell are you?" He was angry. "You are such a whore! I can't believe you took that Army Ranger next door to a hotel. What the hell is wrong with you?"

"What are you talking about, Derrick? How could you possibly know where I am right this minute?"

He went quiet, and Taylor worried he'd ended the call.

"Derrick? You're tracking my phone, aren't you?"

"I guess it didn't take long for you to forget your valiant Mr. Lockett. Convenient for you that I got rid of him. Well, screw your Ranger boy's brains out. He'll be dead tomorrow. Oh, and don't expect to see your precious son any time soon."

This time, he did hang up.

She was shaking all over when she pulled the earbud out and wrapped her arms around herself. She felt a hand on her shoulder.

"You did good," Maggie told her.

Taylor glanced up at her. The woman had the other earbud from Taylor's pair in her ear. She also had Taylor's cell phone in her hands and was still doing something with it.

"Antonio, did you get it?" she was asking someone who was still on the line. "Great. Don't spook him until we know we've got him."

Taylor stared out the hotel's sliding glass door. Maggie's room was on the sixth floor. She thought her studio apartment's view over the marina was beautiful, but this was gorgeous. And yet, she felt...*exhausted*. So completely drained. A little bit scared. And a tremendous sense of loss. She'd just thrown away her one chance to be a part of William's life. Derrick would see to it. He already had such an influence over William's grandparents. Now, he would make sure they thought she was a drunken whore.

Maggie handed her a glass of water. She pulled up a second chair alongside Taylor's. She positioned it so that she was facing the Gulf view and so Taylor didn't have to look the woman in her eyes.

"What did he mean about your son?" Maggie asked.

Taylor had told her about working alongside Derrick in Afghanistan. He was older, always wiser and so charming. He was their surgical team's rock. You wanted him in a crisis.

Stateside, they'd gone their separate ways, but somehow, he managed to keep his hold on her over the years. He was married. He was always married, several times over. And he wasn't interested in Taylor as a wife even if she didn't constantly rebuff him. Taylor didn't have the pedigree to be his wife. But he'd made it clear that he didn't want anyone else to have her.

"Years ago he talked me into giving my son up," she told Maggie now. "My husband, Mike, was killed in Afghanistan before William was born. Derrick knows Mike's father. They're on the same boards and belong to the same country club."

Taylor sipped the water and noticed her hands weren't shaking anymore.

"I thought it was the right thing to do. I didn't realize that they wouldn't let me be a part of his life. I think Derrick told them things. Some of them true. Some of them not.

"Then out of the blue, he called me and said that if I cleaned up my act, he thought he might be able to change their minds. He convinced me to move down here. Got me a job at Baptist Hospital. That was weeks ago, and I still haven't seen William."

They were quiet for a long time then Maggie said, "If he killed John Lockett he's going away for a long time. William's grandparents will certainly see Derrick isn't the stand-up guy he pretends to be."

"Will they? Or will he just convince them this was my fault? That somehow I manipulated yet another man."

Chapter 69

Blackwater River State Forest

Creed didn't wait for dark.

He called CSU tech, Hadley and had gotten no response. No call back either. So Creed left another message asking Hadley to warn the sheriff's deputies that he was coming into the crime scene. Once he was in the forest, he couldn't count on having a cell phone signal. Hadley had been there earlier in the day, but he and the day shift would have left hours ago, replaced by the night shift deputies.

Grace needed very little time with the black ball cap. Creed had decided he'd start where the man was last seen on their property, but before he could guide Grace, she was already headed for the fieldhouse. As they entered the forest, he attached a leash to Grace's new vest.

The vest was a bit heavier than she was used to wearing. He'd slid a couple of thin ice packs inside the vest's pockets along with a GPS device that matched the one in his daypack. If nothing else, he would make sure that they kept track of each other.

Creed knew the man had used this path at least twice: last night and then again in the morning to leave the garbage bag with the tainted steaks. The trail was tamped down. Branches broken. Some cut. Vines ripped away and left on top of bushes.

When they left, storm clouds gathered in the distance bringing nightfall sooner than expected. Inside the forest it was already dark. The extra gear weighed Creed down, and his skin was quickly slick with sweat. He had traded his ball cap for the helmet Benny had provided. The mini-rail held the thermal imaging camera off to his right side. He glanced up at it trying to get used to the dancing colors.

He saw a red mass up ahead and stopped dead in his tracks. One tug at Grace's leash got her to stop. They stood stock-still. Though it hardly mattered how quiet they were. The creatures had already begun their calls and whirs and barks. He'd forgotten how loud the middle of the woods could be after dark.

Creed's fingers inched to his utility belt. There was enough twilight to see shadows. His night vision goggles dangled around his neck. They wouldn't help determine what this heat source was hiding in the bushes.

Grace was watching exactly where the thermal image was lighting up. She didn't strain or whine or seem at all concerned. If anything she looked a bit impatient.

Creed saw the red mass jerk across the camera screen before he saw the raccoon run from the bushes.

Grace looked up at him. He released a long breath, and she wagged as if to tell him she knew it was no big deal.

He shook his head and reminded himself he needed to trust his dog. All this cool equipment couldn't replace Grace's nose.

They hadn't gone far, and Creed recognized the killer's path was taking them to the crime scene. So the man had been sneaking back and forth. Although the deputies seemed to be unaware. When he warned

Hadley, the tech said the deputies hadn't seen any signs of anyone else in the forest. And yet, their boat had been taken and damaged.

They already suspected this guy knew his way around the forest, but Creed wondered if the man had special ops training of some kind. Or was it simply dumb luck? Either way, Creed would need to be better prepared than letting a raccoon startle him.

He caught a glimpse of one of his surveyor flags that he had left a couple days ago. They were just on the outskirts of the crime scene. He was about to call out and alert the deputies when Grace stopped. She sniffed the air. Circled twice. He held the leash so she wouldn't get tangled. She glanced up above him then met his eyes.

Creed tilted his head, but his eyes stayed on the thermal image screen. There was no vibrant pulsating red. No movement in the canopy overhead.

He looked down at Grace. Her nose was back to poking the air. Her front paws shifted. She was ready to continue. This time when she glanced up, Creed slipped on the night vision goggles and tracked exactly where she was looking.

He kept his feet planted, but his stomach dropped to his knees. Even hanging upside down and tinged in the green light, Creed recognized Deputy Danvers.

Chapter 70

Creed put a finger to his lips, and Grace stood still.

His heart pounded too hard. Not far away an owl screeched. A chorus of tree frogs competed with the tick-tick-tick-whir and a round of hisses.

He tried to slow his racing pulse as he kept his feet from moving. The thermal imaging screen followed the movement of his head as he swiveled it as far as he could. First to the right then to the left. He tilted the helmet back and searched the treetops.

A few small blips. Even Danvers registered as a glob of pink and yellow, no red. Creed had no idea how long it took for a body to cool, but he suspected if Danvers was dead, it was likely his partner was too.

He thought it looked like fishing line tied around the deputy's neck, over and over again. Some of Danvers' fingers were stuck inside the line. It wasn't the only sign of the man's panic and last efforts to breathe.

Creed tried to listen over the night sounds. It was impossible. He watched Grace, instead. He nodded for her to continue, but he wrapped her leash tighter around his wrist, giving her less lead and forcing her to stay close at his feet.

The medical examiner had asked him what he'd do if his dog did, in fact, take him to the killer. Jason, Benny and Colfax had spent a good deal of time talking about snares and sniper nests. They outlined how one of them could flush the killer out and send him directly into the other one's hands.

Creed figured he had the element of surprise on his side. That, a canister of UDAP pepper spray and a Ruger .38 Special +P revolver. Years ago he'd bought the lightweight pistol because it could slip into his daypack easily. It was hammerless, compact and fit in the palm of his hand. He liked that the short barrel made it difficult for an opponent to grab it. And yet, it was effective in close-quarter conflicts.

Originally, Creed bought the gun to protect his dogs. But UDAP pepper spray worked better against a bear or cougar. He figured the spray would work against a serial killer, too. That's why the pistol was still in his daypack while the fingers of his right hand were ready to grab the pepper spray canister on his utility belt.

The guy expected the deputies. He had obviously watched them, maneuvered around them, and in the end, tricked them. Creed couldn't help wondering if Danvers had even seen the guy coming.

He was beginning to think Grace was taking him on a wild goose chase. Instead of taking him farther inside the crime scene perimeter she was leading him back deeper into the forest. In the opposite direction of the sandbar and Coldwater Creek.

Trust your dog, he kept telling himself as he kept one eye on the thermal imaging screen.

When Grace turned, he knew they were circling back. He realized the killer's scent could be all over these paths if the man had gone back and forth for the last several days.

Creed was starting to get acclimated to the symphony of creatures. He could tell when a new voice joined the night air. But would he recognize if there were noises that didn't belong?

Then Grace came to an abrupt halt.

Sometimes the humidity in the forest got so thick the moisture dripped from the leaves. Creed heard the drip-drip hit his helmet just as he noticed Grace tilt her head back. He smelled it as he side-stepped out of the away.

Up above was the second deputy.

In the green tint Creed saw the gash in his neck still dripping. Rope was used. One end tied to the trunk, looped over a branch as a pulley with the other end tied around the deputy's waist so he hung over them like he was flying.

Creed forced himself to take deep breaths. His pulse raced again. The humid air was oppressive, and the tang of blood only made it harder to breathe.

This guy was losing it. With both deputies dead, what was next? Had he and Grace missed him?

Then a thought slammed into Creed. What if he was headed to Creed's property?

Before he could react, he suddenly smelled something else. A scent that definitely didn't belong in the forest.

Cigarette smoke.

Chapter 71

Creed didn't need to check the thermal imaging screen. He could see the man clearly with his night vision goggles. He was surprised that he recognized him. Surprised but relieved.

He pulled off the goggles and dropped them to dangle at his neck. Emotion runs down the leash. Even Grace knew she could relax. Creed stepped out from behind the trees and the man stumbled backwards.

"Doc, what are you doing here?" Creed asked.

"Same thing as you, I imagine." He tossed the cigarette to the ground and stubbed it out.

"Did Benny and Colfax tell you about this?"

The man's khakis were stained, and his polo shirt was untucked and drenched in sweat. Creed glanced around. This wasn't right. But in seconds Doc confirmed the uneasy feeling in Creed's gut when he pulled a gun out of his pocket.

"I sent a boy to do a man's job," he told Creed. "I figured I needed to correct my mistake."

"I'm not sure I know what you're talking about."

"I know you didn't bring your sidekick, because I know exactly where he is. Now put your hands out where I can see them."

Creed was confused. He tried to access what he knew about the guy. All he could remember was that he had been an Army surgeon. Had done a tour in Afghanistan.

"What's going on, Doc?"

"I heard you found the dog."

Creed could see him watching for his reaction.

"This time you can be sure," he told Creed. "I won't be so sloppy."

"You shot Hank?" Creed still didn't understand.

"The stupid thing lunged at me."

"Because you were shooting his owner." Creed concentrated on the burn that had started in his gut and was moving up his chest.

"Take that silly helmet off and lay it on the ground. But nice and easy. Put your hands out in front of you."

Creed obeyed while his mind kept racing.

"You killed all these people?" Creed asked as he slowly released and pulled the helmet off his head.

"Put in on the ground. Don't throw it."

"I don't understand, Doc."

"Wives are expensive," the man actually laughed and pushed back at the flop of wet bangs on his forehead. "You can only claim bankruptcy so many times. The helmet, Ryder. Put it on the ground."

Creed kept his movements slow as he bent at his knees and eased his body all the way down to place the helmet on the ground. At the last second, he flung it at Doc's hand. He swiped his fingers over Grace to unsnap the leash.

"Run Grace. Home. *Now.*"

Doc lifted the gun and fired after her. He got off one shot before Creed dived at him. The second shot hit Creed center mass and knocked him to his knees.

Doc felt confident enough to come in closer for a final shot.

"I won't make the same mistake twice," he said as he brought the gun up to place against Creed's temple.

Creed grabbed the man's wrist, twisted and pulled him off balance. The gun went flying but Creed didn't let go. Doc had fallen to his knees. Creed lifted and twisted Doc's wrist then slammed his elbow into the back of the man's arm. The snap of bone silenced the night creatures for a second or two then Doc's scream filled the air.

Just then, Creed caught a glimpse of the thermal image screen still attached to the helmet on the ground. It was pointed back behind him and a red mass was filling the screen.

He felt the burst of pain at the back of his head before everything went black.

Chapter 72

Pensacola Beach

After Taylor left, Maggie called Santa Rosa County Chief Deputy Glenn. She explained to him what had just happened. She told him everything she'd learned. He wasn't happy that she was asking him to bring in a prominent Pensacola surgeon for questioning.

"I'll handle the questioning," she said. "You can let the federal agent be the bad cop. You can be the good cop."

He still wasn't happy.

"If we wait, he has the means to pick up and leave," Maggie warned him.

She could do this herself. Escambia County Sheriff Clayton had invited her in to investigate the storage unit. The medical examiner had requested her to be a part of the case in the forest. But Maggie had learned long ago that it was better to have the locals on her side.

He said he would take care of it.

She hadn't even met Glenn. With her luck, he was a patient of this surgeon or a friend of a friend. She reminded herself this was a small community, and Glenn's resistance only confirmed what Taylor had already said about the man's influence.

Maggie had ordered room service. She hadn't eaten at Walter's Canteen. Hunger and the incoming storm had contributed to the pounding in her head. She'd left the tray on the desk and instead of sitting down and eating, she paced with her phone, stopping for a bite of the fish tacos or grabbing a couple of French fries.

She'd already left a voice message for Ryder. When she got no response, she added a text telling him she had a suspect and to please get in contact with her. She told herself that he might be with Jason and the guys at the hospital. She hoped that was where he was.

Having a suspect might tamp down their urge to trek into the forest themselves and go all Rambo.

She was just about to sit and put a serious dent in her dinner when she got a call from Keith Ganza. Ganza was the head of the crime lab at Quantico. She'd been patient with the man, but she couldn't handle another lecture on how long "these things took."

Still, she snatched the phone back up.

"Hey Keith."

"Looks like your medical examiner friend is sending me more stuff."

He didn't sound happy. But it was difficult to tell with Ganza. He reminded Maggie of a hard rocker from the 1960s with his long, gray hair ponytail and his slow monotone.

"Right," she said, "I forgot to tell you, I found a woman's head this morning."

Alonzo had made a joke about it, but Ganza just let it roll. She smiled at her own bad pun and popped another French fry in her mouth. She was exhausted, physically and mentally.

When he stayed quiet for too long, Maggie added, "We need to see if it matches the body we found in the forest."

"Her samples will be here in the morning, but you know these things take time."

She winced and bit back her frustration.

"I do have some news on the cheeseburger you sent."

Maggie started pacing again, forcing herself to stay put at the patio door. Usually the view would calm her, but evening had brought dark clouds, and even the beachgoers were scattering.

"I was actually able to get enough DNA to do a search."

"That's fantastic."

"Not so fantastic. I didn't find a match."

"He's not in the system at all?"

"Locally, I suppose he could be. Alonzo offered to help with those details."

She knew that meant Alonzo might not be asking permission. The man had a knack for getting into cyber places.

"But then he reminded me of a case we worked six months ago. The killer's DNA was recovered on a victim, but we couldn't find a match anywhere. We started checking those ancestry companies."

Maggie wasn't crazy about the idea. The process had gotten a lot of press when it was used to finally capture the Golden State Killer. After thirty plus years, Joseph James DeAngelo was arrested for as many as fifty rapes and twelve murders in a ten-county area of California. DeAngelo's DNA had never been on record. But investigators used third-party familial DNA from an ancestry company to narrow down the search to find him. When they were finally able to secure a DNA sample from him, they got a match.

The process was controversial, and the results could sometimes be misleading. But most of the ancestry companies already warned their customers in their contract agreements. When they gave their consent to release their DNA and build the profiles that might find ancestors, they were also releasing their DNA to be used for other profiles, including criminal searches.

Maggie held back her impatience with Ganza. In her mind, this track would take even longer.

"Going through family's DNA could take forever," she told him now. "And I actually have a suspect. Hopefully, he's going to be detained very soon."

"What if I told you we didn't need to go through third-party familial DNA?"

"Keith, what are you talking about?"

"The cheeseburger guy actually submitted his DNA directly to one of these ancestor companies. We have a confirmed match."

"You're kidding," Maggie said. "Well, that's perfect."

This would definitely make Chief Deputy Glenn less hesitant about bringing in Derrick Winslow for questioning.

"His name is Ernest Udall Sutton."

"Excuse me?" Maggie asked. "That can't be correct."

Was it possible the fast food bag had been someone else's trash? Or did Dr. Derrick Winslow have help?

Chapter 73

Blackwater River State Forest

"You should have stayed the hell away. I didn't need your help."

Creed didn't recognize this man's voice. He didn't know how long he'd been unconscious. He stayed motionless, squinting enough to see only darkness.

He was facedown on his stomach. The back of his head felt let it had been cracked open. His chest hurt like he had been hit with a rocket. And then he remembered, he had been. The bullet hit him right in the breastbone. Benny's bulletproof vest stopped it, but Creed would have a hell of a bruise.

They thought he was shot. That might be a good thing. But his hands were tied behind his back. With a subtle probe of his fingertips he could feel the plastic zip tie.

"The asshole broke my arm."

Doc's voice. Creed resisted the urge to smile at the pain in his whine.

"He would have broken a lot more if I hadn't saved you. I told you I had things under control."

"You have nothing under control. They identified Lockett. This is the guy who found his dog."

"Hey, that dog and that guy were *your* fault. Didn't they teach you how to shoot a gun in the military? You didn't kill him, remember? I had to finish the job. You owe me. Or did you already forget that?"

This man sounded younger. Much younger. Almost like a teenager badmouthing a parent.

But this was the man who had bludgeoned John Lockett to death. Creed remembered the bloody mess. He was also responsible for delivering the knockout blow to Creed's head. He was the guy who had come onto their property. He didn't think it could have been Doc.

Creed listened and tried to figure out how close they were. Could they see him? How long did they expect him to be out? They evidently hadn't noticed the vest under his T-shirt and the button-down shirt he wore over it. If they had noticed the vest, he'd have another bullet in him. He had fallen face first. The young guy must have simply pulled his hands back and tied them.

"No, I haven't forgotten," Doc told him. "You've been a good partner, Udie, just like your mother was. I miss her sometimes."

"Yeah, right you miss her."

"What's that's supposed to mean?" Doc asked him.

"I know she didn't tell you."

"What are you talking about?"

"That I'm you're frickin son."

There was a silence, and Creed remained still. He listened now, curious.

"Oh, I didn't realize she told you," Doc told him.

"You knew?"

"We were both really young, Udie. Barely out of high school. She knew I wanted to be a doctor. I had to join the military to do that. Look Udie, we can talk about this later. I'm really hurting here."

Another silence. Creed lifted his head. His eyes were adjusting to the dark, but he still couldn't see the men.

"I have some patches in my duffel bag," the younger man finally said.

Creed could hear rustling and crunching. He used the distraction to test the zip tie. He had a bad habit of sleeping with his fists balled up. He noticed that they were still clenched. Whoever had tied his wrists together had left his fists side-by-side, facing out.

"I've never used fentanyl for myself," Doc said.

"Oh man, it'll definitely make you forget your pain."

The zip tie was an amateur's mistake. One that Creed was grateful for. But he soon noticed any movement of his shoulders sent a shock of pain into his chest. He squeezed his eyes shut and slowly turned his arms inward until his wrists were front to front.

"Won't it zone me out?" Doc was still skeptical. "I can't get the hell out of here if I'm completely zoned out."

"It doesn't start working immediately. Geez, I can't believe you. What did you use to overdose all those guys I've dumped?"

"Injecting makes it go faster. Opioids are the perfect killer. Very peaceful. Just slows everything down. And after a few days in rehab and withdrawal, they're begging me for it."

Creed stayed focused on his task. An amateur doesn't realize that when the hands are fisted and the wrists are side-by-side instead of facing together, they take up more room. With that small maneuver Creed had loosened the tie. Now all he had to do was work one thumb under and out. It still was a lot easier said than done.

Chapter 74

K9 CrimeScents

Brodie hated leaving Hank all alone. Dr. Avelyn had stopped by to check on the big dog along with Chance and Winnie, but she had already released them back to the kennel. Dr. Avelyn gave Hank something to help him rest and said that he'd probably sleep through the night.

"Do you think he'll be okay?" Brodie had asked her.

"He's doing really well."

"But will he be able to walk and run?"

"There wasn't as much damage as I expected," Dr. Avelyn said. "We'll have to wait and see. Some of it will be up to Hank. But he's strong and young. He's only two years old."

Brodie knew the veterinarian had gotten the basic information because of the microchip implanted into his subcutaneous tissue. She liked that the she always shared stuff and answered her questions.

Now Brodie walked with Scout from the clinic to the house. She heard a rumble of thunder in the distance. Ryder had completed all the chores before he and Grace left. She glanced up at his loft and didn't see a light. She looked over at Jason's doublewide. It was dark, too. And

Jason's SUV was still gone. But as she got closer to the house, Brodie noticed that Ryder's Jeep was parked in its regular spot.

When she came in the back door, she thought maybe he and Grace might be inside. Thomas and Isaac were having milk and cookies at the counter.

"They think they should get to stay up later," Hannah told her, "because it's summer and there is no school."

"Ryder and Grace aren't back yet?" Brodie asked.

"I didn't know they were gone."

And just then, there was a scratch at the back door. All of them heard it. Brodie was closest. She opened it to find Grace. She was wearing a working vest but it was muddy. Twigs and grass stuck out of it. The dog was panting, but she wouldn't come in.

"Grace!" Brodie said as she leaned out the doorway looking for Ryder.

"What's going on?" Hannah wanted to know. "You said they were gone somewhere? Grace, come on in. You look exhausted."

"Something's wrong." Brodie could feel it.

"I'll call Rye and see what's going on," Hannah said, rushing across the kitchen to get her phone.

"Is everything okay, mom?"

Brodie concentrated on Grace. The dog looked up at her and circled. She was trying to get Brodie to come with her. Brodie grabbed her daypack from where she'd left it on the bench by the door. She raced out trying to keep up with Grace before she realized Scout was right alongside her. She heard Hannah calling for her, but she didn't look back.

Chapter 75

Blackwater River State Forest

Creed squeezed the rest of his hand out from the zip tie, and the plastic slid off.

The men were still talking, but their voices were becoming mumbled. Creed was starting to lose his sense of direction. The pain in his head seemed to be replaced by a muddled fog, and he wondered if it was the cause for the sudden sleepiness he was feeling. His breathing had slowed and an overpowering nausea swept over him, leaving him cold and clammy. Now with his hands free, he wasn't sure he could even lift himself off the ground.

He managed to roll onto his side. Something was tangled at his neck, and he remembered the night vision goggles. It took extreme effort for his fingers to pull the goggles up over his face and over his eyes. His hands were shaking. It was probably from being tied.

But now the green tinged light added to his nausea. The ground felt like it was moving, rolling underneath him. He couldn't see the men anywhere. His head swirled, and the dizziness almost made him vomit.

Creed returned to his stomach. He propped himself up with his elbows. That was as far as he could get. He was too weak to do anything more. Maybe if he just stayed still. At least for a little while.

Then he started to smell something else that didn't belong in the forest. The scent was strong and close.

Gasoline.

Someone was pouring gasoline.

Chapter 76

Blackwater River State Forest

Brodie didn't need to see where she was going. After the last several days, going back and forth, she knew the way almost by heart. She knew Grace was taking her to the crime scene.

She had stopped the dog once, insisting Grace drink some water. When Grace realized Brodie wouldn't continue to follow, she relented then ended up drinking the entire bowl. That was when Brodie considered taking the vest off the dog. It looked heavy and hot. She felt for the release and noticed a patch of fur missing on Grace's shoulder. Brodie's fingers came away sticky. She smelled it and knew it was blood.

She made the dog sit while she ran her hands over her body, neck, and head then each leg. Her fingers had to search since her eyes couldn't see. The wound on her shoulder appeared to be the only one, and it wasn't bleeding anymore. But when Brodie started to take off the vest she hesitated. It wasn't like the others Grace usually wore. She left it in place.

They weren't far from the scene and Brodie tried to slow Grace down. She could hear men's voices. Too many night creatures drowned them out. Brodie didn't recognize either of the voices as Ryder's. She couldn't make out what they were saying. They seemed to be arguing. Could it be the deputies?

As she stood completely still, she tried to watch Grace and Scout. It was dark. She squatted to be closer to them. Touching their backs to keep them in place.

Then suddenly there was a swoosh, and the forest lit up in front of them. Bright red and yellow flames.

Chapter 77

Creed was now on his back. It seemed to help the nausea. He closed his eyes. It took all his strength to peel the goggles off his face. He thought they might be the reason for the swirling feeling and the bright colors, remembering the thermal imaging screen. But even with the goggles off, the colors were still there skewing his vision and making him more confused than ever.

He'd gone from clammy and cold to hot. The heat felt like it would scorch off his skin. Flames licked at the treetops. They couldn't be real. But the heat was.

He rolled back onto his stomach. The pain in his chest had disappeared, but he still couldn't climb to his feet. Instead he crawled using his elbows to pull the rest of his body. It took a tremendous amount of energy to move only inches.

When he saw the big, black dog Creed was certain he was hallucinating. Maybe all of this was a dream. Was that possible?

The dog licked his face, and the wet slobber felt wonderful. Another lick from the other side.

Grace!

He had told her to go home. She shouldn't be here. And somehow, she'd brought Scout with her.

"Ryder, are you okay? Can you stand?"

Someone was trying to pull him up. Nothing seemed to work.

"Are you hurt?"

He could see Brodie was yelling at him, and yet, he could barely hear her.

She grabbed at his arms.

"Brodie? You can't be here. Take the dogs. Go. Please just go."

Then suddenly, she disappeared from his view.

He couldn't see the dogs anymore either.

He had trained them too well.

And now, they were gone.

Chapter 78

Something was wrong with Ryder, but Brodie couldn't figure it out. On the back of his head, his hair was matted with blood, but he wasn't bleeding anymore. Even as he spoke, every word seemed to be an effort.

The fire was getting closer. She needed to move him. There was no way she could drag him using the path to get back home. She wasn't strong enough, and there were too many obstacles. The flames would surely devour them.

She started to gather up one of the tarps the investigators had left over one of the graves. The stakes were hard to pull up. There were bungee cords attached on one side of the tarp stretching it like a tent. The cords were looped through rings in the tarp and took forever for Brodie's fingers to pull them free.

Then she realized they might come in handy.

Grace went back to Ryder. It looked like she was walking around and sniffing him, from head to toe. Scout stayed with Brodie, interested in the bungee cords.

The flames gave her plenty of light. There was a supernatural flickering and an earsplitting crackle that made her fingers work faster.

She assembled a makeshift harness out of the shorter bungee cords and looped them around Scout's broad chest.

"You're going to have to help me, Scout."

Brodie grabbed two of the longer bungee cords and dragged the tarp back to Ryder. Now she had to get him onto the thing.

She stretched out the tarp right next to him. Before she reached out for his arms, she saw Grace sniffing his shirtsleeve. He wore them uncuffed and rolled up. They fell to mid-arm to protect him from bugs and thorny bushes. But Grace didn't appear interested in his shirt as much as what was under the sleeve.

Then suddenly, Grace did something that Brodie had seen her do during training sessions and at the crime scene. She sat and stared up at Brodie.

The dog was alerting.

At first Brodie didn't understand. Was Ryder bleeding? It wasn't soaking through his shirt.

Then it hit her. Grace could detect different scents including explosives and drugs.

Brodie dropped to her knees and pushed Ryder's sleeve up over his elbow. Attached to the back of his arm was a square patch. She pushed up the other sleeve to find two more patches. She ran her hands over the rest of his arms and his torso searching for more.

Grace was alerting to the drugs in the patches. Brodie remembered the garbage bag Scout had found. She made the dogs step back. She ordered them five feet away and told them to stay.

With a glance, she could see the flames dancing between the trees, less than a hundred feet away. Her mind was racing. She couldn't think. She could hardly breathe.

Ryder's daypack was still on his back. She threaded it off of him. She zipped open pockets. Found one of his rolled-up T-shirts, wrapped it around her nose and mouth then tied it at the back of her neck.

In another pocket she found latex gloves, two sizes too big for her. She tugged one up over her sweaty palm. Carefully she ripped off the patches, folding each one to stick to itself. She wrapped the wad of patches into the palm of her latex glove as she pulled it off around them.

She still wasn't sure what to do with them. She was wasting time, but she remembered Scout's reaction from finding the torn garbage bag. In one of the daypack pockets she found some Ziploc bags. Again, she made sure the glove was tightly wrapped around the patches then she stuffed them into the plastic bag and into a pocket of the daypack.

Now, she needed to dig for the antidote.

It was a small pouch. Both Ryder and Jason carried them.

Finally, her fingers found it. But as she opened it she wasn't sure what to do. Jason had said there was a short window of opportunity. Was it the same for people?

She rolled Ryder from his side to his back. His eyes fluttered at her. He choked on the smoke.

"Brodie, what are you doing here?" It was like he was seeing her for the first time.

She tried to remember how Jason held the container, and she pinched it between her thumb and forefinger the same way he did.

"Stay still," she told him as she held his forehead down and inserted the tip into his nose. One steady push until it was all gone.

Ryder's eyes fluttered again, startled then flew open. He was alarmed, but he obeyed.

A second dose won't harm him. Brodie remembered Vickie's words. All handlers carried two.

She ripped open the second and stuck it up his other nostril. Pushed the plunger, one even motion.

She started to pull on his shoulder to roll him over and onto the tarp. Ryder wouldn't budge. She realized his daypack was in the way.

Now she was struggling. It was getting harder to breathe.

"Well, well," she heard a man's voice behind her. "What do we have here?"

Still on her knees, Brodie turned to look at the man. His clothes were sooty. One arm hung limp at his side. He had a small gun pointing at Brodie's head.

"I thought I already killed this guy, but it looks like he has his own rescue team."

She glanced at Scout and Grace then immediately regretted it. The man swung the gun in the dogs' direction.

"No!" she screamed.

The two gunshots blasted through the air.

Scout and Grace dropped to their bellies. Brodie didn't know what had happened until she saw the man fall to his knees. Then he collapsed face first.

She twisted around to see Ryder with a gun. He braced himself up on one elbow. He tried to sit up.

"Don't," Brodie told him. "Don't push it."

She looked back at the dogs. Both were still in "dog down" position. She gestured for them to come to her, and they raced over.

She turned to see Ryder tucking the gun into his pack. Awkwardly, he attempted to lift himself onto the tarp. She helped him, shifting his legs one at a time.

She wrapped the tarp up around him and strapped him in with the remaining bungee cords. The smoke was making it difficult to breathe. She fell to her knees twice, coughing and fighting for air.

Somehow Scout knew exactly what she wanted from him. And so did Grace. She led the way. Brodie hadn't given the little dog any directions. She was relying completely on Grace's survival instinct.

With the flames close behind, Scout and Brodie pulled the tarp. She cringed every time Ryder's body bounced over the gnarled roots and jutting rocks or snagged on fallen debris. At the last minute, she'd stuck one of his extra T-shirts rolled up under his head.

Finally, she could see the tree line ending. They skidded out onto a sandy beach. There in front of them was Coldwater Creek. Brodie could already feel the cool air blowing toward them off the water.

She could now see the sky, too. Black and churning, lightning pulsed from inside the storm clouds. She'd never been so happy to hear the crash of thunder. Within seconds came the downpour.

Brodie hugged the dogs close to her, one on each side. Grace twisted out of her hold and raced to the other end of the rolled-up tarp. Brodie could hear Ryder choking.

Panic set in again. She tugged at the cords then ripped and pulled. Grace and Scout both helped, biting and pulling corners of the tarp.

Finally they had him unwrapped enough, and Ryder pushed himself up onto his elbows. He tilted his head back, closed his eyes and let the rain wash over him.

Brodie searched his face watching for some indication that he was okay. When he opened his eyes they seemed more focused. Grace licked his face. Scout came to his other side and head-butted his shoulder.

Ryder sat up slowly and petted the dogs while his eyes found Brodie's.

Then he said, "That was one hell of a ride."

"Get ready for another," she told him, "because we're going to steal that boat."

Chapter 79

Blackwater River State Forest

Udie cursed at the rain. Too many distractions had delayed him. He had expected to be finished and back home in bed by now.

Things had been going exactly the way he planned. Actually, the deputies had been easier than he'd expected. Each of them had been like a lamb walking into a wolf's den. It couldn't have gone smoother. And now any evidence of their bodies would be burned along with that dog handler.

He'd left Derrick to fend for himself. At first Udie had been angry that he hadn't trusted him to take care of things. Then he found himself embarrassed of the man. He appeared weak and helpless. The guy had a gun, and he still managed to be overpowered by the man he shot. Got his arm broken.

Udie had looked up to Derrick. He thought he wanted to be just like him. A military guy. A surgeon with a fancy house and pretty wife. Udie wanted to have all the money and toys and prestige he had accumulated. Udie figured he deserved it. Deserved to be the man's partner. After he'd discovered that Derrick Winslow was his father, he figured all he had to do was prove himself worthy, and the man would…what? Embrace him? Love him?

All this time he knew Udie was his son. He knew!

Udie wiped the sweat from his face, out of his eyes. It didn't matter. He didn't need a father. Certainly not one as incompetent as this guy. All the whining. And the fancy leather shoes in the middle of the forest. How lame.

Udie shook his head. He was over it. He didn't even care what the guy said or did. Udie had stashed away all the cash he'd been paid every time he dumped a body for the guy. It added up over the years. Maybe he'd pick up and leave. His mother was gone. His father was an embarrassment. He didn't have any reason to stay. Maybe he'd move down to Tampa. Go watch his Buccaneers.

But there was something he needed to do now that the rain had started and the winds had shifted. His beautiful, roaring fire was dying out behind him even as he made his way to the ridge. It would never reach the dog handler's property.

No, he'd have to start a fire inside one of the buildings.

He had left just enough gasoline in the can. By the time he slid down the final stretch, he was soaked to the bone, which only made him angrier. In Udie's mind, the woman and the man and all those dogs had ruined everything for him. If it hadn't been for them stumbling onto his sacred dumping grounds, none of this would have happened.

He hesitated at the corner of the woods. The big house at the far end of the property was the only building with lights, and it looked like every single one was turned on. Several vehicles were parked in front of the house, but there was no one outside. He searched for movement behind the windows and couldn't see through the curtains.

He remembered where the motion lights were and stepped carefully trying to avoid tripping them. If he slid along the side of the buildings, he knew the lights weren't tilted close enough. He could do this, building by building until he got to the one that housed the dogs.

Protected under the eaves, the rain didn't pound him as much. It seemed to be easing up. The thunder rumbled instead of crashed. Lightning still flickered.

Udie slid around another corner. He jerked back startled to find the barrel of a shotgun pointing directly at his face. The black woman was dressed in a dark rain jacket, with the hood pulled up over her head.

He knew he was fast. He thought about diving back around the corner when she told him, "I wouldn't move if I were you."

He did it anyway.

He stumbled and ran into another gun. This one held by a black mechanical hand.

"We've been watching you on the cameras, asshole," the amputee dog handler said to him.

He waved his other hand and triggered the motion sensor then pointed to the small camera snug under the eaves. Udie hadn't even noticed it before.

"Hey, I know you," the man said. "From the Segway House. You're the cleanup guy."

Three Days Later

Chapter 80

Maggie was still gathering bits and pieces of information. Her cell phone rang even as she parked for her appointment. She checked the caller I.D., glanced at the time then left the motor running and the air conditioning blasting as she took the call.

"Antonio, you know it's Saturday, right?"

"Weekends are the best time to hack into computer systems."

"I'm pretending I didn't hear that." She was anxious to find out what he'd learned.

"Looks like our Dr. Derrick Winslow was a very naughty boy," Alonzo had his own flare for telling a story. "I started with that dead veteran you found in the forest, Simon Perry. He signed up for a special drug rehab program Doc started at Recovery Gardens for veterans without families. Very generous, right?

"It turns out Doc had Simon list him as his only contact. Also convinced him to sign over his bank account while Simon was in rehab, so he couldn't skip out of the program. It was for Simon's own good. Problem was, Doc pronounced him better and released him late last week."

"And we found him in the forest on Monday," Maggie said. "Judging by the decomp and all the maggots, he may have gone from the rehab center directly to the forest."

"What's interesting is that Simon transferred money out of his bank account as recently as Tuesday afternoon."

"Winslow couldn't have been reckless enough to transfer money directly to himself?"

"Oh no," Alonzo told her. "He had creative ways to reroute it. He never expected someone like me tracking his cyber footprints. Looks like he's done the same thing with other veterans he admitted into his rehab program."

"How do you know that?" Maggie asked.

"I managed to get a list of them for the last two years. I just started checking, but so far, I have three others who left Recovery Gardens and seem to have disappeared. No one has seen them. There's been no credit card activity since they left. I can't find cell phone numbers or social media accounts in their names. But they are, however, still collecting their veterans' benefits."

"And let me guest, they're transferred through the same routing system as Simon's."

"You got it."

"So this was all about money?"

"Greed is one of the oldest reasons in the world for murder," Alonzo reminded her.

"But Winslow was a prominent surgeon."

"One carrying a whole lot of debt. He's started businesses, or he's been a partner in one or two that have gone bankrupt. One was a pretty successful reconstructive and cosmetic surgical center. Oh and remember UnitedBio? You were right. It was a short-lived company that provided organs and tissue samples for research labs. Winslow was a partner. That one closed suddenly when there were inquiries as to where and how they were obtaining the organs and tissue samples."

Maggie remembered the stacks of containers in the storage unit that had labels with UnitedBio on them.

"Didn't you tell me the only contact they had for Unit B12 was a phone number at Recovery Gardens?"

"That's right. But it was disconnected about two years ago."

"Why would Winslow allow the lease to run out and have all that stuff discovered?"

"Maybe at that point he didn't care," Alonzo said.

"Or maybe he didn't know."

"Now you've lost me."

"Didn't you say the number was for housekeeping?"

She heard him tapping keys before he said, "Yup, that's right."

"From everything else I'm finding out, Winslow liked to have someone clean up after him."

"A shame we can't ask him. This guy sounds like a piece of work."

Maggie had been getting regular updates from Vickie, the investigators and the recovery crew in the forest. One of the bodies had already been identified as Dr. Winslow's, so the man would never be held responsible for his crimes.

"Unfortunately, I have the next best thing," Maggie said. "His accomplice."

"Go get him," Alonzo told her.

Chapter 81

Maggie was expecting to meet with Chief Deputy Glenn, so she was surprised to find Sheriff Norwich waiting for her on the other side of the security check.

"Hello, Agent O'Dell."

"Sheriff, how are you?"

"Tired of lying around."

Maggie must have looked concerned because Norwich added, "The rumor of my demise has been greatly exaggerated." She allowed herself a small laugh. "Much to the consternation of some people around here."

Maggie suspected she meant Chief Deputy Glenn. The man seemed to enjoy the regular press briefings he'd been holding since the night of the fire. With two of her deputies dead, Maggie could understand why the sheriff might feel the need to get back to work.

She had to admit, the sheriff looked good. She was dressed in civilian clothes: khakis, canvas deck shoes and a short-sleeved polo shirt. Her pace was a bit slower than normal as she walked beside Maggie, gesturing which way to go as they walked.

"There's a group of us getting together at Walter's Canteen on the beach later. Maybe if you're up to it, you could join us."

"Thanks. I'd like that."

They walked a bit more then Norwich said, "I have to tell you, I'm surprised he agreed to talk to you. One of our best guys tried to get him to open up, and he just stared at him. Seems he remembers you from the forest."

"Is his attorney here?"

"A public defender's been assigned, but he didn't want him here."

"You have that on tape?" Maggie asked.

"Audio and video. And it's all set up for you."

Maggie checked her phone one last time before she shut it off. She had talked to Ganza earlier, and he had given her the bombshell she was hoping to use on Ernest Udall Sutton.

He was already sitting in the room, chained and handcuffed to the chair. Maggie came in and took the seat across the table from him. The orange jumpsuit was a size too big, making him look thin and gangly. One glance at his lean, muscled forearms reminded her this was the man who had taken down Ryder and had bludgeoned John Lockett. Still, she was surprised at how young he looked. Until his dark, dead eyes met hers.

"I'm Agent Maggie O'Dell." She kept the introduction friendly. He'd obviously seen her as someone he wasn't intimidated by. She'd use that to her advantage. "What would you like me to call you?"

"Udie."

"Okay. You know you're in a whole lot of trouble, Udie."

"But I didn't kill anybody. I just cleaned up after Doc."

"The deputies in the forest?"

"Yeah, I mean Doc just went crazy. He was worried about all of you finding his bodies."

She pulled out a cell phone, and he watched her set it on the table close to her. She gave him a few seconds to see if he'd notice the case and recognize it as the one Jason had taken from him when he patted him down to make sure he wasn't armed. The phone was one piece of evidence Maggie and the FBI were processing.

She glanced at it and said, "John Lockett's phone."

He gave it only a glance. His eyes continued to examine hers.

"You're right," she told him. "There are text messages from Lockett and Dr. Winslow setting up to meet at the boat launch. Doc even gives him detailed directions."

"Yup, that's right." Now his head bobbed, nodding in agreement.

"But there are also text messages after we found Lockett's body. I suspect those are from you and Doc. I mean since you had his phone."

She paused, watching as his eyes darted back and forth. He was trying to remember what he might have said.

"Then you saw all the instructions he was constantly giving me."

It was a good answer, Maggie had to admit.

"How long have you worked for him? I mean, your cleaning service."

"Quite a while."

"Your mother started the business, right? So she probably worked with Doc, too?"

"Yeah." He was trying to rub his neck and shoulder together since his hands were handcuffed and connected to a chain that ran to the shackles on his feet. She knew he was being treated for a nasty rash.

"How long have you known that Doc was your father?"

The surprise flickered across his face as his eyes blinked several times.

She didn't wait for an answer. She wanted him to realize she knew more than he could imagine. "Those ancestry companies," she told him, "when you submit your DNA for the profile, you allow law enforcement access, too."

"Just means he had even more of a hold over me," Udie said.

"And your mother?"

"What about her? Why do you keep bringing her up?"

"I'm just trying to understand your relationship with Doc. If your mother worked with him…I mean, she cleaned for him at Recovery Gardens and probably whatever businesses he had before that."

She recognized the anger setting his mouth in a straight line.

"And yet, she never told you he was your father?" She kept her voice sympathetic. "You obviously didn't know or you wouldn't have gone to the ancestry company."

"She was a wicked woman."

"I'm sure she must have loved you. Maybe she was trying to protect you."

"Protect me?" He let out a laugh that sounded like a squawk. "She expected me to work my fingers to the bone exactly the way she did. All she did was nag and criticize. I'm glad she's dead."

He didn't even notice his slip until Maggie asked, "How do you know she's dead?"

He slouched down to meet his cuffed hands, so he could scratch his face and wipe his mouth as his eyes analyzed hers.

Then he said, "I haven't heard from her since she left. I figure she's dead."

Maggie kept her expression steady, but she was impressed at how calculating this young man was. He was a scrappy survivor and a very good liar.

"We found her," Maggie said and watched his eyes go wide before he had a chance to control them. It wasn't surprise or shock. It was panic. The kind you'd expect to see from an animal when it realizes it's cornered.

"Her body was in the forest," she continued, trying not to be distracted by the sudden tapping of his left foot. Maybe he knew he wasn't just cornered but trapped. "We were able to match her DNA with the one you submitted to find your father."

At the mention of his father, he lit up like he had found a lifeline.

"It was Doc," he finally said with the same bobbing nod.

"And you didn't notice that she was lying out there in the grass?"

"How could I without her head? I just thought it was one of the bodies he put out there before we partnered up."

"So you didn't know anything about her murder?"

"Nope." He was back to feeling in control. The foot had even stopped.

"Udie, we know you killed her. We found her head. In the bucket." Before he attempted another cleanup excuse, she added, "Your fingerprints are still on the bucket. On the outside and the inside."

The foot started tapping again. His shoulder bunched up to his neck to rub at the rash. But his eyes stayed on Maggie's.

"She was a wicked woman."

Chapter 82

Walter's Canteen
Pensacola Beach, Florida

Creed watched Hannah and Walter at the bar, laughing and interrupting the young bartender with their stories. The guy was trying to mix drinks for the rest of them. It reminded Creed of the very first time he met Hannah. She was behind that very same bar. When Creed started a brawl and tried to take on more men than he could handle, Hannah came to his rescue. And she'd been coming to his rescue ever since.

Jason and Brodie were pulling tables together while Benny and Colfax seemed to be directing them. Nobody would let Creed do anything. They were still babying him just because he'd broken a couple of ribs. Turns out, having a bulletproof vest on and getting shot from a close proximity could still cause injury. Tobogganing through the forest, wrapped in a tarp, probably contributed to the muscle aches. That night was still a bit fuzzy in his mind. But the drugs seemed to be out of his system, thanks to Brodie's quick thinking.

He still couldn't believe she had accomplished what she did that night. Whenever anyone attempted to give her credit or praise, she was quick to say she couldn't have done it without Scout and Grace. He always knew his dogs rescued him emotionally and mentally on a regular basis. He never thought they'd actually come to his rescue.

Creed wasn't sure how Jason and Hannah had managed to convince Brodie to come with them. Hannah was full of surprises. Somehow, she had bargained with Walter to close down his place on the busiest day of the week just for their celebration. She knew Brodie might not be ready for a crowd beyond the team that had been in the forest.

At first, he noticed Brodie's head constantly swiveling to look out the windows. He was concerned she might be uncomfortable with the crowds out on the beach. She caught him watching and said, "It's more beautiful than I remember."

He figured Jason, Colfax and Benny needed this distraction. Their friend, Eric Hudson's death was being investigated as one of Doc's murders. Creed could tell the three of them were feeling bad they hadn't suspected a thing. As a consequence the men were doting on Eric's widow and little boy. Jason had told Creed, that more than ever, he wanted to get Sarge ready for Luke.

But Creed knew the real antidote for Jason had just walked in the door. Taylor Donahey turned everyone's head. Creed started to smile at the woman's effect until he saw Brodie's face.

Maggie and Vickie came in minutes behind her, and his sister immediately smiled again at the presence of the medical examiner. He was pleased to see Sheriff Norwich with them.

As the others greeted each other, got drinks or filled plates from the generous buffet Hannah had ordered up, Maggie sat down next to him.

He was at the small table off to the side where he had been happy to sit and observe.

"Why are you here all alone in the corner?" she asked, pulling her chair close to him.

"They wouldn't let me help."

"You hate when they do that, don't you?"

"I do."

He could feel her watching him.

"Sheriff Norwich looks good," he said.

"I know, and she had a heart attack. You just have a couple of bruised ribs."

He allowed a hitch of a smile.

She pulled her chair closer and looped her arm through his. He almost asked how things went at the jail, but he didn't want to ruin his or her good moods. Instead he said, "Taylor looks happy."

Maggie had told him she was going to talk to William's grandparents. Taylor had helped Maggie by forcing a confession from Doc, at the expense of losing what she believed was her only hope of getting back into her son's life.

"There's a lot that needs to be repaired," she told him. "But they now realize Doc hadn't been honest with them. They didn't even know Taylor was in Pensacola."

Creed tilted back to get a better look at Brodie. She was with Vickie and Norwich, but he saw her glancing at Jason and Taylor.

Maggie leaned in and quietly said, "Unfortunately, you can't protect her heart."

She noticed it, too.

"I know you still see her as that eleven-year-old little girl, but the rest of us see a smart, very capable, young woman."

He knew she was right. He remembered how Brodie had steered the boat through the narrow passages in the dark with only his incoherent guidance.

"You asked me to check on something else," Maggie said. "It looks like John Lockett was a loner. Alonzo hasn't found any family or close friends for Hank. I'm sorry."

"Don't be. I think he's found someone he trusts. Someone who might need him as much as he's going to need her." He pointed with a tilt of his head to Brodie.

"Really?"

They watched quietly for a while. Soon everyone would be seated, and they'd be forced to join. But Creed was enjoying this little bit of time alone together.

"Speaking of trust," Maggie said, and he almost winced. He didn't want to talk about what was or wasn't happening with them.

"I've been a real pain in the ass this whole week," she said, surprising him. "Maybe I can make it up to you."

She slid something along the small tabletop until it rested right in front of him. With only a glance, he recognized it was a hotel keycard.

"I'm in 620," she said in a low voice. "I promise I'll be gentle."

Author's Note

Warning! Spoiler Alert.

I started a fire in Blackwater River State Forest.

And wouldn't you know it, a month later a raging wildfire raced out of control just miles south of the forest. In early May, the Five Mile Swamp Fire raged for a week with winds and low humidity fueling it. Over 2200 acres and more than a dozen homes were destroyed. Over 1100 residents were evacuated. It came within a half mile of my Florida home. It was frightening enough for me to readjust the last chapters of my story.

Too many times my stories have ended up coming true. In my novel, *Damaged*, published in 2010, I dealt with the underground cadaver business. Early in *Hidden Creed* Maggie refers to Joe Black. He was one of my favorite characters, a body broker who provided human body parts for medical doctors to practice surgical procedures.

Fast forward to August 2012. A Pensacola man buys the contents of a storage unit (Unit B12) at auction for $900 then finds the grisly remains of human brains, hearts and lungs stashed in plastic food containers and soda cups.

It didn't take long for readers and friends to start sending me the articles. Dr. Michael Berkland was never charged (as far as I can find) with anything other than misdemeanors. It was believed that as a private pathologist, he performed autopsies at funeral homes for families, some asking for second opinions in the deaths of loved ones. The families didn't realize Berkland kept a few parts. Police found remains belonging to more than 100 people.

Even I can't make this stuff up. It made perfect fodder for this book.

Onto the more serious topic of opioid addiction. I can't begin to do justice to this problem, but because it affects the lives of so many of our veterans, I thought it deserved some attention. Each day 128 people die from an opioid overdose. That's around 70,000 people every year. There are some wonderful recovery centers, however, Recovery Gardens is not one of them. It is fictional.

Speaking of real places, most of you already know that I like to include actual locales in my books. I've used Blackwater River State Park and Forest before. The case Maggie refers to where the killer tricked her and Tully into the forest only to hunt her down, takes place in the novel, *Stranded*. It's also the first time she meets Ryder and Grace. *Breaking Creed* is technically the first book of the Creed series, but I always tell readers if they're just starting the series, they really should begin with *Stranded*.

Margaritaville Beach Hotel and Peg Leg Pete's are real places on Pensacola Beach. I recommend the grouper sandwich at Peg Leg Pete's. But you won't find Walter's Canteen or the marina. The Segway House is also a figment of my imagination.

My apologies to the Santa Rosa County Sheriff's Office. I took all kinds of liberties with law enforcement procedures, processes and jurisdiction. I did the same with Florida District 1's medical examiner.

Although Vickie Kammerer is a real person, she is not a medical examiner. Vickie and her dog, Sugar, won my "Get Caught Reading Alex Kava" contest last year. Her prize was for her and her dog to appear as characters in the next Ryder Creed novel. I met Vickie years ago at one of my first book signings, and it feels like a reunion every time we see each other. But I have to admit I had fun learning new things about her. Only those of you who know her will recognize what's true and what came from my imagination.

That is the best part of my job—taking real things, places and people then blending them with fiction, so that my readers can't tell what is real and what is fiction. Always keep in mind that *truth is much stranger than fiction*.

With each new Ryder Creed novel I try to include new and different things I've learned about scent dogs. They are truly amazing. You can probably tell the dogs are my favorite characters. In writing a series, I've learned that all of the characters continue to show me new insights into themselves and their relationships. Some of those insights surprise even me.

I appreciate that you have so generously welcomed these characters into your reading life. And I want you to know I'm already researching and plotting out *Fallen Creed*.

The biggest compliment a reader can give an author is to tell a friend. If you've enjoyed this book, *please share it* with a book lover. And thank you for reading my books.

Acknowledgments

I want to thank all my friends who put up with my long absences and help keep me grounded. Thanks to Sharon Car, Marlene Haney, Sharon Kator, Amee Rief, Maricela and Jose Barajas, Martin and Patti Bremmer, Pat Heng, Doug and Linda Buck, Dan Macke, Erica Spindler, Dr. Elvira Rios, Luann Causey, and Christy Cotton.

Special Thanks to:

My publishing team: Deb Carlin, Linda and Doug Buck, Maricela Barajas, and Joshua Mackey.

Dr. Enita Larson of Tender Care Animal Hospital in Gretna, Nebraska, for her veterinary expertise in helping me figure out where to shoot a dog and ensure he survives. And extra thanks to her and David Appleget for working out what caliber of gun and bullet would keep us from doing the least amount of damage to Hank. Enita has also generously allowed me to use a combination of her children's names for the character, Dr. Avelyn Parker.

Judge Leigh Ann Retelsdorf and her amazing forensic contacts patiently spent an entire evening talking to me about maggots. Thank you Christine Gabig, MSFS, forensic chemist and Dr. Tim Huntington, PhD, forensic entomologist. For many years, Leigh Ann has been my reliable go-to-person for information, advice and working through forensic puzzles.

However, keep in mind, I wander from the facts, because I am a storyteller. So any mistakes in processes or procedures are mine, and mine alone.

Thank you to all the booksellers, librarians, book clubs and book bloggers for mentioning and recommending my novels.

An *extra special thank* you to all of my readers, VIR Club members, and Facebook friends. With so many wonderful novels available, I continue to be humbled and honored that you choose mine. Without you, I wouldn't have the opportunity to share my twisted tales.

A huge thank you to my pack: Deb, Duncan, Boomer, Maggie and Huck. You guys are truly my heart and my soul.

Last, this book is dedicated to my dear and wonderful friend, Sandy Rockwood, who passed away last year, five days before Christmas. Those of you who have attended my VIR Club Luncheons might remember me introducing her. In *Desperate Creed* I used her name as Brodie's therapist, and now, it will forever be a lovely reminder of her. Over the last twenty years, Sandy has been there, celebrating each and every book. This journey certainly won't be the same without her.

CPSIA information can be obtained
at www.ICGtesting.com
Printed in the USA
LVHW011556050820
662470LV00009B/46/J

9 781732 006430